THE SEVEN LIVES OF GRACE

ELENA SHELEST

Cover design by Rob Williams, ILMC

Copyright © 2019 by Shelest Publishing LLC

ISBN: 978-1-7340087-1-5

First, think.
Second, believe.
Third, dream.
And finally, dare.

—Walt Disney

Dear Reader,

I am glad you found this book. It was written from my heart, and I hope you'll enjoy it.

Expect to be taken on a leisurely hike with quiet surroundings, picturesque overlooks, and a summit with a view to relish at the end of your journey. Find a quiet place, grab your favorite drink, a few treats, and let the story speak to you.

I certainly enjoyed the two-year adventure of writing and publishing this book. As a thank you to all my readers, I included the link at the end of the book to download a **FREE novella** about the origins of the main story as well as the **complimentary guide** to embark on your own adventure.

Before starting, download your **reading companion**: www.subscribepage.com/livesofgrace_reading

For updates, new books to read, daily words of encouragement, and to connect with me, click the links below:

WWW.FIVEMINUTEDISCOVERY.COM

WWW.FACEBOOK.COM/FIVEMINUTEDISCOVERY

WWW.INSTAGRAM.COM/ELENASHELESTWRITER

WWW.TWITTER.COM/ELENASHELEST

WWW.GOODREADS.COM/ELENASHELEST

CONTENTS

PROLOGUE

A petite middle-aged woman in loose khaki trousers and a white tunic shirt entered the tent. She walked to the knee-high table and sat cross-legged on a handwoven carpet. Ornamental shadows from iron lanterns flickered on her pleasant face and reddish-blonde curls that escaped the silk headscarf. She opened the parcel with a stack of documents, but a sudden commotion made her look up.

"Stand down, Hassan. He's a friend," she said.

An armed bedouin that guarded the entrance relaxed his rifle and let the visitor pass.

"Greetings, Louise. Still taking precautions?" A tall man walked in, dressed in a travel kaftan, his head and face covered by a white shawl, but not a speck of dust was on his broad shoulders. The rich aroma of frankincense filled the air around him.

"Such is the nature of my calling, Tzali." The woman got up and bowed slightly.

"Please, no formalities. We've known each other for too many years." The man uncovered his face, revealing a smirk behind his gray beard. His blue eyes sparkled like two sapphires.

Louise smiled back. "You haven't changed one bit."

"From the moment we begin our service as Magi, we are no longer bound by time or space. But your bloodline is," he said, taking the woman's outstretched hand. "That's why I'm here—to discuss the next carrier of the gifts."

"My niece?" She startled and pulled away. "What urgent matter regarding her made you seek me out in the middle of the desert?"

"She's finally ready."

Louise sighed. She gestured the traveler to recline on the colorful floor cushions and poured him tea before speaking again. "I love Grace to pieces, but she's too reasonable for her own good."

"We are aware of that," Tzali said. "That's why she will need your guidance."

"I don't even know where the gifts are. They were sent with your courier years ago. Grace hasn't received them yet. I mailed her the key a few months ago like you instructed, but it might be too late now."

"The Sovereign One is never late." The blue light shimmered in the man's eyes once again. "But her time is running out, and we need to take precautions against the rising threats."

Louise shook her head. "There is no way I can get to her. I have to complete my mission, and it will take several more days to travel back to the States. Plus, as you know, it's too dangerous for me given the circumstances. It might cause more harm. I can't compromise—"

"I understand," Tzali interrupted. He sat up and took out the golden pocket watch. "The package with the treasure will be delivered to your niece in exactly twelve hours. Find a way to call her. We'll take care of the rest."

PART I
THE UNDISCOVERED LIFE

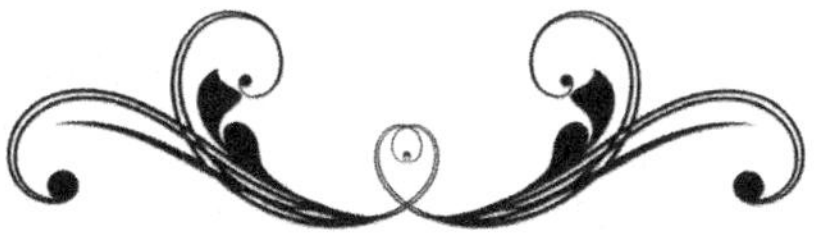

Our only limitations are those we set on our own minds.

—Napoleon Hill

CHAPTER 1

There were no warning signs. No clues. Nothing to prepare me for the events that took place a week before my twenty-fifth birthday.

It all started on Monday. My cell phone buzzed against the uneven surface of the old computer desk with "private number" flashing across the cracked screen. I shoved the despicable gadget under the pillow, but the nameless caller didn't relent.

"Hello?" I croaked.

"Gracie!" My aunt's familiar bubbly voice broke through the static and echoed in my ear as if separated by thousands of miles. Where was she calling from now?

"Aunt Lou?"

"So glad I caught you," she said.

Of course she'd caught me. Where else would I be at four in the morning? But a phone call from my aunt was worth the interrupted sleep.

"Gracie, you there? Wake up, kid. It's important. Get outside now."

"Oh, you came?" I finally found my voice again but logic

was still catching up. After ten years of absence, wouldn't she give us a warning?

"No, kid. I'm not in town. Sorry. Impossible. It's the package. Courier should be at your place in a few minutes. C'mon, quick. Grab your ID, get dressed, and meet them outside. Questions later."

"At this hour? Aunt Lou, but…"

"No buts. Wait. Got my letter?"

I snorted. "You mean your chicken scratch of a note?"

An envelope with a small vintage-looking key and a card had arrived a few months earlier. On the back of the photo of the Alps, my aunt had scribbled: *Time is short. Use the key to unlock your destiny. Love, Louise.* I didn't want to admit that her tiny souvenir had hung around my neck ever since.

"Leave your sarcasm for later, Miss Sassy. Tell me you have the key."

"Yep."

"Thank goodness! Take it and hustle. Out you go. Can't talk. Love ya."

She hung up before I could protest. Postcards from places I'd never heard of, unidentified numbers, and disappearances for long periods of time were the norm for my aunt. I could now add package deliveries at unusual hours to her list of oddities. Nevertheless, to receive mail from her was always a special treat, not something to miss out on.

I shoved away the textbooks scattered over my bed and jumped up. With one foot caught in the blanket, my round frame tumbled over the chair and collided with the desk. The pain shot through my knee and kicked out the last ounce of drowsiness. Thankful for the scant décor, I steadied the lamp that'd survived another fiasco.

The only sizable piece of furniture I owned was a cumbersome double-door wardrobe with a full-size mirror on one side. Its shelves contained more books than outfits. I opened it carefully to prevent the neatly stacked volumes from falling out, snatched a fuzzy sweater from a shelf, and threw it over my *Star Wars* pajamas. Looking like a panda that'd joined the Galactic Rebellion, I rushed down three flights of stairs and hobbled outside.

Frosty air hit my nostrils while I tried to catch my breath. Heavy rain instantly soaked through my clothes. I hid under the carport and hugged myself to stifle the shiver. It was the end of March, but the Seattle area still dropped to the thirties at night. Even my pudginess wasn't enough to repel the chill.

Oh, Aunt Lou, I hope I'm freezing here for something good.

Dimly lit by the street lamps, our large apartment complex stretched solemnly in both directions. Not a single soul was nearby. As I started to question my aunt's sanity, the rumbling sound of a motor broke through the monotone drumming of raindrops. A white armored truck came around the building on the left and stopped at the curb in front of me. A woman in a gray uniform jumped out and headed in my direction, leaving a burly armed man in a bulletproof vest behind to guard the cabin. No company name. No logo. The whole ordeal seemed surreal. I wondered if someone had transported me into the detective story I'd read earlier that week.

"Grace Ainsworth?" The woman said, her voice formal and steady, as though there was nothing unusual about personal deliveries in the middle of the night.

"Yes," I forced out but didn't move closer.

"Can I see your ID? Have a package for you."

After inspecting my driver's license, the woman continued in the same calm tone: "Now, the key."

I gave the courier a sideways glance but took Aunt Lou's present off my neck and handed it over, wondering what all the precautions were for. She put the key into a palm-size mold and then returned it.

"It matches," she said.

The woman walked to the truck and came back with a large package. She put the heavy box in my hands and walked away before I had a chance to ask any questions. Not trusting my overactive imagination to logically sort things out, I headed home.

After blundering past the narrow kitchen and through the crowded living room, I sat the parcel down on my bed and quickly cut through the cardboard. My heart raced. I tore away layers of packing material and unearthed a square container about fifteen inches across that looked like an oversized jewelry box. Polished reddish-brown wood with elaborate carvings of pomegranate fruit covered each side. My imagination instantly upgraded it to an ancient treasure chest.

Why would Aunt Lou hire armed guards for this? Must be something valuable.

I turned the box around and slid my fingers across the smooth varnished grooves of its handcrafted design. The container was solid, with no visible doors or handles; just a letter taped to one side. Bursting with anticipation, I ripped the envelope and took out several pieces of stained and crumpled paper. Each page was filled with my aunt's familiar handwriting.

Gracie.

This letter and the package are for your eyes only. If you are not alone, wait to read further.

A knock on the door caught me off guard. A second after I pushed everything behind the bed, my mother appeared in the doorway, her short stature wrapped in multiple blankets like an oversized burrito.

"What was that noise? I'm wide awake now," she said in a scratchy voice that sounded like nails on the chalkboard.

"I fell off the bed, and then… um, went out to get fresh air. Must have stumbled in the dark when I came back."

I attempted to sound casual, as if to roll off my bed and take strolls before sunrise was a daily occurrence. Could I not have thought of something better? Mother didn't need to discover her only sister had a secret, but her mind was too preoccupied to notice.

"I have chills. It must be flu or some other terrible disease that's going around. I heard on the news—"

"It's probably because I turned down the heat," I interrupted. "Just for the night. I'll fix it."

My heart sank. Another one of my money-saving ideas had backfired. Mother liked to turn the house into the tropics, but every time I received the utility bill, I wished to relocate from Washington State to Madagascar.

My mother moaned. "Oh, Grace, you'll freeze me to death, if this headache doesn't kill me first."

I wanted to say that watching reality TV until midnight would give anybody a headache but kept that theory to myself.

"Go lay down, I'll bring you something."

My mother turned around and disappeared into the dark hallway. Aunt Lou's letter was calling my name. I threw one longing look towards the package, sighed, and headed to the kitchen. After cranking up the heater, I took out the plastic container full of herbs, ointments, and vitamins that I'd labeled and organized into neat stacks. Despite my effort to make things easier around the house, mother still required my personal assistance.

The secret in my bedroom hampered my usefulness. Silverware dropped into the sink with an awful rattling noise, clover tea spilled all over the floor, and ginger powder littered the counters. Shuffling across the linoleum floor in my fuzzy Chewbacca slippers, I cleaned the mess, gathered the remedies, and hurried into my mother's bedroom.

Inside, the ever-present smell of menthol filled the stale air. Contrary to my bare-necessities style, her room was full of mismatched furniture pieces purchased at garage sales and stuffed to bursting within the four walls. I climbed through the barricade my hands itched to put in order, dug Lara Ainsworth from the pile of blankets, and put medicine in her hand. A Himalayan salt lamp threw odd shadows over her pasty face. At forty-six, her once beautiful refined features looked worn out and her blue eyes had dulled.

"If I don't get better in a few hours, poor Mr. Davis will have to handle the store by himself again," she announced.

"Here, take this," I said, finally finding a spot to sit down. So early in the morning, my ability to converse downgraded from "not so talkative" to "practically mute". To make up for the shortage of reassuring words, I let my mother complain without interruption while my mind wandered off to Aunt Lou's present.

I often missed my aunt and her outlandish stories. Starved for adventure, my sister and I had swallowed her every word during her short visits. Independent, fearless, and eccentric, she was the total opposite of her fragile younger sibling who, at the moment, complained about the weather.

It's for the best you can't come to see us, Auntie. I doubt you'd be impressed.

When my mother's laments turned into the rhythmic breathing of a person sound asleep, I snuck back to my room and took out the letter. With a warm blanket over my shoulders, I sat on the bed and continued to read.

I hope to send this soon or give it to you in person if circumstances allow. This gift is of great importance for you and generations to come.

I tightened my lips. My aunt had a tendency for drama—a

trait she shared with her sister. Was she exaggerating again? And what was that formal language for? So unlike the spunky way she spoke over the phone.

At one point, I was in your place, with my aunt Genevieve explaining it all to me. You might not believe me at first, like I didn't believe her, but I beg you to follow my instructions at least once.

"What's up with the long introduction? C'mon, Auntie, get to the point."

Let me tell you everything from the beginning.

I groaned and looked at the clock. It was time to get ready for work, but my aunt's writing seemed hopelessly tedious and covered multiple pages; nothing like the scatterbrained messages she usually sent. It sounded serious, and I didn't want to read it in a hurry.

Reluctantly, I put her letter in my worn-out purse, crammed the box into the closet, and faced the inevitable—the official start of Monday. It was a day when I dragged myself back to a place of brainless activity called work. Forty hours a week felt more like a life sentence, but a grown woman who had bills to pay and a frail mother to take care of couldn't afford to be picky.

After four hours of sleep, my trip to the shower seemed harder than an expedition to the Himalayan Mountains Aunt Lou attempted last year. On the way out, I threw black loose-fitting clothes over my round five-foot-three frame and twisted my flimsy hair into a quick bun. I straightened my oversized glasses and glanced in the mirror. My nose wrinkled at the sight of my pale, tired face with light blue eyes. Nature must have run out of paint when it made me.

"Good enough for a Monday," I told my reflection, then

hurried into the kitchen to brighten my existence with fresh coffee and bacon.

CHAPTER 2

After our stuffy apartment, the frosty air outside was a welcome change. I pulled up the hood of my old jacket and hurried through the puddles that lined the sidewalk.

Spring was exceptionally crummy that year, which, according to my mother, provided an ample supply of various ailments. Under the constant overcast sky, everything looked colorless. The sun tried to break through with some occasional warmth, but stubborn clouds didn't plan to give way. Even in the state of Washington non-stop rains were hard to endure.

At least I don't have to stress over a ruined hair-do or makeup.

To prove the point, I took off my hood and let raindrops sprinkle on my face. A chilly wind made a mess out of my tight bun as I raced to the station and hopped on the tram.

"Hello, Mrs. Jones," I greeted the driver.

"How's your morning, honey?" The woman gave me a warm smile, her bright white teeth contrasted against her dark skin.

After our daily encounters on the tram over the past year, I'd warmed up to the older woman who engaged every regular passenger in conversation. Mrs. Jones had no problem getting into people's private business and had drawn all sorts of confessions from me with ease. She studied me with her deep-set eyes that saw right through my fake cheerfulness.

I shrugged. "All as usual. Mother's not well again."

"Bless your heart, young lady. You oughta take care of yourself too. Wrung out like a sponge, poor thing. I hope you'll have a better day than you had a morning, child."

"Hope so." Blood rushed to my cheeks. Avoiding eye contact with other passengers, I prayed they hadn't overheard the driver's frank comments and moved through the cabin to a single seat in the back.

In some way, Mrs. Jones and her screechy snake of a vehicle had become my respite. Without Mother invading my personal space, I let myself forget reality. During the one-hour commute from the outskirts to Downtown Seattle, my imagination roamed free and lifted me above my dull existence.

I often thought about the time when my plan was to finish a Master's in Education and teach at one of the top schools in coastal California. What would my life look like if I hadn't dropped out of high school and lost the scholarship? I closed my eyes and painted an image I'd seen so many times before. Instantly, the crowded cabin turned into a bright and cozy office. I sat at a desk with stacks of students' homework and my unfinished dissertation for the PhD in Education. Through the large open window, clear sky stretched above the calm ocean. Warm salty air, filled with distant calls of seagulls, rushed into the room and played with the white curtains. A pair of kids, busy with a sandcastle at the nearby beach, caught my attention. Relaxed and content, I watched them for a few minutes until strong arms surrounded me in a familiar hug.

I turned with anticipation but found myself back in the

cold hard seat of the tram, staring at the middle-aged black man in the embroidered shirt and brimless round hat.

"Am I in your way?" He said, shuffling his feet and studying me with a pair of pensive eyes. His weathered face with a short black beard was full of mirth. I shook my head and turned away to hide my embarrassment.

My daydreaming is getting out of hand. I shouldn't do this on public transport or waste my time on it at all.

The temptation to slip back into my imaginary world trampled all logic. To distract myself, I bit into a chocolate bar, doodled on a foggy window, and attempted to study. Aunt Lou's letter in my purse begged to come out, but with so many people breathing down my neck, I couldn't follow her directions to read it alone.

My stop arrived faster than I wanted. After a short walk, I stopped in front of the massive thirty-five story high-rise. The impressive pile of stone and glass reached proudly into the sky. It mocked me with its grandiosity. Once, I considered any job in a place like this an upgrade from the long hours of toil in the retail industry. But after two years, I still saw myself as dispensable, a generic number to fill the gaps and support the important work of others. I pushed those thoughts away, walked past the security guard and joined the crowd.

"Good morning." An attractive man in a business suit smiled at a woman one step ahead of me. He slipped between the two of us and nearly slammed the revolving door in my face.

The story of my life, I thought, stepping into the building. *Dream session's over. Time to go back to reality.*

Squeezed into the elevator with the manicured and perfumed crowd, I stared down at my worn-out flats, stiff and sweaty under the heavy jacket. On the tenth floor, I snuck through the back entrance of Bailey & Partners Law Firm. The swarm of people inside chatted, laughed, got their coffee, talked on the phone, and ran between the offices. I fought my way through the crowd and slipped into my work area. My desk, stuffed into the furthest corner of an open multipurpose area, overflowed with an impressive pile of folders. Even my computer and fax machine were buried under the paper tsunami. Rows of floor-to-ceiling cabinets waited patiently to receive all the displaced files. I addressed my sullen companions with a small curtsy.

"Dusty friends, did you miss me?"

"Grace!"

The sudden harsh tone of my supervisor, Olivia Peterson, interrupted my silly speech. My jaw tightened when a tall, curvy blonde in her mid-thirties stormed to my side and slammed a fat stack of documents on my already overfilled desk. One hand on her hip, Olivia looked me over with open disdain. Was my lack of style too much for her to handle?

"What can I do for you, Miss Peterson?" I peered at her overly plump lips and imagined her inflating them with an air pump.

"I need these reports compiled. Now!" Olivia snapped.

With my eyes focused on the hardwood floor, I shook off the mental picture of my supervisor's trout pout deflating like a balloon.

Focus.

"I'll make sure to get it done first thing this morning," I mumbled.

Put it on top of the million other things I need to finish today.

I took the papers like Cinderella who accepted orders from her evil stepsisters. Only Cinderella never contemplated a few dozen ways to avenge herself as I did at that moment.

"And clean this mess, for goodness' sake." Olivia raised her chin even higher if that was possible, but a fresh Botox injection limited her ability to frown. Not finding anything else to blame me for, she spun around and marched out of my work area. I gravitated towards the mundane work, replaying a few sarcastic remarks in my mind.

Was I expected to have an empty desk on Mondays? The only way to do that was to wish away the paper mountains that my co-workers faithfully built in my corner every Friday afternoon. To clone myself was another option. Our criminal defense law firm was the largest in Seattle, but it had downsized and outsourced most of the support staff. As the only legal filer left, I was destined to become an ancient artifact replaced by a C-3PO droid in the near future.

It wouldn't be that bad if androids took over the world. I would fit right in and maybe even keep my job.

Determined to fight for my rightful place in the workforce, I attacked the mess. While my hands swiftly performed mechanical tasks, the books I recently read and legal concepts I studied for the exam fought for their rightful place in my thoughts. They fascinated me more than the alphabetical order of the filing system. All I wanted was for the day to be over so I could get into my comfy pajamas, finish Aunt Lou's letter, and figure out how to open her present.

"Grace, sweetie," Victoria, the administrative assistant, chirped behind me, instantly filling the air with her sharp perfume.

Startled, I turned around and dropped a stack of files to the floor. The young woman let out a musical laugh. Dressed borderline skimpy, Victoria pushed away her long perfectly straightened copper hair, displaying a flashy set of earrings.

"Oops, sorry I scared you." Her voice was saturated with sweetness, which meant only one thing—she needed something. I adjusted my glasses in preparation for the onslaught.

"Um, would you be a dear and help me with this one super tiny report? I'm like literally drowning. Olivia must be out of her mind to think I can do all these things."

My co-worker lowered her tone to a whisper on the last

sentence. She glanced around and handed me the file with a sappy smile.

"Victoria, you know how busy Mondays are," I said.

"Pretty please." She folded her hands and stuck out her lower lip. The folder was for a recent client of Miles Taylor, the youngest partner at the firm. It drew me like a magnet as if to hold it in my hands would bring me closer to its owner.

"You're superb. I owe you one." Victoria blew me a kiss and skillfully ran off on her high heels as soon as I took the file.

You owe me a couple hundred. When will I learn to say no? I might as well be a secretary myself... if I didn't have to answer the calls. I should at least tell her to stop calling me "sweetie".

Despite my determination to stick to my scope of duties, similar incidents happened with a few more members of the staff who discovered my research and writing skills. Coupled with my pathetic inability to decline frantic requests, I'd become their personal genie on demand with no limit on wishes. But as long as I did everything on time, there was no other reason to pay attention to a quiet file clerk.

Soon, every piece of paper found its place, and every report was put into the hands of the rightful owner. My area was tidy again—just the way I liked it. Despite my tendency to cause unintentional messes, I turned into Mary Poppins's sidekick when it was time to get things organized.

CHAPTER 3

With my work completed by lunchtime, I grabbed my oversized purse and slipped out into the food court. Dining options of all types spanned across the large open foyer of the first floor. The area buzzed with office workers. The smell of smoked barbecue attacked my senses and lured me into the longest line. Over the noise of the crowd, I heard my cell phone's ring. It was my aunt.

"Has the eagle landed?" she asked, half-whispering.

"What?"

"Did you get my package?"

"Yes, but didn't open it yet."

"Make sure you do it soon or it might be too late. And, please, be careful."

She hung up and left a tiny knot in my stomach that dissipated the moment Alicia Bacallao jumped in front of me. It was a relief to see my friend's pleasant face.

"*¡Hola, chica!*" She squeezed me into a tight hug. My nose wrinkled in response. I could never get used to her touchy-feely ways, and she never got tired of bursting my vast personal space bubble. "How's it going?"

I grimaced. "It's Monday."

Alicia ignored my apathetic response and stared at the top of my head. Her hazel eyes narrowed under her long eyelashes. She pushed her cherry red lips into a pout.

"What did you do with your hair?"

Alarmed by the intensity in her voice, a few individuals turned in our direction as if expecting to see green Liberty spikes or an oversized flowery hat. Their interest quickly faded when the spectacle turned out to be a sloppy bun. I shriveled under everyone's glances and picked up an extra cookie.

"It's a new style called 'I don't care about the fancy hair'. The rain would've ruined it anyway. What's the use?"

Alicia dismissed my perfectly sensible excuse with a wave of her manicured hand. "*¡Ay!* And how many times did I tell you not to wear these dreadful clothes of yours? It's like you're Darth Vader's apprentice or something. One of these days, I'll break into your place and throw away all your terrible outfits."

My face twitched as though I'd eaten a lemon, but once Alicia got into her "fix Grace" frame of mind, nothing could stop her.

"We have to work on your mindset," she continued while piling heaps of food on the tray. "*La actitud estodo.* That's what my mother used to say—attitude is everything. You can't hide in these baggy clothes forever."

"I'm not hiding, just being realistic. Nothing fits me. A petite plus-size seems to be an anomaly in the clothing industry. I'm too busy to shop around and, honestly, I don't give a frell."

Alicia cocked her head and stared. She wasn't a sci-fi fanatic like me and hasn't watched *Farscape*, but I wasn't in the mood to explain the terminology. I quickly paid for my lunch and hurried to get away from the curious crowd. Alicia followed me to the lonely little table in the corner.

"I'm sorry. Didn't mean to be so bossy. It's these darn energy drinks, I swear. They wire me up." My friend sat across from me and flapped her thick eyelashes with the most innocent look until the corners of my mouth crept up.

"Fine," I said. "Forget it."

"You know, you have this Drew Barrymore cuteness when you smile," she blurted as though nothing had happened. "We just need to dress up your impressive pair of *tetas* that never see the light of day."

"My what?"

Now it was my turn to take out the dictionary. Alicia put up her hands in defense, her face lit with an impish grin. "All I'm saying, there's nothing wrong with you, *amiga*. A big heart needs to fit into an appropriately-sized body. *¿Comprende?*"

"Your mother said that too?" I gave her a crooked smile.

Alicia clicked her tongue. "Don't make fun of my *mamá*."

Despite our disagreements, my friend had a point. Not a dieting type herself, Alicia wore tight colorful dresses over her full figure. She always looked impressive in high heels, with bright makeup on her olive skin. Her rich auburn curls danced when she walked. I had to admit that next to her, I looked like a gray cloud beside a ray of sunshine.

I sank my teeth into a juicy burger, then picked up the conversation. "Well, I also told you many times not to go shopping until you get paid first. This looks like a spanking new dress. Do I need to break into your purse and take away your credit cards?"

"*Oye*, girlfriend. Don't switch things around. This won't get you off the hook. Plus, I needed this dress. Remember Marcos? The guy I told you about a few weeks ago. He couldn't resist my good looks today and agreed to go out after work. So, my purchase is justified."

She looked at me with self-assured triumph. I stared at

her in disbelief. "You asked him out yourself? Doesn't it need to be the other way around?"

Alicia scoffed while munching on her food. "Oh, forgive me for breaking an etiquette of dating, Miss Ainsworth. Wake up, *chica*. You can't just sit around and wait for a decent guy to fall out of the sky and land on one knee in front of you. You read too many books. If you want something, go and get it. At least try, or you'll never know."

Go and get it... as if it was so simple and easy.

All I ever did was fantasize and ruminate. It was Alicia who'd encouraged me to apply for the open position in the law firm next to the real estate office where she worked as a receptionist. It was hard to argue that sometimes Alicia's methods proved useful, never mind they were mostly about how to get a new purse or a new guy. Her self-confidence was a gulp of fresh air in my stagnant world.

"What are you thinking, Grace, *eh*? You got to talk once in a while. I can't read your mind yet."

"I'm thinking you're right—about trying." I smiled.

"*¡Vaya!*" Alicia exclaimed and clapped. "That's a first."

I gave her a bow of defeat. "I hope you'll have a fabulous date. But let's agree on one thing—on Mondays, you won't say a word about my choice of wardrobe no matter how hideous you think I look. I can't handle any more criticism today."

"Is it that nasty supervisor of yours? Did she get on your case again?" Alicia pointed a fork like a weapon in my direction. "I swear, if you don't stand up to her one of these days, then I will."

"I doubt it'll make her treat me better. But next time I need a bouncer, I'll know where to turn."

Alicia's loud laughter filled the foyer and, for the first time that day, I relaxed enough to join her.

～

I WAS STILL SMILING on the way to the office, imagining Alicia circling around her love interest in the new dress, when I saw *him*. No, not Marcos. I saw Miles Taylor, one of the managing partners at the law firm where I considered myself a humble nobody. The person who caused a hurricane of conflicting emotions inside my chest. The one who'd carved a weak spot in the protective armor around my heart. I wasn't able to stop the disintegration of my defenses no matter how hard I tried. He was the James Bond version of Prince Charming, and I was a very unlucky Cinderella who never went to the ball. Tall, always wearing a well-fitted suit, with his black hair in a perfect wave, he moved with ease and confidence, collecting admiring smiles from the female staff.

I stood in the corner as if in a foggy dream, with everything else blurring away and only one man's handsome face and dark piercing eyes in focus. Spellbound, I stared until Miles's voice with a hint of British accent boomed above all others and jerked me back into reality.

"Hey, Phil. You have the exhibits ready for the Decker's case?"

Phillipe, the young litigation support specialist waved and made his way to the boss. Victoria was not too far behind. She inched herself closer to Miles with a sultry smile.

"I have the papers you asked for," she cooed and handed him the report I'd typed for her earlier.

"Brilliant. You two follow me," Miles Taylor commanded and marched past my hiding spot. No doubt I blended well with the pasty color of the wall. A wave of nausea rose into my throat as the man of my dreams walked by so close, I could touch him. Thankfully, I convinced myself that dumping my lunch on the office floor was not the best way to get the man's attention.

His entourage trotted right behind, Victoria avoiding my eyes. Was her consciousness whispering to her that to present my report as her own wasn't exactly a fair deal?

You're such a coward. A grown woman, but you act like a... like an irrational youth. You have less than minus one thousand chances to ever receive one glance. Why even look at him? You want to get his attention? Go tell him who preps all his paperwork, instead of standing here like a statue. Alicia's right. When will you start living in reality?

But these mental threats were inadequate to persuade me to undertake such radical actions. With my insides in disarray, I swallowed hard and snuck back to my work area. In my haste to get away, I ran into somebody's hard shoulder. The unfortunate individual lost footing, and I watched in horror as the contents of his suitcase spilled over the floor. His companion, lucky enough to escape my rampage, caught my elbow and stood me upright.

"I'm so sorry..." With shaky hands, I reached for a pen that'd rolled in my direction.

Not again! How many things will I knock down today? Maybe I'll set a new record.

"Oh, no. It's not your fault." My savior suppressed a chuckle, increasing my distress. I wanted the floor to open up and swallow me. "My friend should be the one to apologize. We got too distracted trying to find our way around and didn't see you."

Nobody sees me. I must disappear from time to time into another dimension. That would actually be handy right now.

The stranger studied me with a curious stare, and, unfortunately, I had nothing to hide behind. Men in general made me uncomfortable, especially good-looking ones, and he definitely fell into that category. Broad-shouldered, he towered over me like a mountain.

"I told you, Jamal, these law offices are dangerous places." The man winked at me and elbowed his companion.

His lanky friend fixed his glasses and continued to gather the rest of his belongings in silence. He was clearly not in the mood to joke after colliding with a klutz like me.

Unfazed by the lack of input, the stranger continued good-naturedly. "Well, since we had the pleasure of running into you—literally—may we ask for a small favor?"

I lowered my eyes, bothered by the laughter that still danced in the man's blue eyes, but felt obligated to cooperate after the chaos I'd created.

"Yes, of course," I mumbled.

"Would you point us to the office of Mr. Bailey? We have an interview with him, and I'm afraid we're late." His voice mellowed, but I refused to look up.

"Yes, of course," I repeated like a parrot. Breaking out of my stiff stance, I took the men to the right place and slipped away, chased by a cheery "thank you".

At least somebody thought this whole thing was amusing.

I returned to my duties, catching frequent glimpses of Miles while I worked. Even the awkward incident hadn't swayed my preoccupation with the man. This threat against the rationality I tried to achieve in my life was even worse than my daydreaming on the tram. It trampled all logic to the ground. Even the emergency stash of candies I pulled out of my desk failed to create a diversion. But I knew what could help. I took a short break from my duties, sat on the floor between the file cabinets and opened Aunt Lou's letter.

Let me tell you everything from the beginning, my aunt wrote, *I am passing to you a family tradition.*

As you already know, our roots go back to the Zaporozhian Cossacks, a free commonwealth community in Eastern Europe.

They often raided Tatars to loot and free the Slavic people taken into captivity. As the legend goes, after Cossacks attacked a wealthy port on the coast of the Ottoman Empire, one of the officers fell in love with the daughter of a Jewish merchant who traveled through the area. He married her and took her home.

The young woman insisted on bringing along a mysterious jewelry box. She told her husband it contained gifts from God.

Heels clicked on the wooden floor near my hiding spot. I leapt to my feet, slipped the letter into my pocket, and returned to filing.

CHAPTER 4

The rest of the afternoon flew by without any unfortunate encounters. The only thing that kept me excited was the anticipation of digging into Aunt Lou's mysterious box. I itched with curiosity, eager to open the gift that'd been passed through generations. Part of me wondered what her warning on the phone could have meant. At that moment I was still blissfully unaware of the week-long roller-coaster of bizarre events that waited for me around the corner.

By the end of the day, I'd organized my work area to perfection once again. On my way out, a group of my female co-workers gathered around the announcement board and filled the hallway with excited chatter. I got closer and caught my breath. "Paralegal Specialist" was written in big letters at the top of the section for new positions.

"This job opening is to replace Miles Taylor's assistant," Victoria said with an air of superiority. "I overheard it yesterday—old goose Mrs. Thomson gave her notice."

She was always the first to get the wind of things and reminded me of the fox from the fables.

"Time to move over and make room for the younger

ladies," one woman shot out and the group burst out laughing.

"Well, if anybody qualifies for this job, it's me," Victoria announced with a self-assured smile. "If he needs something right away, he always asks me first."

Others protested, but their voices trailed off when I bolted out with my hands clenched tightly over my frayed purse strap. Gasping for air, I ran out into the hallway. Victoria's little speech stung more than I was willing to admit. She planned to use my skills as her ticket to the promotion and it was all my doing.

How could I be so stupid? I've sabotaged myself once again.

I slowed my steps and attempted to subdue the frustration before facing my friend James Chan, an accountant from the firm next door. Over the last six months it'd become our little tradition to walk out together after work. What started as Alicia's attempt to send me on a blind date with her co-worker's brother, ended up as a comradery against their schemes to destroy our peaceful state of singlehood. To get his sister and my friend off our case, we'd pretended to date but bonded over science fiction.

"How was the worst day of your week?" he asked with an all-knowing half smile, his slender frame leaning against the wall. I must have told him at one point how I hated Mondays.

"Amazingly dull." I hid my disappointments behind a playful tone.

With exaggerated gallantry, James offered his arm and led me to the elevator like a princess at the reception ball. My lack of royal upbringing showed itself when I tripped trying to keep up with his strides. I laughed at my own clumsiness.

"Don't ever invite me to a dance. It won't end well for both of us."

James chuckled. "We'll definitely be safer playing a game

of chess. But I bet right now you don't have time for either. How's your final week of school?"

I grimaced and pushed the elevator button. "Well, last night I dozed off while reading *Criminal Law.* And that's after three cups of coffee! But since I slept with my textbooks, I hope all the important information transferred into my brain by osmosis."

"You'll do fine. One thing I don't understand—why don't you study for something else? You're capable of so much more."

I looked up into his soft brown eyes. "Oh, no. Don't read my mind. It's freaky. That's exactly what I thought this morning—or I should say, tried not to think about."

"Well… and?" James let me enter the elevator first and turned to face me.

"What? You know I can't afford to continue my education —my sister Jules is in school. Paralegal certificate is the best I can do right now. It's the only chance I've got to move up at the firm. Plus, I'm using my hard-won associate that took four long years to complete."

James frowned. "As a paper pusher?"

"Hey, at least I push important papers." I glanced at him over the top of my glasses and arched one eyebrow. "It might not be ideal, but I need the money, and right now I make more than a teacher's assistant."

We stepped outside. I shivered from the cold wind and zipped up my jacket. James stood by me with arms crossed, determined to finish our conversation even if it was fifty below.

"It sounds like you're trying to convince yourself. I heard paralegal jobs are hard to get. Don't look at me like that. I did some research."

"Thanks for giving me the cold hard facts of life! I'm already freaking out that communication skills are part of the job description. I love to dig up the laws and type reports but to talk to clients…"

"You can practice on me. I just need to think of a crime to commit. I could pretend to not file taxes or something."

I laughed. "Thanks, Goodie James. That's the worst you can think of?"

I paused for a second, deciding if I should tell him about the job opening, but he noticed my hesitation.

"Spill the beans."

"There is a new posting at my firm for a paralegal job." I wrung my hands. "Don't know if I qualify, but if they don't hire me, nobody else will."

"Apply. It's worth the risk. Make it a calculated risk, and it will all work out. Take the word of an accountant for it."

"Well, if you say so." I let out an exaggerated sigh of resignation and pulled him along toward the parking lot.

James had mastered the skill of playing to my logical side. He could convince me of anything, but one thing he hadn't been able to change my mind about was to think of him as more than a friend. Early thirties, with thick dark hair always neatly combed to the side and cashmere pullovers covering his dress shirts, he oozed stability and comfort. We were alike in so many ways, but my love interests constantly landed way above my league. Was that why I was still alone?

I'D NEVER LET James drive me home no matter how many times he insisted. I put him in his Toyota Camry, said my goodbyes, and crossed the street to the tram station. Suddenly, the back of my neck tingled and my spine tensed. I turned around and caught a stranger's eyes on me, but he disappeared into the crowd of people who were all in a rush to get home. Was my aunt's warning getting into my head?

She wouldn't put me in danger, would she?

While being squashed in the overfilled tram, I thought about what she had said on the phone. Louise had no problem taking risks. Years ago, I heard family rumors about her recruitment by either the CIA or the FBI. Nobody knew for sure what she did for work. Aunt Lou had always called herself an "international relations specialist". Though she was an attractive woman, she'd never married and didn't have any kids, but seemed to be happy with the life she'd chosen. How I wished to have her bravery. On this day more than ever, I needed to hear her say: "Grace, you can do anything. Seize your moment."

Maybe learning about my heritage will give me enough of a confidence boost to apply for the new job.

An hour later, I was in front of our apartment building. The rain had stopped and even let pale rays of the setting sun peek through a thick wall of heavy clouds. Mr. Kent, our new next-door neighbor, greeted me at the mailbox.

"How's your mother?" he asked. I gave him a short civil response, but my tight-lip smile and tired expression didn't encourage any further conversation. I wanted to ask how he'd met my mother who hardly, if ever, stuck her nose outside. Instead, I pulled out a stack of bills and headed home.

When I entered, Mother was at the dining table. By the looks of it, she was in full-fledged sulking mode and awaited a captive audience. Unfortunately, I was the only listener available, and her stage was our tiny kitchen with once-white cabinets and countertops the color of swamp water. Her ash-blond hair was full of disorganized curlers that matched the worn-out beige tablecloth perfectly. She'd given up the blankets but was still in her favorite hot pink nightgown with her makeup half-done. Taking care of herself was no longer on her list of priorities. Everything else had fallen off the list too, including my sister and me, but that was harder to understand or forgive.

We're like two discounted shoes, I thought when I caught her exasperated gaze.

"These constant rains are making me sick," she announced, squashing my hopes of a peaceful evening with Aunt Lou's letter. I braced myself for another crisis to solve.

Once my mother convinced herself of a new ailment, nobody could talk her out of it. Even doctors, therapists and naturopaths gave in and prescribed various treatments that turned into a continuous stream of bills.

"You should rest. I'll make dinner," I suggested. "Go to bed earlier."

"I just got out of bed! You want me to spend all my life there? Why do I bother explaining things? You'll never understand."

Nevertheless, "explaining" is exactly what Mother proceeded to do, giving me a full account of her worries. The evening dragged on while I fulfilled requests and listened to a list of new medical complaints that sounded like a lesson in epidemiology mixed with the latest episodes of *Grey's Anatomy*. Even the grilled cheese and hot chocolate I made for her didn't improve her mood. No matter what I did, the root of the problem was always beyond my reach.

A few hours later, I tucked her in bed with a pile of flu remedies nearby and sunk into a pink antique chair, pretending it was a throne. By the time I solved all the problems in my imaginary kingdom and completed a few quests for the holy grail of patience, my mother was sound asleep.

CHAPTER 5

Finally free, I went back to my room and took out my stash of snacks. Wrapped in a blanket, I climbed into bed with Aunt Lou's letter. My heart made a drum roll when I started to read.

The box contains gemstones of Light. After reaching maturity, the eldest daughter in each generation is honored with the gift. On her twenty-fifth birthday, she chooses one gemstone that will determine the course of her destiny.

The responsibility is transferred to you now. I cannot answer any "why" or "how" questions. There is no explanation. I know that you have a very inquisitive mind, but this time you just have to trust me and receive this as a blessing.

In this box, you'll find the gems that haven't been retained by the previous owners. Try as many as you like, but decide what to do with them before you turn twenty-five. Choose carefully. This can change your life forever. Read the translated instructions on how to keep and pass on this legacy.

I dropped a potato chip and gaped at the words in front of me. "What?! I'll be twenty-five in a week! Oh, Auntie, did you send this package from space? Why did you give me such short notice if it was so important?"

I bit my nails instead of the snack but returned to the letter.

Many women in our family line used this opportunity to make a difference in the world. They were spies during the war, great inventors, political figures, financial gurus, travelers. Some gave up these unique destinies to be good wives and mothers. The choice is yours. All I ask of you is to try.

Please, keep the gems secure and away from prying eyes. Stay safe and don't share this knowledge with anybody else. I can't emphasize this enough, but I trust your sound judgement.

Gracie, you are like a daughter to me. I wish you the best, and may all of your dreams come true.

Yours always,

Louise.

The letter was dated four years earlier. I'd turned twenty-one then. What had stopped her from sending it?

I wish she was more straightforward. She could've just called it a nice tale to pass along... but that wouldn't be Aunt Lou.

There was nothing else to do but to open the gift and see what sort of familial treasure it hid. I retrieved the wooden box, studied the unique design, and turned it around, but once again did not find a way to get in. After struggling for a few minutes, I finally noticed a hidden keyhole. The small golden key with a trefoil handle my aunt had sent me fit right in. My heart pounded in the stillness of my room. I held my breath and turned the key. The top of the box popped up, then one side separated and revealed ten drawers. I pulled one out and counted twenty-five smaller compartments, each with a lid, a golden symbol, and a small handle.

The writing must be in a foreign language.

I examined the strange marks, then pulled one of the

handles and opened the lid. The fragrance of orange and ginger hit my nostrils. Red silk lined up the empty interior. I opened a few more sections, but they were empty as well.

What would I need this for? I don't have any jewelry to keep in this box.

My excitement dwindled until I unlocked a larger drawer at the top. It enclosed a weathered hardcover booklet labeled "Guidance".

This will clarify things... I hope.

I carefully turned the thin yellowed pages filled with pictures of pendants and short descriptions in different languages. The first paragraph instructed the owner to wear these jewelry pieces next to the skin and only one at a time. Other writings contained information on how to use the special powers of the stones.

The carrier of the gift must learn to accept and become one with the stone. If she resists, takes the gem off, or puts another one on at the same time, it will result in a gradual loss of power. The carrier can change out the stones until she makes the final choice that becomes her destiny.

"Whatever that means," I muttered under my breath but kept reading until I got to the last page with instructions on how to keep the gem's ability forever and how to pass the treasure on. Since my only way to contact Aunt Lou was through her P.O. Box, I was at the mercy of her sporadic phone calls. There was nothing left to do but to follow her written request and try on the pendant.

Is it like a birthstone? A nice little tradition, I guess. Maybe it will help me get more confidence for the interview.

I looked at the drawers again. The symbols on the lids matched the Hebrew writings of the manual.

It must be in the original language. First owner?

I leafed through the book and found the corresponding

English translation: "strength", "beauty", "empathy", "hearing", "sight". The last two seemed unusual. Who would want a gem like that? "Flexibility", "intangibility", "flight", "fire", "healing".

It all sounded strange. I scrolled through the pages to find a description of the stone that caught my attention.

BEAUTY

יְפִי

(Jacinth)

Harmony of the body, a balanced composition that makes an outer appearance pleasant to the sight, an irresistible charm, a good taste, charisma, elegance, ability to navigate social interactions with ease and to cause an attraction to happen.

I smirked. If the stone represented the person who wore it that was not the one for me. Everybody always considered my sister the cutie of the family. Even my mother had a certain glamor in her appearance and was a real stunner before the divorce had crushed her. I looked more like my father and loathed our resemblance. At times I wondered if the person in charge of destinies had short-changed me. Did I come last in line to beauty, success, and happiness when all the supplies ran out?

But for some strange reason, my aunt favored me over my adorable and chatty sibling. Loud and energetic, Aunt Lou always threw me into the center of attention and showered me with encouraging words. "Gracie, one day you'll grow up to be an exceptional woman," she used to tell me at every opportunity. "You'll do great things. Remember that."

Oh, Auntie, I wasted my whole childhood listening to your fairytales. Look at me now. Why do you put ideas into my head again? You just make real life harder to digest.

I noticed the clock and gasped. It was almost ten. No time to play with useless decorations. Quickly, I found the lid that matched the Hebrew symbols for the Beauty stone and opened it. The jewelry piece was in its rightful place. It was fascinating to look at—an oval transparent stone about one inch in diameter with an orange-red tint. I rubbed my finger over its cool multifaceted surface and turned it over. The gem was set into the silver base with delicate branches and leaves that enclosed it on the sides.

If I was beautiful, things would've been so much easier. I should at least try this pendant on. Aunt Lou will surely ask if I followed her instructions.

I took the sparkling ornament out of the drawer and, after digging up a small silver chain from my sister's room, hung it on my neck. I had never worn even a simple necklace before, but the intricate piece of jewelry rested against my chest like it belonged there. Why was I already getting attached to this decoration?

There, I've tried it. No need to get personal here. I would never wear something like this. If it has any real value, it'll be nice not to worry about bills for a while. I should stop by the jewelry store tomorrow to find out.

Satisfied with my practical solution for the unusual ordeal, I reached for the necklace clasp to take the pendant off.

"I wouldn't do it if I were you."

Startled, I spun around toward the voice. A tall man stood in front of my bedroom door. He was dressed in a long colorful garment. A blue scarf was wrapped around his head and his face, leaving a pair of eyes to stare me down. I froze, momentarily paralyzed by fear.

"I mean no harm," he said calmly and raised his hand when I was about to scream. My voice seemed to die in my throat. I looked around for something that could be used as a weapon and grabbed my lamp.

The stranger chuckled at my frantic efforts. "You don't want to hurt me. Not that you can. My name is Bongani, and I am here to warn you."

"How…" I stuck my shaky finger in his direction, wanting to know how he got into my room.

"Questions later," he replied.

Great, now he sounds like my aunt.

But this oddly dressed man with piercing eyes was nothing like Aunt Lou. And if he wasn't my long-lost relative, he had no business standing in my bedroom swaddled in a blanket.

"I am here with a proposition," he continued. "You can either follow your aunt's advice or give the pendants to me."

So, he does know her!

"Yes, I know Louise," he said, as if reading my thoughts. "I figured you'd be as stubborn as she is."

He folded his arms, still blocking my door. My knees were getting weak, but I clenched the lamp tighter and peered at the man. This whole situation seemed surreal. Was I already asleep and seeing a dream?

"Did my aunt send you?" I wheezed, glancing around for my phone to call 911 in case she didn't.

"Let's just say we're both after the same thing." He took a step forward, and his eyes lit up like liquid gold. Their glare made me shiver and retreat closer to the opposite wall. "Now, listen to me, Grace. You're either going to wear the gems or hand them over to me. You can try to discover your destiny, but if you fail and miss your timing, everything will be lost. It might be more than you bargained for. Are you sure you're ready to be responsible for the safety of the gifts?"

"Who are you?" I managed to stammer. "Why would I trust you?"

"You'll find out soon enough. So, what's your decision?"

"I'm not giving you anything," I said, raising the lamp higher.

"Take the pendant off, and we'll see," the stranger murmured.

I looked down at the gem on my chest. When I raised my eyes again, the man was gone. It took a few minutes to regain my ability to think. Finally, I put the lamp back on the table and peeked out of my bedroom, then made sure our front door was locked. Our apartment was quiet. Nothing was out of place.

What in the world was that! First, a package, then a stranger in my room. What would be next? An elephant from Africa?

I took a big breath in and shook my head, but decided to keep the necklace on. Apparently, I was now bound to have these things hang around my neck all week long. I didn't want to give that man a reason to return. But why wasn't he able to just take Aunt Lou's treasure from me?

My nerves were too unglued to study and too wired up to let me sleep. To distract myself and calm down, I sorted through the day's mail. My mother's chiropractor's office sent us the final notice, and another collection letter came for "the miracle remedy" she ordered a year ago. Medical charges, rent, utilities, and a partial payment of my sister's tuition not covered by financial aid usually took the bulk of my paycheck. Even with my mother's meager salary from her part-time job at the thrift store, I wasn't able to pay for everything and still buy groceries.

I got up and turned on my ancient computer. My work page took a few minutes to load. I scrolled to the new job openings and looked over the qualifications for the paralegal assistant. Would they even consider me? And how would I manage to work with Mr. Hottie without burning alive or turning into a blubbering mess? No matter how hard I tried, I couldn't imagine myself next to Miles Taylor. Why would he ever want an assistant like me to stomp around, knock into his office furniture, and embarrass him in front of clients? Victoria would definitely fit that role better, but I winced at the thought.

Miles doesn't need a pretty assistant but a competent one. Mrs.

Thomson was no model. He is smart and knows what's best for his practice. All I have to do is prove to him I can perform the job well.

Doubts bombarded my mind, but I pushed them aside, filled out the form, and sent it before I could change my mind. I had to try. It was my ticket out of financial struggles. Exhausted but hopeful, I got ready for bed. Every slight sound in the house startled me, bringing back memories of the unexpected visitor. After what seemed like hours, I finally fell asleep.

PART II
THE ALLURING LIFE

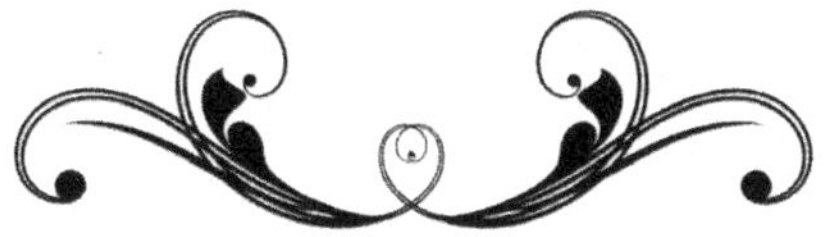

Beauty begins the moment you decide to be yourself.

—Coco Chanel

CHAPTER 6

The rapid beating of a bird's wings against the window woke me early on Tuesday. It interrupted an unpleasant dream.

I usually sleep hard and don't remember where my mind had traveled during the night, but that morning was different. My consciousness became trapped in a nightmarish vision. I could clearly recall being hopelessly late to a very important appointment, but each step was like a slow crawl through the mud. Gigantic stacks of papers blocked my path, and I could barely climb over them in my long fluffy skirt. Olivia Peterson, dressed as the Red Queen, dumped more obstacles in my way and laughed hysterically. I tripped over the last pile, fell into a hole, and landed in the middle of a large bright room full of nicely-dressed people. They twirled around in a dance but stopped abruptly when I made my sudden appearance. I spotted Miles Taylor, who turned in my direction, leaving his dance partner behind to follow the crowd of people gathered around me. Everyone laughed and pointed. I glanced at myself, appalled to discover that my beautiful dress had turned into a collection of dirty rags.

How silly. I'm petrified by something that's not real.

With my eyes still closed, I lay in bed, drenched in a cold sweat, and waited for the sensation of panic to dissipate. Warm rays of sun rested on my cheek, but I wasn't ready to face the world. I yawned and rubbed my neck. My fingers caught the necklace with the delicate jewelry piece.

That's right. The letter. So odd. These trinkets, family traditions... Did my ancestors have nothing better to do? Now I can't even turn it into money, cause Aunt Lou sent some guy to watch after me. Maybe, I made him up. Ugh. This is too much!

I opened my eyes and watched the bright sunshine slip through my moth-eaten curtains. In the cheerful glow of the morning, even my shabby quarters appeared cozier. I jumped out of the bed with ease and wrestled the window open. Fresh air flew in with the songs of birds. It smelled of wet earth awakened after the long cold winter.

Surprised at my excessive energy, I sprung up to the bathroom only to be startled by my reflection in the mirror.

Something was off.

Leaning over the sink, I wiped the glass, traced the reflection with my fingers, then blinked and jerked back. The person in front of me repeated my movements, but it wasn't me... not exactly.

The more I stared, the faster my heart raced, until it ran out of steam.

This is what happens when I don't get enough sleep—I imagine things... again.

I waited for an explanation that never came. No matter what I did, a radiant young woman confidently glared back at me from the mirror with a healthy glow on her cheeks and brightness in her crystal-clear blue eyes. A lush wave of honey-colored hair fell over her shoulders, as if she'd just finished posing for a shampoo commercial. I stood and stared at my features in her face, afraid to look down to the rest of the body.

"Ok, Grace, you are just having a little... breakdown?" I

whispered. "To wish you looked like that is not enough to make it happen. Your denial of reality went way too far, missy. You can thank your aunt for putting ideas in your head."

I stomped into the bedroom, opened the closet and observed the same delusion in the full-length mirror. Perplexed, I looked down at my legs, peeked under the night-gown, and gasped.

"Holy Sithspit! Son of a Blaster! What in the world…"

The good old *Star Wars* style swearing didn't restore my faulty perception. It seemed the extra weight that I'd carelessly added on and that'd bothered me so much had disappeared into a thin air. If it was really me, then my body had received an overnight upgrade. With curves intact, I now possessed bikini-ready abs and Photoshop quality skin. Models from the magazine covers that usually made me cringe in the grocery line, would've been jealous.

I sat on the carpet and hyperventilated pathetically until my head got dizzy. Wiping my sweaty cold palms, I tried to reason things out.

"Don't worry. There's always an explanation. What if extreme dieting caused me to lose memory and forget a few years of self-starvation? It's not a bad way to go crazy. Think, Grace. Did you eat something strange yesterday? Was the chocolate bar spiked?"

I got up and paced between my bed and the closet, but it became even harder to find logic when I tried to get dressed. My clothes sagged helplessly, and the idea of wearing something so ill-fitting made me queasy. I tried on a few more outfits, but an irresistible inner impulse pushed me to rip my meager wardrobe off the hangers and stuff it into a disposable bag. My mind silently protested against such recklessness. Nevertheless, I couldn't lift a finger to save even my favorite sweatshirt with a large logo on the front: *I'd Rather Be Reading.*

Trembling inside, as if undiluted coffee ran through my veins, I held up the last article of clothing—a simple but elegant cream-colored dress purchased for my first job interview. Despite my inability to squeeze it past my shoulders for years, I'd kept it hidden in my closet as a relic of my once slender form. The idea of putting it on made me chuckle, but that quickly turned into a silent cry when I slipped right in.

"Don't panic," I commanded myself.

I covered the closet mirror with a blanket, but it didn't help. Finely shaped parts of my body constantly came into view when I moved around the room. The possibility of being stuck in the Matrix of an alternative reality seemed less absurd with each passing minute.

With no time to process the sudden change, I mechanically continued to get ready for work. Things got more complicated as the morning went on. Any leftover logic abandoned me when I borrowed my mother's makeup and knew exactly how to put it on. Thankfully, she was too preoccupied to notice and even let me borrow her bracelets, which for some reason became necessary to complete my outfit.

"Take all my jewelry. What's the use. I never go anywhere," she muttered but didn't break eye contact with the TV. Her employer opened the store later on Tuesdays, giving her a chance to watch the morning shows. For once, I was thankful it kept her attention away from the real-life drama I faced at the moment.

Great! I should sell all the jewelry in this house. The funds can go towards my visit to a psychiatrist. Looks like I'll need one soon.

As if injected with a mind-control serum, I proceeded to ransack my sister's closet. Mother insisted that we keep a three-bedroom apartment so Julie could come home to her perfectly intact room during school breaks. My sister didn't visit much, but she'd left behind some of her clothes. I grabbed a colorful scarf, a matching purse, and a pair of shoes with five-inch heels because my comfy flats were deemed unfit to wear. These strange items looked like weapons of mass destruction in my hands.

"How will I walk in these contraptions? I'm either completely nuts or stuck in somebody else's form!" I moaned but obediently slipped into the horrendous stilettos. My body now had a mind of its own.

With the temperatures rising by the minute, I didn't need my hideous jacket. This, unfortunately, didn't save my old companion from the same fate as the rest of the outfits. My intellect protested while my hands put perfectly functional things into a dumpster.

Alicia will do a happy dance around me when I tell her.

INSTEAD OF BASKING in the long-awaited sunshine and enjoying a peaceful stroll on the way to the tram station, I caught the stares of pedestrians. Complete strangers smiled and greeted me, and a few even followed. Such excessive attention from the human race dried my throat and sent my self-consciousness through the roof. Although my uneasiness went no further than the heatwave to my face. With my chin high, back straight, and steps light, I confidently strolled down the street while my higher brain functions tripped over the fact I could walk on the heels at all. Even though these heinous devices had the potential to elevate me to everyone's eye level, I'd always avoided them with passion. Apparently, Tuesday morning was a good day to reverse my lifelong conviction and make me a slave to the necessities of fashion. I was so distracted with my new ability to carry myself that the question of why my vision had improved without glasses didn't cross my mind. It was not until the tram approached the platform, that I realized I'd left them behind in the commotion of the morning.

"Hello, Mrs. Jones," I said, stepping into the cabin. It took the good woman a few moments to recognize me.

"Well, I declare! Look at you, sweetheart," she exclaimed. "You're pretty as a peach! I'm glad you took my advice so seriously yesterday."

I thanked her and moved to my usual seat, contemplating the likelihood of Freaky Friday happening in real life. In the movie mother and daughter exchanged bodies. Since my only parent was still intact in her sulky self, I was left to figure out which unlucky person got my sad form.

Soon my thoughts were interrupted by a steadily growing crowd of male passengers that gravitated in my direction and blocked the flow of people. I stiffened when a few of them tried to get my attention. Throwing weary looks at the invaders of my personal space, I wondered if this was the plight of all pretty people. To become a human magnet wasn't on my wish list, and I breathed a sigh of relief when my stop came into view. Mrs. Jones, on the other hand, couldn't contain her excitement for my sudden popularity. She caught my distraught glances in the rear-view mirror, winked at me eagerly, and gestured her approval.

"The butterfly is finally out of her cocoon," she whispered on my way out, her face spread in one big smile. But at that moment I desperately wished to hide back in that cocoon and never see the light of day again.

My walk to work was no better. When I reached the building, a fine-looking security officer by the entrance jumped to open the door for me.

"Have a good day," he spilled out in one hasty breath.

"Don't work too hard," I replied, startled by my playful response.

At the elevator, a young man stole glances in my direction. When the doors opened, he let me walk in first and pushed the floor buttons with a trembling hand, a lost puppy expression plastered over his face. His eyes traveled to the pair of the nicely shaped legs I now owned.

Can this day get any more awkward? Darn this Barbie body. Although technically I'm not tall enough to qualify... and I do have hips...

Before the doors closed, another person ran in. My elevator neighbor looked disappointed, but I breathed with ease and stopped pulling on my dress. Unfortunately, my celebration was short-lived—the newcomer was my accidental acquaintance from yesterday. Memories of papers flying in different directions filled my mind and put a deeper shade of blush on my already overheated cheeks.

"Thanks for waiting." The man pushed the button and took a relaxed stance by the wall.

Unknowingly, he'd saved me twice, but our first meeting was a blur. Curiosity took over, and I allowed myself to observe him. With my recent five-inch elevation from the ground, he seemed less of a Thor and more of a regular athletic guy. He was casually but tastefully dressed, with chestnut blond hair in disarray and five o'clock shadow over a strong jaw. Catching my gaze, he returned it with a big smile that softened his somewhat rugged features.

"Are you late for another interview?" I asked, surprised by the cheerful tone of my voice and shocked I was talking to him at all. I secretly wished he'd ignore my comment.

"Oh, I'm so sorry. Did we run into each other somewhere?" He gave me a puzzled glance.

"Yes, I literally ran into your friend yesterday."

I laughed. It was a pleasant new sound like a backyard wind chime, not the snort that usually came out of my mouth. The man cleared his throat and stared at me for a few seconds.

"Oh, you must be my guiding angel from that law firm. I am glad you... feel better today. Thanks for showing us around." He smiled again. "I didn't even introduce myself.

My name is Greg Miller. Journalist. I work a few floors above your office."

Darn it, I thought your job was to destroy the evil invaders of the Earth. I scanned the impressive set of muscles under his shirt but thankfully didn't vocalize that thought. Instead, I managed to make a few less obnoxious statements and even joked about my "illness" and his tardiness. How he'd made a connection between the pasty creature in baggy clothes and the colorful shiny being currently in possession of my body was beyond my understanding.

Well, makeup and nice clothes can do wonders. What if yesterday was my "woke up with a headache" look. More like woke up with a massive allergic reaction.

"Being late is a bad habit of mine, but I promise to fix it for you," my new acquaintance said before I exited the elevator. He stretched out his hand to shake on it.

"Don't make promises you can't keep," I teased and strolled out like a model on the runway.

Instead of being confined to the imaginary catwalk, I wanted to jump and skip around like a little girl. At that moment even stilettos couldn't stop me. To shed all my extra weight in one night was in itself a good enough reason to do a few somersaults. Was it really me? Just a day earlier, I'd avoided all eye contact with people, and now I'd managed to have a light conversation with a complete stranger. I touched my neck and followed the silver chain to a pendant under my dress.

Are you doing this? Are you the one that changed me into this ridiculously attractive humanoid?

The idea seemed absurd, but there was no other explanation.

I shouldn't try to figure this out. I should just enjoy this, even if it's only a dream. But what will I say at work?

My heart squeezed inside my chest once again.

CHAPTER 7

Despite my inner worries, this new Grace was determined to come through the front entrance of our firm instead of crawling through the back door like usual. I walked past the glass entry and looked around noticing, for the first time, that our office space was bright and tastefully decorated. At least I worked at a place that looked nice.

My heart skipped a beat after I passed the reception area and walked through the main hallway. That morning I didn't keep my eyes glued to the floor to study the carpet and its various patterns that were already etched in my memory. Instead, with my head high, I greeted my co-workers and to my surprise found a lot of friendly faces. I felt like a Hollywood star on the red carpet. Puzzled glances and smiles followed me to my work desk, but with so much turnover of the support staff, nobody questioned a replacement of the file clerk.

Out of the few who recognized me, Olivia Peterson seemed the most shocked. She handed me the papers with her mouth half open. My new self-assured demeanor and radical change of appearance must have rendered her speechless. Not that I minded.

I started my work as usual, only the day refused to fit into the normal routine and put my unprepared mind into overdrive. Within an hour I caught Frederick Bailey, the founding lawyer of our firm, amidst an angry fit, his face as red as a boiling kettle. All the silly cartoons I watched in my childhood ran through my memory and I found a few matches.

"Do I have to do everything myself?" he roared, loud enough for the entire office to hear.

People scattered, but instead of hiding in the furthest corner, I found myself next to my raging boss.

Mind your own business, Grace, I told myself, but it was too late.

"Mr. Bailey, you definitely hold this place together, but we're all happy to help." My honey-drenched voice came out before I could bite my tongue. This new Grace was out of control.

Mr. Bailey looked at me with surprise. The deep lines on his forehead cleared. A short, overweight man in his fifties with a receding hairline and a white perfectly trimmed beard, he appeared relatively benign close-up.

"Mr. Bailey, what can I do for you? I promise we'll get it all fixed." I took him by the arm and smiled pleasantly, sheltering his paralegal assistant, Mrs. Williamson, from his furrowed gaze. The woman that'd triggered his distress appeared lost for words. With grayish-blond hair and an amiable face, she resembled a younger but less upbeat version of Betty White. I liked her instantly and even gave her a conspiratorial wink.

A few minutes later, this strange new person that invaded my body calmed the storm with compliments and a hot cup of coffee. To everyone's relief, after a short investigation, the misplaced report was retrieved.

"That's much better," Mr. Bailey said. He took the papers and smiled in my direction. "Watch and learn, Mrs. Williamson."

Not in the least upset with my interference, Mrs. Williamson thanked me heartily behind the closed doors and promised to return the favor.

"It's getting hard for me, dear. My memory for things is not as good as it used to be," she confided. "Don't think badly of Mr. Bailey. He is a nice man, but he likes things well-organized."

I offered to help whenever possible and got the woman so excited about it, she taught me a few things right away and even shared her stash of candy.

The rest of the morning proceeded with an unusual number of visits to my humble work area. Male representatives of our office staff suddenly found themselves in need of various documents. At first, I suspected the migration was due to Mrs. Williamson's chocolates on my desk but quickly realized the true cause. Men lingered longer than necessary, asked about the weather and other irrelevant topics. Even Olivia, no doubt burning with curiosity, ventured in my direction and gave me a silent once-over.

My capacity for daily human interactions soon maxed out. So many conversations with individuals who were not my close friends should have drained me, but I seemed to enjoy myself and listened intently to the smallest and silliest details others shared. Finding subjects to talk about was no longer hard work. I asked the right questions and watched with amazement how people eagerly opened up about themselves. My interest grew. I observed myself as though from a distance, the whole ordeal taking a flavor of a wacky science experiment.

Do they want to talk to me or this charming woman who's taken over my life without asking permission? She sure is delight-

ful. I pondered this question as I listened to a young man who came to ask for another document he didn't need.

Despite the distractions, I finished my work on time and left for lunch. I walked around the corner and suddenly found myself face-to-face with Miles Taylor. My heart did a triple flip inside my chest and hid somewhere in my left heel.

"Alright?" His soft baritone spread like honey through my veins.

He looked pleasantly surprised by our abrupt meeting, and since it was too late to turn in a different direction, I lingered and soaked in his presence. Proximity to that man and his fresh woody scent made my thoughts hazy, but my body was in an obvious discord with the rest of my person. Instead of trembling like a dry leaf on a windy day, I boldly offered him my hand with an elegant gesture. Openly meeting his gaze, I smiled and said in a pleasant voice:

"Mr. Taylor. So nice to see you today. You're looking exceptionally well."

No, you look unacceptably well, and I'm seriously considering passing out.

My thoughts raced but my lips held a charming smile. To my astonishment, he returned it with a satisfactory grin that caused strange sensations in the pit of my stomach.

"Thank you. You look lovely yourself." He kept his inquisitive dark eyes on me as he squeezed my hand.

My insides melted like plastic in an oven when he pressed my fingers into his warm palm and held them captive. Despite my mind becoming unhinged, I wished him a successful day at the office and gracefully escaped down the hall followed by his gaze.

Can I scream now?

Afraid I might combust if I kept it all inside a minute longer, I rushed to the lobby. I urgently needed to talk to somebody about what was happening to me.

Alicia.

In the main foyer, I caught a glimpse of my reflection on the glass wall. It was hard to believe that the dazzling shapely blonde who strode happily across the hall with a carefree smile on her bright lips was me. No matter how much I wanted to run to our regular meeting place, I kept a steady pace, still in awe of my high-heel-walking ability. This new Grace wouldn't let me have my way, but slowly I started to appreciate her choices. If the bizarre experience of that day made Miles Taylor notice me, it was worth losing my mind over.

In the cafeteria, I spotted Alicia and snuck up behind her. "Boo!"

"*¡Ay, Dios mío!* That's not..." My friend stopped in mid-sentence when she turned around and took one good look at me. Frozen in half motion, she dropped her jaw and her big hazel eyes blinked uncontrollably. I laughed.

"*¡Oh, vaya!* Is this the end of the world?" She finally said. "Did aliens kidnap my friend and replace her body? Am I in a dream? Who is this creature?"

"I've already considered all of these options, but unfortunately, it's still a mystery. We have to sit down before I tell you anything, or I'll have to scoop you off the floor, and it won't be an easy task." I grinned.

"You can't joke about my weight looking like this," Alicia complained with an exaggerated whimper.

We tried to find a quiet spot to talk and picked a bench outside. The weather was still nice, and a crowd of people spilled onto the sidewalk in hopes of absorbing some vitamin D—a sure deficit in Washington State. A few more degrees above fifty and men would go shirtless.

Alicia shooed away a few guys that wanted to join us, took a bite of her taco, and looked at me expectantly.

I hesitated, remembering my aunt's warning. "I don't know if I'm allowed to tell you."

"*¿Por qué?* I'm ecstatic for you. How many times did I tell you to take care of yourself? Did you see a plastic surgeon, a beautician, and a stylist at the same time?" She said in one breath.

"I haven't seen anybody." I laughed. "I'm not sure you would even believe me."

I pulled the pendant from under my dress and let it glimmer in the sun for a moment, but slipped it back when a few eyes turned in our direction.

"*¡Oh, madre mía!* Such a beautiful stone. Why did you hide it? You should show it off."

My friend's eyes lit up with delight. She was all about sparkly things. I looked around with caution and shifted uncomfortably, still sensing someone's gaze on me. Was it my visitor from the night before? The thought made me frown.

"Please, keep it down, Allie," I hushed her. "I have to wear it next to my skin or it won't work. A shorter chain—"

"A bigger cleavage! *Chica*, I'm glad you finally figured out how to show off your assets, but such a big change! What happened?"

"I don't know. I'm in shock myself. It's all so sudden and so unreal. Not sure what to make of it."

I chewed my lower lip, but the desire to share was too strong. After making Alicia swear on her mother and grandmother to keep the secret, I told my friend all about my aunt's letter and the jewelry box. She sat quietly for a minute and drank her soda.

"Well, here's what I think. If after wearing an amulet, you turned into this, who cares why or how it happened! If your aunt asked me to carry a dead skunk in my purse or take a plunge in the Ganga River, I wouldn't hesitate. You've got to be *loca* not to keep this."

"Allie, you already look great," I interrupted.

She gave me a warm smile. "I can't complain, but we're talking about you, girlfriend. *¡Eres muy bonita!* I almost peed my pants when I saw you. You can't let this chance pass you by."

I touched the gemstone on my chest. "But why me? I've done nothing to earn this. Didn't do a single squat. It's almost not fair."

"Nonsense! Stick your Robin Hood tendencies in… somewhere far away and enjoy your life for once. Trust me, you needed this makeover more than others. Real or not, take all you can from it. Try everything your infamous fairy godmother of an aunt told you to try. I bet she spied on you and saw that without supernatural interference things can't be helped. I wish she'd sent this thing earlier. She would've saved me lots of grief."

It was exactly what I needed to hear. I let out a big sigh and gave my friend a hug. "Thank you, Allie."

"Oh, boy, free hugs today too? Is it part of the extreme makeover?"

Alicia often called me *erizo* or hedgehog, but my alter ego had crossed the touchy-feely threshold with ease.

"You deserve a hug." I gave her a quick smile. "The funny thing is that I looked down on pretty women, and now I'm stuck in one of these bodies. Payback time, I guess. I still think that smarts are more important than good looks."

"*Chica*, one doesn't exclude the other. Take me for example."

Alicia flashed me a cocky smile and proceeded to ask a dozen more questions about what I found in the mysterious box. We concluded that I should take full advantage of the peculiar family inheritance. Preoccupied with my transformation, Alicia even forgot to tell me about her date the night before. She let me go only after I promised to keep her informed.

I had finished my work a little earlier than usual with the help from my newfound friend, Mrs. Williamson. Thankful I saved her from Mr. Bailey's rampage, she refused to leave my side. Victoria also hovered nearby and pestered me with questions about my stylist. A few other people persisted in seeking my company and even offered to give me a ride back home, which I politely declined. With my things gathered, I headed to the front reception area. No more sneaking out of the back door. In the hallway I bumped into Victoria. She was chatting with another legal secretary, Maria.

"I heard they're going through the candidates within the office first." Victoria stopped as soon as she saw me. Her lips curved into a half-smile. "Here's our Wonder Woman. Isn't she a stunner today? Fooled us all."

"Thank you," I said calmly.

"Are you applying for a new position with Mr. Taylor too?" Maria asked.

"Actually, I am. Just in time to use my paralegal certificate."

Victoria's plump lips stretched into a thin line. She

crossed her arms and looked me over. "Oh, I see. That's what the sudden transformation's for? How much dough did you shell out for this? Pretty looks ain't everything, you know. Mr. Taylor needs someone with experience. Like me."

"Yes, *sweetie*, pretty looks are *not* everything. His assistant needs to have a brain too," I said before I could catch myself. "Good day, ladies."

A perplexed expression spread over the young woman's face, but I walked away before my words had a chance to sink in.

Looks like Beauty has teeth too!

James was held up with a work project and couldn't meet me on the way out, but Alicia was already waiting outside. We agreed to go shopping after work to replenish my vandalized wardrobe. Before I could escape, Greg met me in the main hallway. He paced by the front entrance of the firm, but stopped and moved in my direction when he spotted me. His lengthy strides quickly covered the distance.

"We're closed, and Mr. Bailey already left for the day. I can find out when he'll be at the office tomorrow," I said, confused by his overwrought appearance. Had he missed another meeting with my boss?

"Oh, no. I'm all done interviewing him. Actually, I hoped to speak with you. If you're not busy that is." He ran a hand through his unruly hair.

I held his gaze trying to read the expression on his pleasant face. Was the stone affecting him too? "Sorry, my friend's waiting. We have plans."

"Would you have a cup of coffee with me afterward? Unless you're tied up all evening. It won't take much of your time, I promise. Just a few questions for my article."

I breathed a sigh of relief. So it was for his work. "Not sure how I can help."

"We want to interview people who play different roles in

the office. I already asked Mr. Bailey for permission to do that."

"Ok then, but it'll be a few hours," I said, mentally kicking myself for agreeing. Couldn't he interview somebody else?

"That's the nature of my job." He smiled and handed me his business card. "Call me when you're free. I'll wait and try to catch a few more of your co-workers in between."

Jump in front of an angry boss, go out with a stranger... What else is on my agenda for today?

My attempt at mockery had no power over the spontaneous, social woman that'd held me hostage all day. She conspired to ruthlessly break through all the limits of my comfort zone and march across my safeguards like an army of elves. Not able to resist her, I put his card in my purse.

I called my mother to make sure she was doing well and to tell her I was coming home later than usual. After meeting up with Alicia, I headed to the stores nearby. My friend's eyes grew large when she saw the clothes and accessories I'd picked. Within a short hour, my radical improvement in taste convinced her I was truly under a magic spell. I couldn't agree more. My heart squeezed uncomfortably inside my chest when my one and only credit card passed from my hand to the cashier. My mind quickly calculated how many months it would take to pay off the debt, but that didn't stop the catastrophe. Although, according to Alicia, having nothing to wear was the only true disaster.

"Mission impossible is finally accomplished," my friend proclaimed when we walked out with several new outfits and other accessories that tagged along.

Alicia left and I texted Greg. It started to drizzle, and I moved under the covered area by the front entrance. A minute later, a yellow Chevy Camaro stopped by the curb. Greg came out, opened the passenger door, and waved.

"There's a nice coffee shop nearby," he said when I got closer. "I hope you don't mind if we take my car."

"As long as it doesn't transform into a giant robot."

I laughed, all the while reassuring myself that this agreeable young man couldn't possibly be a hitman.

If he is, at least I'll die pretty. Plus, I can't walk around with all these bags.

Any discomfort I might have felt quickly dissipated at a small café a few minutes from our work. Dim lighting and quiet music in the background matched well with the heavenly smell of coffee. I ordered a piece of cheesecake with my cappuccino, deciding that a few extra carbs wouldn't hurt my magically perfect body. Greg stepped in to pay despite my protests. We sat at the corner table and chatted away. Looking up after a big bite of the velvety cheesecake, I caught his gaze. The man studied me, his tall form stretched out on the chair, indigo eyes full of merriment like the day before.

"So refreshing to see a girl not on a diet. A rarity these days," he said.

I managed a nervous chuckle but made a mental note to watch my calorie intake in the future. Good looking or not, a little self-control wouldn't hurt. But for one evening I wanted to enjoy myself.

"I thought we came here to talk about law firms, not the meal choices of modern women," I said with a smirk and took another mouthful of my favorite treat.

"My bad. I need to learn to hold my tongue. Another one of my terrible habits. At this rate, you'll soon know all my weaknesses." He flashed a wide smile and showed off a row of perfect teeth. "So, tell me about your work?"

"My work?" I echoed, recoiling on the inside.

"Don't worry. It's confidential. You can be honest."

What could I tell him about my work? I didn't do anything important or interesting. Today was probably the only exception. To rescue Mrs. Williamson was the highlight of my two years at the firm. Greg must've read hesitation on my face.

"I should probably tell you more about the article. A lot of law firms underwent restructuring. For the company to be successful, each employee needs to know how they fit in and see themselves as part of the big picture."

A tiny sting of guilt pricked my consciousness. I certainly didn't view myself as part of anything. All I wanted was to move up in paygrade and get closer to Miles. Were my motives really that trivial? Greg patiently waited for the answer, but the new talkative Grace must have taken a nap.

"My role is very small," I finally said. "I don't make any important decisions, just organize paperwork."

"But it's very important." Greg leaned forward with a sparkle in his eyes. Closer to the light, they looked like the clear sky we'd enjoyed earlier. "Can you imagine what would happen to this big machine of an organization without a good filing system? What if nobody found the documents they needed? It would be a hot mess!"

I laughed. His excitement was contagious. The man moved his hands like a windmill when he talked, and the comparison added fuel to my unexpected giddiness.

"That's true," I admitted. "Mr. Bailey is on the verge of a heart attack every time he can't find some piece of paper."

I impersonated my grumpy boss and reenacted the morning incident. My new acquaintance rolled with laughter. He asked me a few more questions about my work, and I started to feel like the firm would fall apart without me.

"I detect that it's not what you wanted to do with your life." His gaze, suddenly serious, caught me off guard.

Silence fell between us. Then something unusual happened. Maybe it was the friendly face across the table, or the subtle influence of the gem, or the cozy atmosphere. Whatever the reason, I opened my heart and told Greg about my dream to become a teacher. I shared how my father's sudden abandonment and my mother's inability to cope with the breakup had thwarted my plans.

His warm hand rested over mine while I talked about the heavy responsibilities that'd fallen on my shoulders at a young age. The stream of words I didn't know I had seemed to lighten up the burden that lay silently on my chest.

"My mother completely fell apart back then." I studied the table lamp and crumbled the napkin with my free hand. "I can't really blame her. She depended on her husband for everything... dropped out of college to marry him and was a stay-at-home mom. My father was older. He'd taken care of all the finances. When he left, she didn't even know how to balance a checkbook. She still doesn't."

I managed a watery smile. Creases formed over Greg's forehead and put a shadow over his sunny features. He leaned over the table, his cordial face close to mine, eyes darkened to a deep ocean blue.

I cleared my throat, which suddenly felt tight. "I'm so sorry, not sure why I told you all this. I don't usually dump my life story on every stranger."

"Then let's not consider each other strangers," he replied quietly. "Let's be friends."

I thanked him but my eyes burned. Greg squeezed my hand and let go, relaxing back into his chair.

Is this part of the beauty act? Be vulnerable, get sympathy... Blast this stone! Never cried in front of a man and never will. Keep it together, Grace.

"There is nothing in life that a good cake can't fix," I proclaimed a little too cheerfully and put the last bite in my mouth. "Too much about me. Now's your turn. How did you end up a journalist?"

I must have hit a favorite subject. The somber cloud that'd gathered over us dissipated. Greg was instantly back to his laid-back agreeable mood.

"Oh, wow. That's a long story," he said. "Like you, I studied to be a teacher, but then decided that journalism had a broader influence. I wanted to share my thoughts with the world. That was when I was young and green."

"What kinds of thoughts?" I propped my elbows on the table, ignoring the slight sarcasm in his voice.

Greg scratched his head.

"Mostly about social issues. My first job was more rogue. I was what you'd call a backpack journalist. Traveled the world, got into impoverished areas, places torn by war. Wanted to make a difference. Instead, I got burned out." His expression hardened for a second, but he erased it with a smile. "Now I'm stuck behind a desk, writing cozy articles for a business magazine. It pays the bills."

"Can't wait to read something of yours," I said sincerely. "I haven't been anywhere outside of the States. It must be so exciting to travel and write."

"That's what I thought, too. Turns out it's not very romantic." A bitter note slipped into his pleasant voice once again, but he hid it behind a chuckle.

We stayed a little longer discussing books, environmental problems, and predictions for the next *Star Wars* movie until Greg offered to drive me home. He shook my hand after dropping me off.

"You are an amazing, strong woman. Glad I ran into you twice."

He saluted me and drove away. I wanted to ask what was so amazing about me when all I did was gripe about my life.

Does the Beauty stone make other people so blind they can't see my flaws?

BACK IN OUR APARTMENT, my mother was already asleep. I tiptoed to my room and studied, then sat at the computer and looked up Greg Miller. There he was, on the front page of his blog, sporting a carefree genial smile. His blue eyes shone brightly against his desert-baked skin. Barren land stretched behind him. In traditional African clothes, with disheveled hair and a full beard, he looked as if he belonged in that sun-withered place. His last article was posted a year ago, but I was instantly drawn in. The story followed a fourteen-year-old boy, freed by the UN from fighting for the military group in South Sudan. It described his struggle to integrate back into society. Greg wrote so vividly, it drove me to tears. Why would he leave that lifestyle if so much of his heart was in it? I stepped away from the screen, thankful to get to know a person like Greg. But was he able to see the real me beyond the perfect skin?

To meet new people is not as scary as it seems. This stone was good for something after all.

"Ok, Auntie, what's next?"

I pulled the box out of its hiding place and then remembered the instructions in the book: *taking the gem off or putting another one on will result in a gradual loss of power.* Was I willing to give up the ease of social interactions and my good looks to try a new ability? I only had several days to find out what else was in store for me.

There must be a more useful attribute than beauty, something that can change my life. I can't turn down a chance like this for the sake of vanity.

I got up and peered into the mirror. My new striking appearance made me uncomfortable, but I had to admit that my ability to connect with others had been rewarding. Over the course of one day, I'd lived a completely different life and enjoyed it. For the first time, Miles acknowledged my existence, and what if I got invited to the interview?

It's time to take care of my body. Goodbye, chocolate-filled croissants.

Determined, I got up and went around the room collecting my hidden stashes of snacks—enough to sustain me through the zombie apocalypse. Playing the funeral march in my head, I lowered my favorite treats into the garbage and returned to my room.

I hope I'm done throwing things away. But what do I do now? I can probably ask a stylist to throw in some magic in place of this gem. And it wouldn't hurt to force myself to talk more with others. Hopefully, when the "side effects" of wearing the stone fade away, people will still be interested in me.

With a firm decision to put some effort into keeping these newly discovered skills, I took the pendant off, placed it safely back in its section, and opened other lids. Containers labeled "agility", "speed", "imagination", and "memory" were empty. There was a clear gemstone under the name "invisibility".

No, thank you, I have been invisible enough all my life.

I closed it and looked through the lower drawers. One lid labeled "hearing" caught my attention. It contained a polished irregular opaque stone with various patterns of gold, brown, and red splattered all over its surface. The stone sat inside a sturdy metal frame. I opened the book to read the meaning.

HEARING

שֶׁמַע

(Jasper)

Ability to discern other people's thoughts, capacity to hear conversations at a great distance or through obstacles, power to understand what is on another person's mind as well as to interpret his or her intentions.

I closed the page with frustration.

This is insane! I can at least partially explain the changes in my appearance, but this...? I can't possibly believe this. Otherwise, I'll have to believe in time machines and fire-breathing dragons... and unicorns.

My thoughts quickly pulled me into a downward spiral of

doubt. Suddenly, I lost sight of the self-confident woman that had guided my actions earlier. Did the effect of the Beauty stone fade so quickly? Maybe it was all part of my overactive imagination.

My phone buzzed, and a text message from a long-distance number appeared on my screen.

Follow my instructions, kid. Don't let the doubts keep you from trying new things. You know I love you. Louise.

Frantically, I texted back with a handful of questions that burned in my mind only to receive the "not delivered" notification. I got up and paced the room. My aunt was right. After a glimpse of hope, to turn back was not an option. I couldn't let this happen to me or let my aunt down. I desperately wanted a change, in whatever shape or form it came.

This new ability, if it's real, will help me do something different with my life. To understand others is exactly what I need to do well on the interview and to be a successful paralegal.

I tried to appease my logic. This tornado of strange events had entered my ordinary life and threatened to whisk me away into the uncharted territory like Dorothy in the *Wizard of Oz*. But what if this was true? What if it was possible? To read the thoughts of others was not something I got to do every day.

It might give me an edge at work, but would I be able to handle this new ability?

"Ok, Auntie, I'll try this. It all sounds crazy, but if this is what it takes to bring me out of my boring life, I'll do anything."

I quickly fed the stone through the chain and put it on. Its weight tugged on my neck. With a slight sting of anxiety, I curled under the blankets and listened to my heart beat steadily underneath the pendant. Wondering what tomorrow would bring, I fell asleep.

PART III
THE MINDFUL LIFE

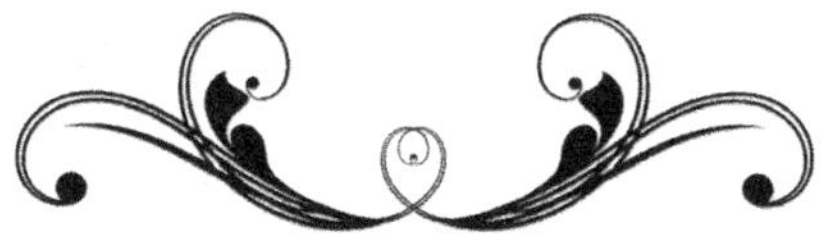

It is more blessed and brings more joy to give than to receive.

—The Bible

The rumble of thunder and the clinking of heavy raindrops on my window woke me before the alarm. I shivered under the covers. Even with my eyes open, the chaotic dream world lingered fresh in my mind. During the turbulent night, Aunt Lou and I traveled across an African safari and down a muddy river to hide the pendants from secret service agents. Our small canoe tipped, and I fell into the crocodile-infested water. I swam away in panic, but the beasts surrounded me. Out of nowhere, Greg appeared next to me on a boat with Aunt Lou in tow. He extended his hand and pulled me out. When we reached the shore and stepped onto dry land, a group of agents in black suits and sunglasses sprang out of the bushes. They chased us through the jungle. I woke up not knowing whether we'd reached the secret hiding place.

That's what I get for stuffing myself with sweets yesterday... and what was that journalist doing in my dream?

I got up to close the window. Outside, the wind lashed and pulled tree branches in different directions. I stood and watched the lightning cut through the rugged sky. My thoughts cleared. I remembered the events of last night and how I'd exchanged the Beauty stone for the Hearing stone. Would I still be pretty? I rushed to the closet mirror, but my worries quickly dissipated. The drastic changes from the previous day were still in effect. Even crinkled from the sleep, my face glowed, and my body—slightly heavier than the day before—kept a healthy form.

At least the cellulite isn't back yet. I need to do something to keep in shape before this gets out of control.

The storm lightened up, and I decided to benefit from my early wake-up call. I borrowed my sister's t-shirt and sweatpants and escaped outside.

Having never been a sporty person, I wasn't sure how to start. Physical activity meant stinky PE lockers and ridicules from classmates when I'd run from the ball instead of catching it like a normal child. But to go back to the same neglected state of affairs was not an option, and a short jog seemed like a safe alternative.

I breathed in the crisp air and picked up the pace down the sidewalk. "No more excuses. I can do this!"

It only took a few minutes for my resolve to diminish. Every muscle in my body ached and burned as though I'd run a marathon. I stopped to catch my breath.

"Good morning," I wheezed when Mr. Kent ran past me, dressed in a striped sweat suit that must have been popular in the nineties. He stopped and scratched his head. It took him a minute to recognize me in the form-fitting workout clothes instead of my usual Lord-of-the-Ring style robes.

"What a pleasant surprise," he finally said while jogging in place. "You like to run in the morning? It's unfortunate the weather isn't that nice today."

"Actually, it's my first time, and it feels like some sort of medieval torture."

I bent forward, desperate to make the sharp pain in my side go away, and wishing the pendant for physical agility hadn't already been taken.

"Ah, but you'll learn to enjoy it." The neighbor smiled through his mustache. "It's good you started your day on a healthy note. You made the first step."

Easy for you to say.

Mr. Kent was in great shape. He looked barely fifty. Silvery strands in his dark hair and a few deep wrinkles in his agreeable face were the only giveaways of his senior status. Compared to him, I was a puny weakling. Squatting to tie my shoes, I secretly longed to stretch out on the ground.

"I wonder how Lara is doing. She looked unwell yesterday," Mr. Kent said.

I raised my head and met the man's kind dark eyes.

"I came home late last night and haven't seen her yet," I mumbled, instantly feeling guilty for abandoning my mother.

"Who?"

"My mom. You said she looked ill."

"Did I? I didn't realize I said it out loud." The older man scratched his head.

For a minute we stood in silence. Confused by our disjointed exchange, I wondered what to say next. Mr. Kent recovered first and offered to jog with me. I tried to decline, afraid I'd collapse, but my friendly neighbor insisted. With a few of his tips on how to control my breathing, the pain in my ribs eased. Distracted by his encouraging comments, I finished my run in a much better condition than when he found me. Mr. Kent and I agreed to meet again the next morning to continue the exercise.

Refreshed by the jog, I flew into the apartment and found my mother at the kitchen table with her face covered by her hands. My heart sank when I heard her quiet sobs.

"I am such a nuisance," she moaned.

"Please, don't say that," I interrupted.

She raised her eyes, surprised. "Don't say what? Where

did you go? And what happened to you? You look…
different."

"I ran. It's time I take care of myself. Come out and get
some fresh air too. It's not good to sit at home all day."

I turned to get water when my mother spoke again:

"That's absurd. I can't go outside. It's too cold. Why did
she say it? She wants me out of her sight. Is this why she
came home so late yesterday? One of these days I'll get sick
and die with nobody around to help. Who even cares?"

I spun around and faced her. "How can you say stuff like
that?"

"I didn't say anything, but I can't go outside in this
weather. I'm already sick. Why did you come home so late
last night?"

I peered at my mother in disbelief. She knew how to get
under my skin, but to repeat her tirade twice seemed a bit
over-the-top even for her. Unless…

The new realization hit me.

Am I hearing her thoughts?

Suddenly, my odd exchange with Mr. Kent made sense.

What did I sign up for? Should have kept the Beauty stone…

I escaped into the bathroom and stood under a hot
shower until the nagging discomfort in my chest eased. My
hope for a better day thinned out, and I faced the closet full
of new outfits with an anxious heart.

Why did I waste money? Soon I won't fit in these fancy things.

Thoughts of defeat knocked at my door, but I took
another deep breath and shooed them away.

*I can replace supernatural ability with a natural one or give up.
Return the clothes and join my mother's sulk club or try. I have to
give it a chance. For my aunt. For my health. For this lovely outfit.*

I took an elegant half sleeve A-line dress off the hanger
and ran my hand through the soft material before slipping it
on. It fit perfectly around my curvy figure. The deep blue
color made my eyes shine brighter. My mood lightened, and

I swung around in front of the mirror, twirling the knee-length skirt.

"Well, well, Grace, look at you. It only took one day to abandon your philosophy that appearances don't matter," I chastised my reflection, but a hint of a smile spread over my lips.

I argued with myself all the way to the tram station but decided there was nothing wrong with looking good. By the time I got to the stop, my high-heel shoes felt like circus stilts, the top of my dress had transformed into a tight corset, and my long-distance vision blurred.

What's happening? Am I losing the power of the Beauty stone? I hope I won't be featured on the local news if my clothes rip at the seam.

Humor didn't help. I sucked my belly in and tried not to wobble or suffocate. While I was distracted with the changes in my body, the world around me erupted in noisy chatter. The power of the Hearing pendant was in full force and bombarded me with the thoughts of every passerby. Inner-voices blended into a headache-inducing murmur when I joined the crowd at the station. I tried to ignore them until one particular comment rose above the others.

"Nice booty," someone said behind me as I climbed the steps to my ride.

I turned around in a fury, but I couldn't tell which man had the audacity to think that. My cheeks burned. I wanted to return home and change out of the dress which had become so snug that it accentuated what Alicia called "assets".

"Ah, aren't you looking sharp today, hon!" Mrs. Jones beamed in her usual warm manner.

Her motherly greeting dissolved my embarrassment. I sat in the back of the tram and fought the urge to loosen the zipper in the back. To undress in public didn't seem like a good idea, especially with all the attention I'd been recently receiving. To distract myself from the increasing tightness around my chest, I attempted to study. But with the constant hum of inner conversations around me, it proved to be an impossible feat. When an older woman in front of me mentally recited her grocery list for the fifth time, I wanted to curl into the fetal position on the floor and cry.

Ugh... I can survive without knowing she needs to buy Rhubarb! And who in the world eats that vegetable?

I turned away and stared at the middle-aged woman to my right. Her inner-voice became louder than the rest.

"Where did she get this dress?" she thought. "And this purse? When was the last time I went shopping?"

She gave me a short civil smile when our eyes met. I switched my attention to the young man next to her who was interested in something other than my clothes. I crinkled my nose and turned to his neighbor.

"I'd give her a ten," he thought, making me question whether male brains were filled with anything else. Soon the constant buzz became unbearable, and my mind was ready to explode from the non-stop stream of thoughts about daily plans, problems, and conflicts.

Son of a blaster... I need to learn how to control this before I go insane! That's what I get for wanting to be a Jedi...

For the rest of the ride, I kept my eyes averted. Eventually, everyone's inner monologues dissolved into a murmur in the background. By turning my attention inward, I learned to tune them out and even managed to get through a few chapters in my textbook. When my stop came into view, I catapulted out, relieved to put distance between myself and other human beings. At that moment, the idea of getting stranded on a deserted island for the rest of my life had the greatest appeal.

After a short walk, a familiar security guard greeted me at the building entrance.

"I should ask her out," he thought while smiling politely. I hurried past him, but it wasn't any easier to maintain my composure in the elevator. I pinned my eyes to the floor and studied everyone's shoes. When the person next to me contemplated whether to pass wind, I scrunched up my face and held my breath long enough to pass out. That caused a few sideway glances in my direction and mental conclusions that I was guilty as charged. Thankfully, most of my neighbors meditated on more reasonable topics, but one inner voice caught my attention.

"This Richard Bailey will finally pay for everything."

I glanced around to figure out its originator in the crowded cabin. A middle-aged man in a tailored black suit with hawk-like facial features caught my attention. When I looked at him, his inner-voice came out loud and clear.

"It's about time we bring him down, the proud old fool."

The man's dark eyes caught mine, like a predator who'd spotted its prey. Turning away, I held my hands together to keep from fidgeting and remained in the elevator until the man made his way out onto the fifteenth floor. He walked fast, his back stiff. I trotted right behind on my high heels. My ability to walk in them had worn off faster than the skill could be mastered, and I stumbled trying to keep up. The stranger entered through the glass door of another law firm, walked right past the receptionist who stood up to greet him, and disappeared inside the arched entry.

I need to get inside. But how? I don't even know his name.

A hand grasped my shoulder, and I gasped like a child caught with her fingers in a cookie jar.

"I'm sorry. Didn't mean to startle you." Greg shot me a guilty smile when I turned to face him. He wore a navy shirt with his jeans and smelled refreshing like Irish Spring soap. "Glad to see you, though. Whatcha doing here on my floor?"

"N-nothing."

"She's even prettier when caught off guard," he thought while I attempted to regain my bearings.

*Oh, no! Don't want to get into **his** head... I have to stop this. Quick.*

"Remember, when you said we should be friends?" I spilled out, unsure where this was going.

"Yes, of course. By the way, wanted to tell you, I had a great time yesterday. What you shared—"

"I need your help," I interrupted, afraid of changing my mind.

His face lit up. "Anything you want."

"Can you get me inside this law firm? I have reason to believe somebody in there plans to undermine Mr. Bailey."

"Really?"

How could I explain things to Greg without appearing crazy? Why would I even ask for his help? But it was too late to back out.

"I overheard something on the way to work, and I need more information before I bring this up to my employer."

I decided it was wise to omit the fact the information was obtained from another person's head.

"I guess that makes sense. It's a competing law firm." Greg rubbed his chin, his expression turning serious. "I would hate for anything bad to happen to your place of work."

"So, would you be able to arrange an appointment for me to get in? An interview for your newspaper?"

"Let me try to figure something out," he said in a casual tone of voice, as if I'd asked for a double order of fries instead of a fake interview.

I glanced at my watch. "Have to run. Let's meet here at lunch."

I bit my lip and caught Greg staring. It was time to leave before my new friend had a chance to think of anything else silly. I scrambled with my goodbyes and walked away as fast as my ankle-twisting shoes allowed.

CHAPTER 10

My co-workers met my rushed appearance with friendly greetings. Some commented on my outfit in their minds, but most focused on the day's work. Mrs. Williamson, still attentive, was not as cheerful as the day before. Worries about her son filled her mind. She offered to fix the stifling top of my dress. While she worked on it, I decided to find out what was bothering her.

"Is everything okay at home? You seem worried," I probed,

"Oh, yes. I'm fine. Thank you," she reassured me with a faint smile. "There. I opened up your zipper and pinned the scarf over it. Nobody will notice.

"Thank you so much." I took a full breath. One problem solved. At least for the moment, my body had stopped expanding. I focused again on my co-worker. "Is anybody ill in your family?"

She hesitated for a second, but my persistence paid off, and the barrier of formality crumbled down. Mrs. Williamson sat next to me and dabbed her eyes with a napkin.

"My son is disabled, and he got the flu yesterday." She sighed. "I have a caregiver, but it still makes me uneasy. He's prone to pneumonia. I'm sorry. I shouldn't bother you with my personal problems, dear."

"Can't you ask Mr. Bailey to give you a day off?"

"But how can I leave? There is so much to do. He needs me," she lamented.

"Let me handle that," I said without the slightest idea of what I planned to do. How would I convince our boss to release his personal assistant? Who was I anyway to ask for things like that?

Well, my life is already crazy. What's one more thing?

I stopped by Mr. Bailey's office, hoping I had enough left-over charm from the day before to advocate for my new friend. The man was talking on the phone. He paced between the massive mahogany desk and tall built-in cabinets that were filled with fat volumes of law books. His voice came through the soundproof glass wall loud and clear, thanks to my new ability.

"What do you mean our credit is overstretched? It's your job to handle these things!"

Not the best time to ask for a favor, Grace.

I tried to escape, but Mr. Bailey slammed the phone down and saw me. He motioned for me to come in.

I hesitated in the doorway. "I didn't want to interrupt. You seem upset about something."

"You're a superb observer, Miss Ainsworth." He scoffed and threw his arms in the air.

I stood still, unsure of what to do next. All I wanted was to disappear like Bilbo Baggins with his ring. Mr. Bailey dropped into the big armchair, rubbed his forehead, and thought: "I can't even get a cup of coffee from anybody."

A little light bulb went off in my head.

"I know what I can do to make things a little better, although it's not much. Be right back."

I ran out and returned with a hot cup of his favorite brew.

"You're the only person in the entire world who knows what's on my heart," he exclaimed with delight. "Even my wife doesn't take such good care of me like you have lately."

I glanced at my boss with caution, but he gave me a fatherly smile and no second thoughts. I continued to read his mind and fetched a few more things he needed that morning. After he calmed down, I gathered enough courage to ask for Mrs. Williamson to go home early and take care of her sick son. The man fretted and complained that everybody had left him to do all the work himself but eventually gave in to my pleadings.

"I will honor your request if you continue to be as helpful as earlier," he declared, like a king who'd just knighted me and sent me on an impossible quest at the same time. How was I going to help him? I couldn't do paralegal work... or could I?

There're other paralegals in the office. I can always pick their brains... literally.

It was time to cover the red panic button and push the speed lever instead. Wasn't that what I wanted? A chance to prove myself?

"I'll be happy to assist you, Mr. Bailey."

"Hurry. We have lots to do," my boss grumbled.

I ran out of his office to deliver the good news. Mrs. Williamson squeezed my hand with fervor and left in a rush. On my way back to Mr. Bailey's office, Olivia Peterson caught me. She finally got enough courage to approach me after my metamorphosis from the ugly duckling to a much prettier specimen. Had annoyance overpowered the initial shock? With her lips tight and arms folded, she gave me a loaded stare.

"What's going on?" She puffed. "What are you doing over here? You need to file yesterday's reports."

"Find somebody else to do it, Olivia," Mr. Bailey said as he came around the corner and stood between us. "Leave her be. I need her. Let's go, Grace. Remember what you promised. Better not disappoint me."

I am starting to like this place.

I coughed into my hand to cover the smile that threatened to escape and stole a glance at my supervisor. Olivia's face changed from red to pale. She stomped her heels hard into the floor and left me to spend the rest of the morning solving a puzzle called "what does the boss need". Fortunately, seven months of the paralegal school and my freshly acquired mind-reading abilities proved useful. My wish to do meaningful work came true. Ready or not, Mr. Bailey had catapulted me into the new role head-on.

As I sorted through the reports for the upcoming cases and willed my blurred vision to focus, Victoria came into Mr. Bailey's office to drop a message from a client. The girl's eyes turned into narrow slits from which she shot suspicious glances in my direction. The ideas in her head frantically jumped around while she searched for an explanation for my sudden proximity to the boss.

"She is nobody, a freaking filer. That paralegal position will still be mine."

Overwhelmed with my new responsibilities, I had no time to dwell on her enmity. Thankfully most of my co-workers were happy to assist and answer my questions. Our new litigation support specialist, Mr. Betzalel Abeles, was simply indispensable. For some reason his thoughts were beyond my reach. I peeked over his shoulder at the mind-boggling spreadsheets on the computer and wondered if his gray heap of curly hair formed a protective layer over his inner world.

"Are you listening, Miss Ainsworth?" He turned and peered at me through his thick glasses. I nodded. His bushy eyebrows came together above his light eyes and made him look like Gandalf without a hat.

Well, technically, his beard needs a few more inches to qualify for the comparison with a great wizard, but the bulbous nose would do...

"Miss Ainsworth. Grace."

"Yes, Mr. Abeles." I attempted to gather my wandering thoughts. "I'm listening. This is helpful, just a bit overwhelming."

The older man studied me for a few more seconds. "What is it that you want?"

"I want to do this job well, but it's so unexpected. I'm just helping for the day, and there's a lot to learn."

"There are people who want something and there are people who have what it takes to achieve it. Which category do you fall into?"

He turned and faced the computer, leaving me to ponder over his words.

Mr. Abeles started yesterday and stepped right in where the other person left off. If I do the same, maybe Mr. Bailey would recommend me to Miles. That is if I survive trying to fill Mrs. Williamson's big shoes.

Humming the chorus of Kelly Clarkson's *Stronger* made my morning go faster. Despite the business, I anxiously waited for lunch. Would my journalist friend be able to come up with a plan? Had he found a way to get into that law office? When my break approached, I hurried to the meeting spot with Greg. He was already waiting with a triumphant look on his face, his thoughts filled with foolish nonsense about me. I spoke to interrupt them.

"Did you figure something out?"

"Did you have any doubts?" he said with a big grin. "I had to pull a few strings and utilize some serious investigative maneuvers like flirting with the receptionist and the secretary."

My cheeks flushed. Why couldn't he take this seriously? Was it a mistake to trust him? I stared in disbelief, annoyed by his nonchalant attitude until Greg raised his arms in surrender.

"I'm sorry. My mouth got away from me again. I had a few friendly conversations with the staff. It was all business-related, promise."

Why would I care if it was business-related or not? I think you just enjoy being amused at my expense.

I caught a curious glance from Greg, and the darn heat wave spread to my ears. Was he trying to read my mind too?

His thoughts entered my mind louder than if he had spoken. "Miss Serious blushed. Is it good or bad?" Before I could react, he said aloud, "I got an appointment. You'll be my associate, and, of course, I can't go anywhere without you. Here's your badge."

"When is the interview?" I asked, assuming he'd gotten a conference set up with one of the lawyers.

"Right about now."

A minute later, we entered the empty lobby of the law office, in front of which I'd stood hours earlier. The receptionist greeted us with smiles and chatted with my "partner in crime". I squared my jaw and tried to ignore them. Suddenly, Greg pushed me towards the hallway while the girl behind the counter turned away to find something for him. He motioned for me to go and continued to distract her. I picked up my pace, turned the corner, and escaped through the door. Without slowing down, I passed the main hallway, security desk, and a few other offices until a voice through one of the walls got my attention. It was the man from the elevator.

"You know very well it will only take a couple of months before the whole thing falls like a deck of cards."

"That's why Mr. Bailey looked so frantic in the last few days… But how can I do something so sudden? If I leave the firm now, it'll make things worse," another person said.

"Are you willing to stay and take the risk? When Bailey

goes to bankruptcy court, all of you will be dragged down with him. It's just a matter of time. As a partner, you'll be implicated. Why would you want to go down with the sinking ship?"

"I thought we were doing well. Are you sure this information is accurate?"

"One hundred percent. You saw the evidence with your own eyes. Alex Pentovsky already told me about his decision to work for us. You can ask him yourself, but I can't extend my offer for much longer."

"You're right. I have my family to worry about. Get the paperwork ready. I'll sign it tonight."

"Now we're talking. Trust me, you're making the right decision. Let's meet here at seven."

I stood far away enough to stay unnoticed when the two men came out of the room. The voice of the second person was unfamiliar, but I immediately recognized his face. Mr. Murphy was one of the managing partners of our law firm. I waited a few more minutes until they were a safe distance away before walking back to the main lobby.

"I was searching for the ladies' room and got a little lost," I told the receptionist, forcing a smile. She pointed to the restroom. I walked in, stared at my flustered face, took a few deep breaths, and came out to the main hallway. Greg was already waiting for me.

"You said you had an appointment! Why did you push me in?" I fumed after we moved a few feet away.

"I had an impromptu appointment with Sarah at the front desk." He gave me a disarming grin and continued before I could protest. "Did you find what you were looking for?"

"Yes."

I told Greg about the conversation I'd overheard thanks to my unusual ability and about the partners leaving. We grabbed a couple of sandwiches at the kiosk and sat in the common area between the offices to figure out what to do next.

"I don't understand how a few people can hurt a big company like ours," I said. "Mr. Bailey started it twenty years ago."

Greg rubbed his chin. "It can. When I did my research for the article, I'd read about large law firms that collapsed in a matter of weeks. That's because these entities are owned by partners. If one or two withdraw, the company loses clientele and finances. Others may try to leave as well, and that quickly leads to bankruptcy. It's like a downward spiral."

I winced. "That's terrible. Our company is the best in the state, but I guess that doesn't mean it can't fall apart."

"It seems this man already talked to several people and persuaded them to swing over."

"What can I do about it?"

"You should talk to your boss. I'm sure he'd figure something out. I wonder why the other guy wants to bring him down."

"Don't know, but we've got to stop him," I said with a sudden resolve.

"I admire your enthusiasm. If everyone else stood up for what's right..." Greg shook his head and thought: "Only there's way more unfairness in this world than good people can tackle."

Pain shot through his face, but he forced it behind a smile.

"Please, tell me," I said before realizing that my response was to Greg's internal conversation.

"What?"

"Well, I just... you looked upset about something."

Greg sighed. "It's a long story."

"You heard mine. Might as well tell me yours." I bit my sandwich and tried to sound nonchalant.

"It's something that happened at my previous job," he said.

"Is this why you stopped traveling?"

Greg's jaw tightened. "Not sure this is the right place."

My curiosity went through the roof, but I didn't want to pressure him. "Ok. Maybe next time. I have to go back to work anyway."

I got up and shook his hand with a sincere "thank you". I might have imagined it, but Greg looked like he was holding his breath when his eyes met mine. Not wanting to know where his mind would travel next, I ran off.

CHAPTER 11

The failing partner was already back at the firm when I reached Mr. Bailey's office. Behind closed doors, I told my boss everything I'd overheard. His face turned ashen grey. He sat on his chair and held his chest, then got up and paced around the table. For a moment, I was afraid he might have a heart attack and tried to remember the first aid course I'd taken in college.

"Go get Miles Taylor!" He ordered.

Why Miles?

The mention of his name overpowered my concern for Mr. Bailey and caused my chest to tighten too. It wasn't the right time to think of my personal issues. I scurried out with a raw mixture of simmering emotions and ran into Miles in the hall.

"You need to go talk to Mr. Bailey right now. It's urgent," I shot out in one breath.

"What a woman," he thought with a peculiar smile but complied immediately.

His steps echoed right behind me as we walked out. My heart pounded so loud, it drowned every other sound, even Miles's thoughts, which mostly lingered on the view in front of him: me. Carefully placing each step, I silently pleaded with the safety pins in my dress to stay put.

Why am I feeling so lightheaded? It might not be such a bad thing to pass out. Miles could perform a rescue ki... um, breathing.

Fortunately or not, I made it to the office in sound health and in one piece. Mr. Bailey closed the doors and asked me to stay while they discussed the situation. The two men voiced the same concerns Greg had brought up earlier. I didn't understand most of what they said, but one fact was clear—there was no immediate solution. I hid in the corner and observed them, my brain too disrupted from being in proximity with Miles to participate in the conversation.

"Why does this person want to hurt our firm?" I finally ventured to ask.

"He doesn't care about the firm. He wants to hurt me," Mr. Bailey said wearily. Suddenly he looked much older.

"Somebody's giving him information about the state of our affairs. Otherwise, he wouldn't have any grounds to approach our lawyers. I wonder who that is. Did Alex Pentovsky get this mess started?" Miles's hands clasped into fists. His dark eyebrows gathered into a fierce stare. He swore under his breath.

"Miles, nobody knows about the fraud investigation except for you. I hope that unauthorized withdrawal gets cleared soon. The bankers are just dragging their feet."

"Mr. Murphy mentioned concerns for his family," I half-whispered, but both men turned in my direction. "He was worried about his income. Maybe if you show him that his fears are baseless, and the company is well off, he'll change his mind, and then Mr. Pentovsky might change his mind also..."

The longer I talked, the less sure I was about the soundness of my idea. Miles's face relaxed and the intense glare in his eyes dissipated when he focused his attention on me. My logic tangled up every time our eyes met.

"I can listen to her all day," he thought.

"Well, we certainly can't force them to stay," Mr. Bailey said with a sigh that blew away the little cupids I imagined floating in the air between me and Miles. "But if both of them leave at the same time and withdraw their capital, it'll cause a big problem. Especially now."

"And if they stay?" I inquired.

"If they stay, we will get over this bump in the road just fine. We're in a tight spot, and Robert Kowalski somehow got wind of it. Spiteful man!"

"Miss Ainsworth made a good point," Miles interjected. I was surprised he even knew my name. "We need to meet with them individually and try to persuade them that our business is on the upswing."

Miles agreed to conduct an informal meeting with the two partners to convince them that to leave now would be foolish. For the next several hours I played detective and scanned the minds of my co-workers in an attempt to figure out who was responsible for the information leak. I also lingered by the offices of Mr. Pentovsky and Mr. Murphy and listened to their internal struggles. I decided to make suggestions to Miles about the two men. Such audacity on my part surprised me, but a decision to put my personal needs aside gave me the courage to meet the man face-to-face again.

For over two years, I had successfully avoided his office, but now was the time to cross the invisible barrier I'd created for myself. Resolved to build up an immunity to his appeal, I walked through the door with Miles Taylor's name and credentials written on the golden plaque. Miles sprang to his feet and came around the desk the moment I entered. I couldn't help but notice how he seemed to belong in the stylish and cozy room filled with custom-made furniture. He invited me to take a seat on the black leather couch and, settling next to me, listened to my findings with a look of amusement. His undivided attention made my mouth run dry.

"She's clever," he thought. "And quite a looker. Why haven't I seen her around here before?"

Our closeness was intoxicating, and I stopped mid-sentence to gather my runaway thoughts.

"I do believe women have an internal intuition, but you, Miss Ainsworth, are a true mind reader," he said when I finished blundering through my speech.

If only you knew...

I stood up to leave. "All the best in your negotiations."

"I'll do all I can, Miss Ainsworth." His smile made my heart skip a beat. "I'd be happy to hear more of your insights after this whole turmoil is over."

He got up and shook my hand a little longer than necessary, saying "cheers" in his enchanting accent.

"I won't let this one get away," he thought as I walked out, feeling dazed and wondering what he meant. I wanted to pinch myself to make sure our conversation was real, but my sudden collision with Olivia was painful enough to prove it was not a dream.

"Watch where you're going!" my supervisor snapped. Her eyes narrowed. "What were you doing in Mr. Taylor's offfice?"

I hesitated, trying to come up with a convincing explanation. As always, I couldn't think of anything feasible to say on the fly. Where was yesterday's Grace who always had the right words readily available?

"I delivered something he wanted," I stammered.

"Delivered something he wanted? What might that be?" Olivia smirked. Malice danced in her green eyes. "Listen, sweetheart, let me give you a piece of advice. Don't bite off more than you can chew. Trust me, none of this will land you a paralegal job. But neglecting your duties will make you lose the position you have right now, so I suggest you stay put while I still have some patience left."

I gasped. "How did you know about my application?"

"Let me make it easier for you to stick to your job description—I saw your pathetic resume, and it will not get past me. Or did you forget that I review all the applicants first?"

A mocking smile curved the corners of her plump lips, and I imagined myself crushed under her giant high heel.

"This will teach her," Olivia thought and turned away. "I should keep an eye on this one."

I stood in the middle of an empty hallway, paralyzed. What did I spend my time and the gift for?

Why am I trying to save this place? I can't even save myself from a streak of bad luck. Olivia will never let me be more than a file clerk, if she'll even allow me to work here at all.

I covered my face with both hands and tried to wish it all away. Unfortunately, that did nothing to change my situation, and I had to get back to my duties. The idea of hiding in the bathroom for the rest of the day crossed my mind, but my pity party had to wait until I was done assisting Mr. Bailey. Unwillingly, I came out into the main area of our office. People were busy with their tasks. Nobody suspected that in a short time they might end up with no income.

I should probably start looking for a new job myself.

But after learning so much about my co-workers in the last two days, I could no longer stay a distant observer or desert them. There was Lily, a single mother of two; Janis, who'd just had a baby; and Steve, who took care of his elderly parents.

I have to keep our firm from closing down. I have to do this for all of us. Resolved, I sat down to finish Mr. Bailey's report.

CHAPTER 12

The rest of the afternoon was uneventful. Olivia made an appearance once again when I was about to leave.

"Now that you've finished flattering the bosses, go do the work I've hired you for," she hissed. "Don't think you can run around the office and neglect your duties for long."

She threw a stack of files on my desk, sent a few mental curses in my direction, and left.

"To be, or not to be, that is the question." Should I anger her more or stay overtime? Um, I think I'll choose the latter.

Mother was not expecting me until later. I'd already warned her about a scheduled proctored exam that evening for my paralegal certificate. With a few hours to spare, I took out my study notes and glanced over the material while sorting through the never-ending pile of papers.

Ugh, back to my sorry Cinderella life. At least she had a fairy godmother to rescue her, but it doesn't look like my aunt's gift will help me out of the mess I'm in. I have to figure something out on my own. But what can I do when Olivia is determined to stand in my way? Would any of it even matter if Mr. Kowalski accomplishes his plan?

Some files had to go into a separate storage unit, and that required climbing the ladder. I would have much rather cleaned the chimneys, but it wasn't an option. I walked over to the back room with a cart full of paperwork and set up the ladder. With shoes off, I squared my jaw and climbed up the despised steps. The progress was painfully slow. I calculated every move as though I were on a tightrope. Suddenly, the ladder tipped. A loud yelp escaped my lungs. I grabbed the handles of the nearest drawer and hugged the cabinets for dear life. My mind raced. Had I secured it wrong? How would I get down? With eyes tightly shut, I held on as if it were a deadly cliff and tried to steady the metal step with my toes. To me, six feet off the ground was as terrifying as sixty.

"Miss Ainsworth, are you all right?" Miles inquired below. "I heard you scream."

"Please, help me," I forced through my teeth. Every muscle in my body tightened in a futile effort to stay still and not lose my footing completely. My boss walked closer. The ground under my feet straightened and became firm.

"You can climb down now."

With eyes focused on the steps, I made my way to the ground with the speed of a sloth and found myself in Miles Taylor's arms. He held on to the ladder behind me, enclosing me on every side. Even though I was back on a steady surface, the dizzy sensation became worse.

His minty breath brushed my cheek. "Are you all right?"

"Yes, thank you," I whispered, afraid to look up at the man. My voice sounded raspy and I tried to clear my throat.

"A good moment for a kiss," Miles thought.

My thoughts scattered like startled wild animals. Stuck between the ladder and Miles's chest, I was afraid to breathe. I clasped my shaky hands and concentrated on the buttons of his well-ironed shirt, anticipating being burned alive if he got an inch closer.

Keep your head on, I told myself, but it was too late. My brain flew away to Neverland the minute our eyes met. An associate walked by and broke the enchantment. My savior stepped aside. With the escape route wide open, I dashed to the door.

"I should go now. Thank you for your help," I gabbled without turning to look back and fled, leaving unfinished work and unanswered questions behind.

I'm such a wuss, I lamented in the empty elevator on the way down. *I should have kissed him while I had the chance! What's the point of having supernatural abilities if I don't use them? My aunt should've given these pendants to someone else instead of wasting them on me.*

The emotional rollercoaster of the day had worn me out, and in the end, I had nothing to show for it. I wanted to stomp on the jewelry box, then make a fire in the middle of the kitchen and burn it. After taking a few deep breaths, I decided that selling the stones would be more reasonable.

Once outside, I headed to the library down the street to take my exam.

Olivia will make my life hell, and Miles... he'll never speak to me again after I ran off like that. At least Cinderella left a shoe behind. How will I ever look him in the eyes, not to mention work in the same office after hearing his thoughts?

The rational part of my brain eventually woke up from its slumber and attempted to reason things out.

Miles Taylor's attention is only as good as the influence of the Beauty stone. I can't let a temporary fling ruin my chances for the job. He can't be serious. It was so much easier when he'd ignored me! Ugh, these stones are complicating everything.

As I entered the building, my phone vibrated and interrupted the flood of my frenzied thoughts. Alicia left a message to complain about my no-show at lunch. Greg texted to ask for an update about our little endeavor, and James inquired why I'd disappeared two days in a row. I powered the phone off without answering. All I wanted was for everyone to leave me alone.

I signed in with the proctor and entered my exam cubicle, willing my mind to leave Miles Taylor alone and concentrate on the questions. But his face kept lurking between the lines. Despite that, I passed the exam. It didn't excite me anymore. What was the use of a certificate without a job? If I couldn't be a paralegal at Mr. Bailey's law firm, nobody else would hire me without any experience. It all seemed like a waste of time and money.

I dragged my feet to the tram station where a homeless person on the sidewalk contemplated food. He sat with his head down, covered by a blanket, with an empty hat in front of him. His disheartened thoughts made me turn around.

At least I have a place to stay and enough food to eat. I should get off this train Aunt Lou put me on and be happy with my current destination.

I took all the cash I had out of my wallet and handed it to the man. He looked up, first at my necklace, then into my eyes and grabbed my hand. Startled, I recognized him as a person who'd stood by my seat on the tram two days ago. I gasped and pulled away, but his grip was tight.

"You have a good heart," he said, golden light of the street lamp reflecting in his amber eyes. Their fiery gaze pierced through me. "Be careful what you choose."

He released his grasp. Shaken, I dashed away.

What does he mean choose carefully? I don't even have a choice, crazy man. Everything I do is destined to turn into a disaster.

I took the furthest seat on the tram and imagined myself locked away inside a tall castle for the rest of the ride home. A young woman next to me was full of anxious thoughts about college and living expenses that penetrated through my imaginary barrier. I couldn't handle her disorganized flight of ideas any longer and struck up a conversation.

"Did you have a stressful day?" I asked. The girl raised her big dark eyes at me with surprise and pushed the tightly coiled short hair out of the way.

"Why? Do I look it?" She gave me a timid smile.

"Oh, I don't know. I had a heck of a day at work myself." I tried to sound natural. Why would I talk to her in the first place? I'd already had enough trouble with mind reading to last me a lifetime.

"Well, I wish I had work. That's the problem. I've been looking. Don't even know if I'll be able to pay the rent." She choked on the last words.

"Do you have any family to help you?" I asked.

Instead of answering, she burst into tears. "I'm out of state and came here to study."

Now you've done it, Grace Ainsworth. This will teach you to not stick your nose in other people's business. What will you do now, miss-know-it-all?

"Why don't you give me your number. I'll see what I can do to help," I muttered.

The girl glanced at me through her tears. "Would you? I have some office work experience. I applied to a bunch of places but haven't heard anything back. The relative I stay with said I have to move out of her place next month, and I can't ask my Grandma to send more money. She's already helped me so much."

"I'll try to find something. You're brave to venture out on your own. Don't give up and don't let these difficulties stop you."

We exchanged phone numbers. The girl jumped up and gave me a tight hug before I exited at my stop. On the short walk home from the station I felt more at peace with myself.

At least I did a few useful things for others. This is an interesting way to live a life but not a very practical one. I don't think I need to be a mind reader to do what I did today. I just need to learn to pay attention to the people around me.

I stopped at the mailbox and found a letter from my aunt.

It contained one photo; Aunt Lou posed in front of an impressive mountain range that spread all the way to the horizon with a lavish green gorge at its feet. She stood with a backpack and a walking stick, her petite figure erect, a big smile spread on her tan face. Her curly reddish-blonde hair caught the last rays of the sun. On the back of the picture was her usual short scribble.

> Keskenkja Loop Trek.
> Jyrgalan Valley, Kyrgyzstan.
> Your journey is just beginning.
> Don't stop now.
> Climb that mountain.
> Cheers,
> Louise.

Back home, my mother sat in the living room with the TV on full blast. I took my shoes off and tiptoed down the hall. As I got closer to her small lonely figure, wrapped in a blanket, my feet grew heavier until I could no longer take another step. Her weighty thoughts filled the air and made it tangibly thick. I couldn't ignore them. She ruminated about her husband leaving, her health declining, and her life being a burden to her children. Caught in a never-ending circle of misery, she was crushed by self-pity and helplessness. Any resentment I might have held toward her melted away. After a glimpse into her disconsolate, hopeless inner world, all I wanted was to brighten her day. I walked up behind my mother and touched her shoulder. She flinched.

"Oh, I didn't expect you so early. You've been coming later every evening," she sniffled and then thought: "Better get used to it. She might soon leave altogether, like Julie."

"Mom, I'm here," I said, dismissing the bitterness in her voice. My heart ached. "I'm not going anywhere."

"I don't want to be a bother. Do your own thing." She brushed me off and flipped the channel.

I ignored my mother's comments and sat on the couch beside her. How I longed for her to cuddle me like a little girl. How many times I'd wanted to cry on her shoulder. That evening I had to be the one who brought comfort.

"Mom, I'm glad to have you in my life," I murmured. My eyes stung. "You're not a bother."

Her eyes darted in my direction and her lips trembled. She sighed several times and then patted my arm.

"And I'm glad I have you, Gracie." She sniffled. "Mr. Davis… he said he's too old to do things on his own and that… that he needs a reliable cashier. I'm sorry. I lost my job."

My mother broke into tears. I handed her napkins and let her talk. When her words ran out, for the first time I found the right things to say. Seeing through her insecurities, I told her that she was still beautiful. I reassured her that life was not over yet, and I needed her to take care of herself for me and for my sister.

"That job with Mr. Davis was the longest I've ever had. Six months. At least I made progress." She gave me a sad smile.

"Just wait. That old Scrooge will come running after you once all the male customers stop coming to his store. He'll think twice next time before firing a good-looking cashier."

My mother laughed but became somber again. "I can't wait for Julie to be back home again. Is spring break next week? Do you think she'll visit us this time? I was so sad when she missed Christmas."

"You know how college life is. She's too busy." I turned away. Making up excuses for my sister was not my favorite thing to do.

"I'm just not used to her being away for so long, and sometimes she doesn't even answer her phone. Why did she have to go to college in another state?"

"Mom, we already talked about this. She's eighteen and

enjoying her independence. You know, doing fun things like learning how to put her own socks in the laundry. She might even solve the mystery of the dishwasher. It'll be good for her." Suddenly, I had an idea. "Why don't you go dress up a bit? Tonight, we'll have a guest. I'll be right back."

I got up and ran out of the front door before she protested. Dashing across the hallway, I rang the neighbor's doorbell. Mr. Kent appeared in striped trousers and slippers with a protein shake in his hand. He nearly dropped it after seeing me in the doorway.

"Grace, what a surprise!"

"Mr. Kent, are you doing anything this evening? I want to invite you over for tea in about half an hour."

"Oh, that's such a grand idea! I would love to." He hesitated for a moment. "Is Mrs. Ainsworth better today?"

"Yes, thank you. She's well. I think she would enjoy some company."

"I'll be there momentarily."

"In half an hour, Mr. Kent. I need to get a few things ready." I laughed at his eagerness and ran to the store.

An hour later, we all sat at the dining room table. Mr. Kent had a neatly ironed long-sleeve dress shirt on and brought a box of chocolates. Lara Ainsworth looked lovely as well in an elegant yellow dress, with her hair pinned up into a curly bun the way she used to. She talked up a storm after the initial shock of discovering who our guest was. It turned out that I'd invited an older brother of her childhood friend.

"I'm sorry we didn't reconnect earlier," Mr. Kent apologized for the third time. "I saw you a few times but didn't get outside quickly enough to catch you. And to just come and knock on your door..."

"Don't blame yourself, John. I hardly leave the apartment unless I go to work. I'm surprised you even knew I lived here."

"My sister told me." Mr. Kent loosened up the collar of his shirt as though it choked him.

"Oh, that's right. April came to the store where I work... worked. It was a month or so ago. Such a surprise. To see her after all these years... If I'd known you lived so close... Should have tried to find you both."

She lowered her gaze, fixing the pins in her hair and shredding the napkin in her hands. Her thoughts echoed even louder than her words. "I didn't want you to see me like this. I'm such a mess."

Mr. Kent shifted in his chair and turned to me with a pleading expression. His thoughts flopped around helplessly, searching for things to say.

"Did your mother tell you, Grace, that she was the most beautiful girl in school?" He announced when I was about to offer him another piece of cake to break the uncomfortable silence. "All the boys fought for a chance to talk to her when she walked down the halls."

"You're exaggerating. Where did you hear that?" Lara shook her head, but a small smile brightened her face. "If I remember correctly, you graduated before your sister and I even started Ballard High."

"April told me stories. She was quite jealous of your popularity."

My mother thanked him for the compliment, all the while thinking, "I bet she's not jealous now."

But the mood at the table lightened, and the rest of the evening continued with lively conversations about happier days. I left to wash the dishes while my mother and Mr. Kent browsed through photo albums. They chatted, laughed, and remembered old times. I made a mental note to try and get her out of her own world more often.

It was late when Mr. Kent left and my mother went to bed. The familiar exhaustion swept over me. I had given myself to others until there was nothing left. That last leap had drained me, but I couldn't afford to fall apart—nobody was there to catch me and put the pieces back together. Alone in my room, I took the multicolored stone off my neck and turned it in different directions under the nightstand light. It didn't sparkle like the Beauty pendant. Instead, the light reflected off the crystal and revealed variations of color, pattern, and shape.

Every person is a unique combination of thoughts and feelings. Like this gem, sometimes it takes time to see the true beauty inside a person. Everyone wants to be heard and understood. Even my mother was more cheerful today because someone took the time to listen. I hope one day someone will be there for me.

To care for others wasn't easy, but it was worth it. And it wasn't all about physical needs. My mother's starved emotions proved that, and I was thankful to the pendant for that realization. The gift of Hearing had turned out useful after all, but I didn't think I could handle it for more than a day. It was time to put the gem back and try something else. I decided to complete my aunt's request, even if it didn't bring me any material gain. The small changes I'd experienced in the last two days were valuable enough.

I read all the labels again and opened the drawers that interested me until my eyes stopped at the word "courage." I skimmed through the booklet to find the meaning.

COURAGE

אֹמֶץ

(*Emerald*)

Ability to stand against one's own fears and overcome them, bravery in the face of danger, endurance and perseverance during difficult times, inner strength, decisiveness, boldness, ability to take risks and believe in oneself.

A wave of anguish washed over me. I got up from the chair and walked to the window. Staring into the black sky, I tried to subdue the storm inside. If there was anything I needed in my life, it was courage. Courage to do the things I wanted to do. Courage to try new things. Courage to pursue my dreams and climb the mountains in my life. Even courage to be myself. My rational mind kept me inside the walls of safety and prevented me from stepping out of my comfort zone. I had gotten into the habit of going through all the "what ifs" before I would venture out into unknown territory. Yes, my family relied on me, and I couldn't gamble with their livelihood or toy with a stable income. But the fear of failure, fear of what others will think, fear of what might happen paralyzed me and kept me in the shadows.

"It's my time to step out," I thought with determination. I opened the lid and looked down at the perfectly round emerald with silver trimming at the perimeter.

After putting the gem on, I resolved to have the best day yet and turned my phone back on before going to bed. I quickly scrolled through the messages from my friends and played a voicemail from my sister.

"Hi. Um, so I gotta tell you." Julie hesitated. "I had something happen. Hate to do this over the phone, but I need help. So, like I tried to drop a class, but it was too late, and they gave me a fail instead. Anyway, I think I have to pay for it or something 'cause there is some kind of rule. Financial aid won't cover it. It's ridiculous. And, um, I got kicked out of my dorm room. Totally not my fault, I swear. So, like I'm couch-surfing with my friend, but she said I can't stay long. I want to come home for the spring break until I can sort this crud out. That's why I'm calling. I need money for the ticket…"

PART IV
THE DARING LIFE

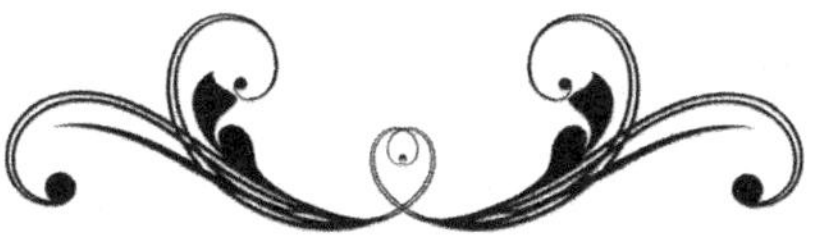

Only those who will risk going too far can possibly find out how far one can go.

—T. S. Eliot

I set my alarm for five o'clock in the morning, the outrageous hour Mr. Kent and I had agreed to meet for our daily run. Thankful for the snooze button, I immediately put it to use. Savoring a few more minutes in bed, I thought about the nightmare that'd haunted me during my sleep. It was an old dream I'd seen many times before, the only one I could ever remember except for those from the last two nights. It always started inside a large airplane. As if on cue, turbulence shook the cabin. Oxygen masks dropped down in front of frenzied passengers, and my gut twisted in knots as we plummeted to the ground at breakneck speed. In my childhood, I'd wake up screaming seconds before the crash. My mother always said that to fall in a dream meant I was growing. Our doctor disqualified her theory years ago when he told me I wouldn't add another inch.

My procrastination over, I jumped out of bed and into my workout clothes, which consisted of my sister's leggings and my baggy *Jedi in Training* T-shirt. Somehow it'd survived the closet purge. Despite the disastrous night, I felt energized and ran out to meet my neighbor. He was already stretching on the sidewalk.

"Morning!" He greeted me with a smile. "Are you ready for this?"

"Ready or not, here I come!" I laughed and ran past him.

When I returned home, my mother was already awake. She'd filled the kitchen with the long-forgotten buttery aroma of pancakes.

"Mom, you should've slept in today." I eyed her with suspicion.

"John offered to take me for a walk to the nearby park this morning, so I have to get ready. Looks like it'll be sunny," she said without turning from the stove. Her voice sounded unusually mellow.

"Great idea!"

"And he mentioned he misses our famous zucchini pancakes, so I decided to make some. Your grandmother used to make them all the time when he came over. I should teach you the recipe too."

"M-m." I nodded, already munching on one. "Zucchini is healthy, right?"

The traces of the hearing gift must have lingered, and I heard my mother's regrets of not spending more time with my grandma Pauline before she died. She'd been taken by cancer prior to our move back to Seattle.

"It's nice to have a day off, but tomorrow I'll search for work," my mother proclaimed.

Watching her cook pulled forgotten strings in my heart. Memories clouded my vision, and for a brief moment, I was back in the big bright kitchen of my childhood home, where my mother hummed while she baked. Those carefree times might have been long gone, but on that sunny Thursday morning, Lara Ainsworth hummed a tune once again. While she poured the batter in perfect circles in the frying pan, I stayed silent, afraid the peaceful scene might disappear in a cloud of smoke.

One thing was amiss. I stepped forward and put both

arms around my mother's shoulders. She stiffened against my sudden embrace but turned to face me. Her eyes glistened. After so many years, physical touch was like putting a foot in the wrong shoe. Why I decided to take that step, I couldn't tell. Was it the pendant?

"I missed your cooking," I said.

She's so isolated, stuck in this little place all day with no one to talk to. A knot developed in my throat, but I washed it down with a big gulp of coffee. I threw another warm pancake in my mouth and escaped to my bedroom.

I wanted to dress up. Even though my figure had gotten fuller, I resolved to put on a pair of slim-fit black slacks. Thank goodness they were stretchy, but in my world of oversized clothes, wearing them still equated to donning a spacesuit. The elongated silky yellow blouse complemented my form and smoothed out my curves. I dug up old contacts to use instead of glasses for my faltered vision. High heels, dangly earrings, and red lipstick completed the look. The green stone sparkled boldly on my chest. The woman in the mirror beamed with confidence and I liked her.

Today I'll break through all the barriers that are holding me back.

I glanced at my phone with my sister's message still saved in the voicemail. My headache-inducing pondering about possible solutions the night before hadn't produced any results. Julie's work-study money would never be enough to pay back the whole term, and my salary was eaten every month by bills with no leftovers. My credit card wouldn't provide enough funds either, especially after I'd used it for my new clothes. It was a dead end, but I couldn't let Julie quit her college education.

I'll figure something out. A few more days with Aunt Lou's present might make a difference. A stone to multiply money would've been nice to have. But since I'm in this land of fairy tales,

I snorted at the idea and hurried out of the apartment.

On the way to work, I showered complete strangers with smiles and compliments. Instead of hiding behind a large Agatha Christie volume during the transit, I chatted with people next to me. Was it the gift of courage or my decision to be more sociable?

When I got to the office, Mrs. Williamson met me at the door with another box of chocolates, and Mr. Bailey gave me a big hug.

"Our plan worked," he whispered in my ear.

"Are we out of deep waters now?" I asked.

"Definitely. We won a big case yesterday too. It should help. Here, this is for all your hard work." He put an envelope in my hand, then gathered everyone for an office meeting.

"Today we'll close early to celebrate our success at the Supreme Court," he announced.

The crowd cheered and threw papers in the air. I laughed at their excitement, but Olivia's appearance cut my enjoyment short. The woman was pale, her lips in a tight knot and her hands clenched into fists. A few disjointed thoughts I caught from her were full of anger and disbelief. She gave me a furious stare as if trying to burn me alive. I remembered a pile of unfinished work from the day before and escaped to my corner. Perhaps Olivia discovered the mess and was about to unleash her displeasure. But why such an extreme reaction?

I was flying through the hallway when Miles Taylor blocked my way. My face instantly flushed at the memories of yesterday's hasty escape. He looked striking in a dark gray shirt and slacks. Nicely trimmed black hair and a clean-shaven sculpted chin gave him a fresh appearance. His sweet cologne enveloped me, and his soothing low voice sent my heart into overdrive.

"I wanted to congratulate you on the success of your plan." He got terribly close and lowered his voice. "Until yesterday, I didn't know a thing about you, and here you come and save all of us from impending doom. You're a mystery."

Sending a mental SOS to the gem on my chest, I expected to panic, to lose my senses, to run away like the day before. Instead, I looked steadily into his dark captivating eyes.

"Mr. Taylor," I said. "A woman might be a mystery, but a determined man can solve it."

Oh, laser brain! Are you flirting with him?

Miles's eyebrows lifted for a second and his attractive grin widened, revealing a dimple on one cheek. I stifled a sigh. How could he possibly get any better-looking?

"I'd love to do that," he said in a way that made me forget my name. In his mind, he'd already drawn me close.

I could swear at that moment music played in the background and little sparkling hearts fluttered in the air above us. Unfortunately, it all abruptly disappeared when I spoke.

"I'm sorry, I didn't mean for you to take this literally."

What?!

My voice sounded cool and controlled, as if the hottest guy alive wasn't hovering over me. For some insane reason, I acted like his charm had no effect on me. Even worse—I brushed him off!

"Now, if you could let me go through," I continued. "I have lots of work to do before we all leave."

Who cares about work?! Is the pendant making me say these horribly reasonable things?

Miles seemed as confused and surprised as I felt. He straightened up to make room for me to pass, but my knees felt so weak I wasn't sure I could move at all.

Miles cleared his throat. "Your wish is my command, even if it's to work when everyone relaxes. After what you've done—"

"I've done nothing extraordinary. It was my duty." Despite my quivering heartbeat, my voice was annoyingly steady. I held his gaze without wavering.

"Still, I'm your debtor," he insisted.

"I did it for everyone here, but if you're taking this so personally, then consider us even—you already saved me yesterday."

No, no, no! Feel indebted to me forever. Blast this stone. I inwardly groaned. How could I sound so nonchalant when my insides melted away like a marshmallow in a bonfire? But hadn't I decided to stuff my feelings away and extinguish his temporary infatuation for the sake of reason?

I guess it's best to discourage him.

Miles was surprisingly relentless. "That's not a fair comparison, you need to let me thank you. At least give me a clue—what can I do for you?"

I shook my head and slipped past him, then glanced back. Miles Taylor, who'd towered over me just a minute ago, now stood silently in the corner. My strange behavior erased the usual smug look from his face. For a moment, I was tempted to throw myself into his arms, but something held me back, something new that had awakened within me. Was it self-worth?

"Surprise me," was all this new sassy Grace said.

"It might be impossible to do with a mind reader like you," he protested, but I already strode away with a flood of concerns filling my mind.

I must have read the instructions wrong. Did I miss the part where the Courage stone makes me a stuck up? I already have a hard time with Miles without the pendants messing things up. Why am I pushing him away? What if he's in earnest... No, I can't think about that. It'll drive me nuts and will ruin my plans. I have to figure out how to make him view me as his future assistant. Although this kind of behavior won't do.

I needed a plan. What did I know about Miles Taylor?

Yes, he was attractive, rich, and successful. But what qualities was he looking for in his assistant? What if my curt ways piqued his interest instead of scaring him off? What if the pendant was right, and it was the best strategy?

To even think clearly about the person who usually turned my mind into a tangled mess was progress. A sense of confidence and independence slowly filled me. My steps lightened, as though I'd traded heavy-duty work boots for comfy crystal slippers. The burdens and anxieties that lay heavy on my heart lifted. Relieved, I flew around the office and helped my co-workers finish their tasks.

After organizing my work area, I opened the envelope from Mr. Bailey and found a check. The note inside explained that it was a bonus for extra work I'd done the day before and for my "contributions to the well-being of the firm". The generous sum was enough to cover Julie's round-trip ticket. I did a little dance around my desk and texted my sister to tell her the good news.

An hour later, I found myself in Mr. Bailey's office delivering documents. He was busy reading. I snuck in and put a stack of papers on his desk. Startled, my boss nearly jumped out of his seat.

"I'm sorry, Mr. Bailey, I didn't mean to disturb you. Here are your reports for today," I said. The title of the document he was so engrossed in caught my attention. "Whittaker vs. Kowalski" was typed in big letters at the top of the paper. Was it the same Kowalski that had tried to bring him down? Mr. Bailey intercepted my gaze and slammed the file shut.

"Well, Grace, now that the risk of closing is behind us, tell me—what can I do for you?"

"You've already given me extra pay. I wanted to say how I appreciate—"

"I haven't done anything yet," he interrupted. "The money was for the work you did so smoothly in Mrs. Williamson's place. Now I want to personally thank you for preventing a disaster."

"I simply did what is right," I said.

"Nonsense! I want to do a few things for a faithful employee. Don't interfere with that. I know a valuable person when I see one."

I don't even recognize my own value. Well, time to change that.

"Ok. There is something..." I swallowed hard, but the stone pushed the words out of my mouth. "I can do more in this place, and I'm willing to learn. You saw yesterday, I pick up new skills on the fly. My current position is very limited. I have so much more to offer."

My mouth became as dry as a desert. To talk about myself was like taking a breath underwater. I clasped the pendant with my hand and tried to squeeze more courage out of it. Mr. Bailey was silent, so I continued.

"Yesterday I passed the exam for my paralegal certificate. I submitted the application for the job opening to be Mr. Taylor's assistant, and I was wondering if you could ask Miss Peterson to consider me for the interview. There are people with more education and experience, but I understand how this office functions. All I'm asking is a chance to prove myself."

The more I talked, the bolder I got. My back straightened and self-assurance made my voice steady. I didn't care anymore what Olivia Peterson might do. I needed that job and knew I could do it well.

Mr. Bailey listened with interest.

"That's fair," he said. "For now, I'll discuss with Olivia the options to expand your scope of duties. Give me some time, and I'll find a proper place for you in the office. You're a bright girl. I don't want to lose you. And besides, who'll take care of me next time documents get lost in this worthless place?"

Mr. Bailey's conversation with my supervisor happened

rather quickly, and the woman threw vengeful glances in my direction for the rest of the morning.

"Don't think Mr. Bailey can protect you much longer," Olivia snarled as she dropped an outrageous number of files on my desk. "Finish these before we all leave."

I calmly held her gaze, restraining myself from sticking my tongue out. Her open disdain and threats didn't bother me anymore. She must have read "just dare me!" in my eyes and left me alone to hustle through the paperwork. Mrs. Williamson came to check on me and, seeing my paper-disaster, rolled up her sleeves next to me. She chatted about Mr. Abeles and his high praise of my skills, and I wondered what I'd done to impress the peculiar gentleman.

CHAPTER 15

Our office staff decided to eat lunch together at Loulay Kitchen & Bar, which was just a block away. To my relief, Olivia declined to join us because of a headache. Normally I would've done the same, but the pendants had turned me into a socialite who wouldn't miss a chance to mingle. Mr. Bailey was in such a good mood that he reserved the whole place. Inside the cozy establishment with wooden floors and warm lights, I caught Miles's gaze on me and walked toward the table where he was sitting.

"Trying to catch two fish at once?" Victoria hissed in my ear.

She stood next to me, turning heads in her skin-tight black dress with how-low-can-you-go cleavage, her shiny hair falling over the round shoulders. Before I could answer, the young woman walked past me and took the last seat next to Miles. Her eyes met mine with a challenge before she turned to smile at our boss. I squared my jaw and walked over to another table.

She won't ruin my day. Miles can come and sit with me if he wants. There'll be other opportunities to smooth things out between us.

Instead of getting discouraged, I talked to my co-workers, enjoyed the food, and willed myself to ignore Miles Taylor. I couldn't completely keep him out of my sight. Soon, everyone left the confines of the tables and scattered around the bar area. Was it my imagination or had Miles made several attempts to get closer to me? If so, our co-workers made it quite impossible. Victoria didn't leave his side, and a few other women surrounded the young lawyer in a tight circle everywhere he went. Men also grabbed his attention with conversations. When he made progress in my direction, others pulled me away.

The sarcasm that usually occupied the inner crevices of my mind found its way out and caused quite a stir. A loud crowd gathered around the bar stand where I fired away jokes about attorneys and courts. Everyone burst with laughter, but I noticed a crease on Miles's forehead. He stood nearby with a different group. His eyes followed me, as if I was attached to him by an invisible string. Each time I caught his intense gaze, I smiled and nodded but didn't take a single step closer. Everything inside me longed to get near him, to hear his voice, to be one of those women who hang on his every word. But the emerald stone on my chest formed an invisible barrier. It stubbornly pulled me away from my boss and into other social interactions.

After the meal, we spilled outside the restaurant onto a sunny sidewalk. The air buzzed with conversations, and we dispersed to let the pedestrians pass. Out of the corner of my eye, Miles's tall figure once again moved in my direction. A group of ladies stopped him. I chuckled, watching him push through the barricade of bodies. When he eventually came closer, I couldn't suppress my laugh.

"Mr. Taylor, are women always fighting for your attention?" I teased.

"Miss Ainsworth, you're very observant as usual. As you can see, popularity with the opposite sex has its drawbacks," he replied, matching my tone.

"Really?" My eyebrows curled up in an exaggerated surprise.

"Yes, but I haven't discovered how to deal with this issue yet. Perhaps you can help me. Seems like you're good at solving problems."

"Oh, you think too highly of my abilities. This is an area where I have no expertise."

"That's hard to believe." Miles looked me over. "You're either too modest or too good at playing the game."

"I'm not playing any games." My face burned, and my jaw tightened. This conversation wasn't going the way I'd hoped.

"Then I just can't figure you out," he said.

"What if I don't want to be figured out?" My voice was chilly. I caught a few frustrated thoughts that escaped Miles's mind. Unfortunately, with the power of the Hearing stone slipping away, his inner world was beyond my reach.

"At least you're being honest..." Miles rubbed his neck. "What should I do, then? I'm afraid, you have to tell me."

"Just be yourself, and we'll get along perfectly."

My heart squeezed as I watched his usual composed demeanor melt away. It was alien to be so blatantly frank, and I suspected the stone had something to do with my boldness. But was it a wise route to take?

While Miles tried to formulate a response, Mr. Bailey came and pulled him away. I was left alone with my tormenting thoughts.

Look at all these women—they would do anything to get his attention and fulfill his every wish. Why would he ever want to work with me if I give him such a hard time? Even Mr. Bailey won't be able to convince him now.

Away from the crowd, I tried to comprehend this new spunky streak in me. Was it arrogance? Would Miles be intrigued by a prude who constantly gave him the cold shoulder? I had to find a middle ground. Fast.

He did say he likes my honesty, but a little diplomacy on my part wouldn't hurt.

What would happen to me without the power of the pendant? To speak without reservations and to stand up for myself was unknown territory. I didn't know how to navigate it.

As I turned to join the group, I noticed a man staring at me from the storefront nearby. He was middle-aged, tall, and dressed in simple clothes. Curly jet-black hair and a short beard framed his attractive face with the elongated nose, dark eyes, and olive skin that seemed to glow in the sun. When our eyes met, he turned away and pretended to be interested in the window display. Was he looking at my necklace? It wasn't a good idea after all to ignore my aunt's advice about keeping the gem covered. I took the scarf out of my purse and wrapped it around my neck.

Don't be paranoid again.

"Grace!" A familiar voice shouted close by. Seconds later, Greg crossed the street and stood next to me. His cordial face beamed with satisfaction, as though he'd just discovered Santa was real. Relieved to have a six-foot barrier between me and the curious stranger, I greeted him with a smile.

"Didn't expect to see you," Greg said. He shook my hand. "I'm glad you can enjoy some sunshine instead of inhaling the dust under a pile of boring paperwork. How did you escape from that bureaucratic dungeon?"

"Greg, don't say that. My whole company is here." I glanced at my co-workers behind us, but they were too far away to overhear.

"Greg always says the first thing that comes to mind," interjected a stylishly dressed striking brunette. She leisurely sauntered closer and put her arm around Greg's elbow as if she owned the man. Tall and lean, she looked like a model from the cover of one of those fashion magazines I'd never read. Next to her, I felt like a plump little pumpkin. Another man stepped up when Greg turned to introduce us. I recognized him as a victim of my clumsiness.

"Grace, this is Sandra, my associate. And this is Jamal. You had the pleasure of knocking him off his feet a few days ago."

We both laughed and shook hands. Sandra stayed at Greg's side, making me uncomfortable with her stare.

Stuck to him like a piece of gum on a shoe, I thought while exchanging friendly phrases with Jamal. *Ok, Grace, today is apparently the day you get to do all kinds of unconventional things. What will it be this time?*

I knew in an instant. Turning to Greg, I put my hand around his free arm.

"If you would excuse us, Greg and I have something important to discuss. I hope it's okay if we leave you now."

Greg glanced at me with surprise but, seeing the mischief in my eyes, quickly caught on.

"Oh, yes, I completely forgot," he exclaimed. "I'm sorry to leave you guys, but I have to do this first."

It took the clingy woman at his side a few seconds to let go of his arm. She tried to give him a goodbye hug, but I'd already pulled Greg in the opposite direction.

Too bad I can't do this with Miles and just pull him away from everybody for a longer chat. Friendship is so much less complicated.

I smiled. At that moment I felt like a child who'd just won a big pile of candy at the city fair. I would have skipped around on the sidewalk but remembered I was an adult woman in grown-up shoes.

"Ok, I'm ready for another adventure," Greg said.

We walked past the restaurant entrance and a few people waved goodbye. Miles stopped talking to Mr. Bailey and stared. His lips held a silent question when he watched me walk away holding on to Greg's arm. My mind-reading days had come to a halt, and I strained to get a glimpse into

Miles's thoughts. Was he jealous? Did his reaction indicate I actually meant something to Mr. Perfect? The idea seemed too bold, even for a girl with the stone of Courage on her chest.

Once we turned the street corner and were out of sight, Greg spoke again.

"How long are you going to hold me in the dark about your plans? My curiosity will burn me alive if you don't satisfy it right this minute. Do we have another conspiracy to solve?"

"There's nothing planned," I replied.

Greg stopped in the middle of the sidewalk and faced me with his arms crossed.

"You disappoint me, Grace Ainsworth. I was expecting another mind-blowing adventure."

"We'll get into some kind of trouble, I'm sure. With you, it's just a matter of time." I laughed and pulled him along. A momentary sting of guilt hit me. "I hope I didn't take you away from anything important."

He winked. "Nothing a boring business magazine can't wait for."

We turned to a quieter street, took a shortcut to the waterfront and walked along the pier. The weather was perfect. Gentle sunshine sparkled on the metal rails and in the calm silvery-green waters. A barely noticeable breath of cool air with a scent of seaweed came from the bay area and played with my still healthy golden locks. Seagulls busied themselves on the sidewalk, spooked occasionally by pedestrians and bikers. I ran up to them and watched the birds fly in different directions. My soul followed them. It wished to rise above all the limitations into the open sky of possibilities.

We continued to stroll in silence, afraid to ruin the moment, then Greg spoke again.

"So, an unexpected day off?"

"Yes! Good news. The partners are not leaving, and Mr. Bailey threw us a party. I suspect it was another way to show that everything is great at the firm."

"I'm glad to hear that. Although, I recall you don't enjoy working there much."

"Well, I might've changed my mind… slightly. Actually, a lot of things happened in the last few days to make me change my views," I reflected.

"How so?"

I paused to think. We leaned on the cold rail and watched the calm waters underneath.

"For years I believed I had to put away my dreams and take care of the necessities of life first," I finally said. "Like in Maslow's hierarchy of needs. I was always at the bottom, worrying about food and shelter. I believed it was selfish to want something more for myself. But it's time to move up the chain and get out of survival mode."

"You know what's next on Maslow's ladder?"

"Accomplishment and self-actualization."

"Nope, you skipped one."

"What?"

"Affection and love."

I opened my mouth to say something, but no sound came out. My bewilderment must have been entertaining because gaiety oozed out of Greg's bright eyes. He tried unsuccessfully to suppress a smirk.

"Did I hit a taboo topic? Is it why you skipped to self-actualization? Or is this step already behind you, your heart taken by the dashing man of your dreams?" His mouth spread wider in a disarming grin, but the more he talked, the more uncomfortable I became.

"It's not funny," I fumed. "Next time I might think twice before sharing anything with you. And to answer your question—it's none of your business."

"Ouch, I stuck my foot in my mouth again. Would you forgive this nosy journalist?"

Abruptly he dropped to one knee in front of me with a comical expression on his face.

What did Alicia say a few days ago? Guys won't "fall out of the sky and land on one knee in front of you." Well, here is the first one.

That realization made me laugh, and I motioned for Greg to get up.

"Ok, I forgive you, but now you have to make it up to me."

"Anything you want."

"The problem is, I don't really know what I want. Today my plan was to step out of my comfort zone."

"That's a fantastic plan, and I'm just the right person to assist you."

"Ok, good."

"You can disclose all your deepest darkest fears. I'm ready. Go ahead."

Greg made an effort to pull the corners of his lips down and be somber for once, but his eager anticipation of amusement was too obvious. He offered his elbow for me to hold. I pushed him away.

"What are you so giddy about? I'm not sure I should tell you anything, Greg Miller!"

"Oh, no, trust me, I'm the perfect candidate for this job." He grinned.

He is having too much fun with this.

"I guess there is no turning back now. But I have a feeling you're a big risk-taker, and you'll have me do more than I signed up for." I narrowed my eyes and watched with growing concern as Greg nodded. "Well, I don't see any other option. Let's get this over with. Number one, I'm afraid of heights."

I regretted my confession as soon as it came out of my mouth.

Greg's face lit up with excitement. "I've got the perfect solution."

And with that, he grabbed my hand and pulled me toward our office building. Reluctantly, I followed his lead. After a few minutes, we were in the parking lot. Greg put me in his car and stepped outside to make a phone call. My hands got sweaty and cold. I didn't even want to imagine what kinds of ideas that adventure-hungry reporter would pull out of his hat. When I started to plan my escape route, I caught sight of the man who watched me earlier on the street. He got closer, and I slid lower in the chair, covering my face with a copy of the business magazine Greg left in the car.

Don't be ridiculous, Grace. He probably works here too.

A minute later, I peeked through the window, but the stranger still hovered close by. There was no way I would risk leaving now. When I was ready to lose my last nerve, Greg jumped into the car and sped away with a satisfied expression on his face.

I'd probably survive on top of the Space Needle, but virtual bungee jumping might cause the evacuation of my lunch. I would hate to waste good food.

"Are you going to tell me where we're headed?" I demanded.

"Nope," Greg answered without turning in my direction. "But you're welcome to disclose your other fears on the way there."

I gave him a sour look. "I'm afraid of sport cars and adrenaline junkies who drive them."

"Let's help you overcome it right now." And with that Greg stepped on the gas.

CHAPTER 16

We drove until the city was behind us and nothing but open countryside lay ahead. The sun was in full force. With windows open, I closed my eyes and let the wind throw my hair around. I sensed Greg watching me and turned, but he shifted his attention to the road with both hands steady on the wheel.

He should've been a farmer, not a reporter.

I studied the man's broad shoulders and muscular arms under a simple plaid shirt with rolled-up sleeves. His messy straw hair and five o'clock shadow over his concrete jaw completed the scruffy look. He glanced in my direction and smiled, ruining the "tough guy" mold I tried to fit him in.

"What else do you need for happiness but sunshine and wind on your face?" he said.

Was that truly all a person needed? I thought about my life. What was I looking for? Why did I agree to go to an unknown destination with a person I'd met just a few days ago? Especially the man who seemed to harbor secrets from his past life. Was this stone of Courage making me reckless? With supernatural powers messing with my head, I gave up any attempts to make sense of things. But in all honesty, I couldn't blame it all on the pendant. Greg had a way of putting people at ease and made me feel as though I'd known him for a long time. Although, to trust him with my fears was probably still a bit too forward.

After what seemed like hours, we turned onto a private road with tall cedar pines flanking both sides. Greg stopped his car at the curb, and we stepped out.

"It's more beautiful here during the summer, but I still like to walk through this area," he said.

We strolled along the trees, then through a garden that was not fully awake after its winter slumber. Coming through the pruned shrubs, we finally arrived at the front of a large colonial style two-story house. I stopped to admire the natural-looking pond with a fountain and a grand entrance with stone arches. A middle-aged man with straw-colored hair and a full beard appeared at the door. He rushed towards us through a manicured lawn like an armed Viking running into battle. Instead of throwing an ax, the Scandinavian-looking giant gave Greg a big bear hug, lifting him slightly off the ground.

"Hey, buddy."

"Josh, you'll squeeze the lunch out of me." Greg chuckled and broke out of the embrace. "Meet Grace. Grace, this is my older brother Josh."

"Very nice to meet you," Josh said. Despite his size, the man had a gentle smile. "So, I heard we're going to cure your fear of heights today?"

"Hey, don't give out too much information or she'll try to escape." Greg lifted one brow and pulled me into a side hug. I shot him a nervous glance.

We walked around the house, past the wooded property in the back, and came to a clearing. A tall building resembling a shop stood in our way. In front of the largest garage door I've ever seen were two small airplanes. A stretch of concrete spread behind them far into the grassy field.

Realization dawned on me. "Oh, no, no, no!"

I turned to run, but Greg's broad chest blocked my way.

"Grace, how else would I fix your fear of heights without taking you up high?" Greg raised my chin up and forced me to look into his eyes, his expression adamant. "You can do this. I'll be with you."

I couldn't tell if my heart was beating fast from the sight of the aircraft or from our sudden proximity. I closed my eyes and tried to calm myself. With the green stone tightly in my hand, I remembered what the booklet said: "ability to stand against one's own fears and to overcome them." Then why was I freaking out?

"You don't understand," I pleaded. "I've flown on an airplane only once as a child. A big one. I hated it. Then we got into turbulent weather. It was terrible. I still have nightmares about it. I'm not sure what will happen if you force me to do this. You might have to scrape my lunch off the floor."

"Let me show you my jet first," Josh offered. He led me to the airplane and lowered the steps for me to get inside.

Reluctantly, I climbed up and peeked through the oval door. The interior looked more like a fancy lounge than an aircraft cabin. It had folding tables and even a minibar. The smooth beige-colored leather was soft and comfortable, but that didn't ease my anxiety.

"My brother is a private pilot. He gives rides to people who don't like to drive," Greg said behind me.

Josh chuckled, but I wasn't in the mood for jokes.

"I don't mind driving at all," I said and made the two of them laugh.

"We'll be going on the smaller plane," Greg said.

"You mean that tin can on wheels?" I frowned. The smaller aircraft a few feet away did not look very sturdy. "I like that idea even less. Why can't we go on the nice one?"

"It's a solid airplane, and my brother is a great pilot. He'll be gentle, I promise. But first we need to gear up."

I searched for ways to escape, but Greg followed me around like a bodyguard. He took me inside the hangar, handed me a full-body jumpsuit, made me switch my shoes, tie up my hair, and put on eye goggles.

"This looks like a rebel flight suit." I pursed my lips. "So much for dressing up today."

"It'll be cold up there."

I wanted to ask why it would be cold in the airplane and why his brother wasn't wearing the same outfit but figured the guy must have done it too many times to care. Greg put a backpack on himself with straps around his arms, waist, and legs, then placed similar straps on me. I grabbed his hands.

"Wait! What's this for?"

"It's for your safety, Grace. You've never flown in an airplane like this, so trust me that I know what I'm doing."

The straps were uncomfortable, and he made them even tighter, but I complied. I tried to walk and nearly fell on the ground.

"Are you also trying to cure my fear of appearing clumsy in front of others?"

Greg seemed to enjoy watching me hobble along towards the aircraft. He fastened a strange device on his wrist and tried to explain how it showed the airplane's altitude.

"Thank you very much, I don't want to hear this kind of information," I said wearily. "If I wasn't a hobbit against you two trolls, I would've ran away by now."

"I always wanted to meet a real-life hobbit. I think you're about the right size."

Greg laughed and lifted me up into the airplane's cabin like I was made out of feathers. I stumbled over a groove on the floor and practically fell into one of the chairs. The cabin was much smaller, with just four seats. Greg closed the door and helped me buckle up. His brother prepared the airplane for takeoff. I pressed my back against the cushion and squeezed the handles on both sides. Greg peeled one of my hands off and took it in his. He rubbed my cold fingers and spoke into my ear over the noise of the engine.

"You'll be ok. You're brave."

All of his friskiness disappeared. His voice was calm and reassuring. A strange sweetness spread around my chest like warm syrup. My muscles relaxed. I licked my dry lips and tried to peek out of the window. Repeated waves of nausea hit my stomach, and I stared straight ahead while the airplane picked up speed on the runway. There was an uncomfortable sensation in my head when we lifted off the ground. I closed my eyes tightly, waiting for it to pass. We finally leveled out, but the ride was bumpy. Greg's voice continued to hum in my ear. I sensed his warm breath on my cheek but didn't understand a single word.

"Grace, listen," Greg urged. He must have repeated himself several times before it registered.

I opened my eyes. Oval windows showed nothing but a patch of blue sky. We must have been in the air for over ten minutes, but I'd lost all concept of time.

"Ok, not that bad. At least I survived the takeoff. When can we land?" I said with a weak smile.

"Landing is exactly what I want to talk to you about. We'll have to jump."

"We have to do what?!" I straightened up in my seat and grabbed his arm. If I'd had fake nails, I would've pierced his shirt.

"You'll be attached to me, so there is not much for you to do. Trust me, you'll enjoy it."

I finally understood what those strange outfits were for. How could I've been so gullible? "Trust you? You can't do this to me!"

Panic choked me, but I had nowhere to escape. Stuck in the tight airplane cabin, I felt betrayed and helpless.

"Grace, I'm not giving you a choice. We'll fly around until

you're ready. Remember, if we run out of fuel and crash, it'll be much worse than to land with a parachute on."

"You're crazy!"

Greg folded his arms. There was not even an ounce of the usual playfulness in his features. I was looking at a man who wouldn't back down.

No, no! I can't do this, my mind raced. *Today is the worst day of them all! Why did I ever tell him about my fear of heights?*

Greg didn't say anything else. His brother circled around the drop zone and threw puzzled glances in our direction. I looked out from the window, imagined leaping off the plane and almost fainted.

"Grace, don't let the fear get the best of you," Greg finally said. "Just do it. You can thank me later."

"Thank you? You tricked me into this!" Anger rose in my chest. "Why does everyone think they can make decisions for me?!"

I covered my mouth, surprised by the fiery words that'd burst out. It seemed I was bound to speak my mind all day long.

"I'm sorry." Greg rubbed his forehead. "I guess, I overstepped my bounds. It's just you wouldn't have agreed to do this if I gave you a warning. I'll tell my brother to land if that's what you want."

Yes, I would've fought him tooth and nail, but it was still my choice. Too many times a simple ability to choose had been taken away from me, and now the stone of Courage urged me to take it back. But why wouldn't the pendant help me overcome my fear of heights? I pressed the gem into my palm and held it so tight it hurt. Had it run out of batteries? Then I remembered. *The carrier of the gift must learn to accept...* That was it! The stones respected my free will! I had to stop resisting. My inner protest was so strong, it must have overpowered the pendant's influence.

Let go of your fear, Grace.

I took a deep breath and my nerves instantly calmed down. When my head cleared, I spoke again with a steady voice.

"How many times have you done this?"

"Enough to have a license."

"Fine. But if you kill me, you'll have to do all my paper filing at the office tomorrow."

"Deal." Greg put his hand out to shake on it, but I didn't take it. He ran it through his hair instead. "Would you forgive me if I promise to never force you to do something you don't want to?"

"You make too many promises, Greg Miller." I attempted to give him a scornful look, but couldn't suppress a disobedient smile that pulled up the corners of my lips. Greg let out a breath he was holding, his features relaxed.

"I was supposed to give you instructions ahead of time, but was afraid you'd bail out on me. So we have to do it now."

He told me about the things I didn't want to hear—our jump, descent, and landing. He had me repeat it all back, then motioned to his brother. We stood up.

"I'll have to look out first before we jump. Just relax," he murmured in my ear. "Are you ready, little penguin?"

It all happened so quickly, I didn't even have time to get mad about the name-calling. Greg strapped himself behind me, the door slid open and the cold wind rushed into my face. The harness pulled tightly around my body and we jumped.

The rush of air assaulted my face and muted my screams, pushing my voice back into my throat. After the initial shock, I opened my eyes, surprised at the absence of the gut-wrenching sensation the airplane ascent had given me earlier. Greg's sturdy hands forced my arms out and spread them like wings. We were like a pair of birds floating in the air. Wasn't that what I'd wanted earlier? An exhilarating rush of emotion swept over me. It was intoxicating, overwhelming, indescribable, and it liberated me.

A loud noise and a sudden jerk upward made my heart leap. Our parachute opened, and the straps tightened around my body again. Silence enveloped us like the clouds that covered the outlines of the land below. The earth spread for miles beneath us. Soon I was able to see the winding strings of roads in the brownish-gray patches of land.

"Hold on to these," Greg ordered.

I grabbed the two loops he placed in my hands.

"Now you're in control." He put his hands on top of mine and moved them in different directions making the parachute rotate.

The surface beneath us grew closer by the second.

"Now, remember to hold your feet up," Greg said as the ground rapidly approached.

A few minutes later we landed on the grassy field. I fell into the weeds and pretended to kiss the earth.

"I'm alive! We did it! And it was amazing!" I yelled.

I jumped around as soon as Greg took off our harnesses. My overwhelmed heart expanded in my chest and threatened to explode. Greg followed me silently with his eyes and smiled while putting our parachutes back together.

"Oh, my goodness! Why didn't you tell me it would be like that? I was flying! It was just you and me and the whole sky," I shouted, unable to contain my excitement. "I can do anything now."

"Well, I'm sure glad you survived. I wouldn't want to be stuck cleaning up Mr. Bailey's paper messes for you," he said coolly.

I grunted, threw a patch of grass in his direction, then chased him down the field. My legs were too short to get anywhere close, but Greg suddenly stopped, turned around, and caught me in his arms. I laughed and struggled to get out of his iron embrace, but he held me tight. With adrenaline still rushing through me and suddenly self-conscious of my body pressed against his, I broke away, breathless.

"You're going in the wrong direction, little penguin!" Greg yelled after me, instigating another fruitless chase.

GREG WAS UNUSUALLY quiet during our walk back to the house. The sun began its descent and birds flew closer to the ground, their melody weaving with the sweet fragrance of the wild grasses. The peace that filled me in the quietness of the atmosphere settled in my heart. Strolling through the country scenery with a friend brought an unfamiliar contentment.

"So what's *your* biggest fear?" I said, walking side-by-side with Greg. "It's only fair if you tell me yours."

Greg frowned. His jaw lines tensed. "My biggest fear is to see injustice and not be able to do anything about it."

I bit my lip. Was it the story he didn't want to tell me? I couldn't resist asking for an explanation. "What happened?"

Greg became silent for a while. We continued to walk, and I looped my arm around his elbow to keep up with his stride. He finally broke the silence, his voice dull. "It was in South Sudan. I was involved in the effort to reduce the recruitment of child soldiers. We spread the word, looked for ways to integrate the boys back into society, reached out to the government… It was like a drop of water in the ocean. I watched these kids try to return to their villages only to be recaptured. One boy got beaten in front of me. All I achieved by intervening was getting a few broken ribs myself…"

My heart squeezed in my chest. "Was it the boy from your last article?"

Greg nodded, his expression hard.

"What mattered is that you tried," I said. "Even the smallest person can change the course of history."

Greg gave me a sideway glance. "Says who?"

"Lady Galadriel in *The Lord of the Rings.*"

He gave me a humorless smile that didn't reach his eyes. "Maybe in a fantasy world. Things are not so easy in real life."

CHAPTER 17

Josh, his wife, and their two school-age daughters waited for us in their beautiful home. We spent our evening at the large dinner table with plenty of laughs and chatter. Josh made fun of my now forgotten fears and told stories of Greg's younger years. The two girls didn't leave their uncle alone for one minute, filling the room with their giggles. After our meal, the kids pulled Greg and me into their playroom. The girls insisted on being pilots "like dad", and we proceeded to have a few great battles for the rebellion, swiftly transported on their makeshift X-Wing. All too soon we said goodbye and were back on the road. It was already dark outside, but I wanted to stay there forever.

"Your brother and his family are very nice," I said while we sped down the highway.

"Yep, they're the best."

"I can tell the two of you are close. Do your parents live in the area too?"

"Not really. They live a little farther than Josh and I can reach, even on the airplane," Greg pointed upward. "Died in a car crash when I was still a boy. They moved here from

Australia, so no close relatives around. Josh practically raised me."

"I'm sorry to hear that. I would have loved to meet them."

Greg gave me a fleeting smile. "I bet they would've liked you. But at least you met my brother."

"I had a great time. I wish my sister and I had the same relationship. I didn't do as good of a job."

"How so?"

I shrugged. "I don't think she enjoyed having a sibling that turned into a rule maker. It didn't go well with a free-spirited girl like her. She even picked an out-of-state college to get away from me. I don't blame her. She was too young to understand how hard it was to save every penny for housing and meals."

"You did the right thing."

"I still wish I wasn't such a bore." I let out a short laugh.

"You don't bore me." Greg grinned.

I shook my head. "She'd never believe me if I told her what I did today. Thank you for infusing a dose of adventure into my humdrum life."

"We're not done yet." He gave me a pointed look. "You still need to give me the rest of the items on your list."

"There are no more lists," I said.

"Then you're fearless." And his eyes were serious this time.

THE DRIVE back to the apartment went by quickly. Greg parked by the entrance and we sat in silence. He reached for the phone brushing his hand against mine and sending an electrical current up my arm. I looked up. In the dim light, his attractive features softened, his eyes became dark and drew me into their endless depths. My breath caught like it had during the free fall. The air grew heavy when his gaze traveled over my face. It stirred up the longing inside me to be touched, to be held in his arms again. If only I could read his mind...

What's happening to you, Grace? You had too much excitement today. Be rational, don't ruin this friendship.

"Thanks for everything. I had lots of fun. Goodnight," I rattled as I jumped out of the car.

I didn't stop until I ran into the apartment. Back in my room, I opened the curtain. Greg was still parked below my windows, his silhouette motionless inside the cabin. I leaned on the windowsill and fogged up the cold glass with my feverish breath. What just happened? What had I run from that even the stone of Courage couldn't stop me?

If I'd stayed a little longer and asked myself again what I wanted to do... No. I would've ruined our perfectly good friendship and made a fool out of myself. Greg hasn't given me any reason to think... It was bad enough to say a bunch of nonsense to Miles earlier and mess everything up. I can't just act on a whim. I need to focus on fixing things with my boss and getting the job interview. This stone has caused enough trouble for one day.

Greg finally drove away. I opened the window and listened to the crickets outside. The night was clear and stars shone brightly around a full moon. I played with the pendant on my neck, lost in thought.

Oh, Greg, you called me fearless, but I'm so far from it. I shouldn't rely on a superpower to be empowered. I just need to take a few steps out of my comfort zone once in a while. I should stop limiting myself and stand up for the things that are important to me. Stand up for what I want.

Pacing the room, I tried to come up with a plan. Ever since I could remember, I'd put my needs on the back shelf and never returned to pick them up. My personal desires lay dormant and covered in dust. I kept waiting for the right time when my mother's health would improve, my sister would finish college, or I would finally have enough money. But what if that time never came?

I need to stop saving things for later and start living now. Otherwise "later" might not happen. I need to enjoy my life today.

I swore to myself to live differently from that moment on, but something had to be done right away, even if it was small. What had I put away that I could accomplish in one evening? I opened my enormous closet and dug through the boxes. One of them was full of unused scented candles and other essentials for a relaxing bath. I'd gotten them as gifts over the years but never used a single item. Showers were always a practical alternative, and I'd never had the time to indulge in the luxury of sitting in a bathtub.

Well, today is the day.

I scooped all the candles and placed them around my tiny bathroom. They filled the space with a soft glow and a pleasant fragrance. I emptied a whole bottle of bubble bath into the tub, turned on quiet music and lowered myself into the hot water.

"Today I'm getting rid of another fear," I proclaimed and held up my backscratcher like a sword. "The fear of being wasteful when I do things for myself. Yes, I banish you from my life forever. From now on, I'll enjoy my life, and that's my decree."

I lowered the backscratcher into the foamy water and knighted the fizzy bath ball.

After taking my time in the tub, I changed into comfortable clothes and went into the kitchen. My mother made coffee and had a batch of freshly baked cookies piled on the table.

"I made them with Mr. Kent this evening," she said, looking at them with pride.

"Wow, Mom! You're on a roll today. I haven't smelled your cookies for years."

I gave her a hug and caught her by surprise again. The

layer of ice between us had started to melt, but it would take longer for the water to flow freely.

"The walk this morning gave me extra energy." She smiled. "Plus, John shared a new healthy recipe with me. It's oatmeal cookies. I just had to try it."

We sat down to enjoy our favorite brew and the treats, but I stopped myself after several of them swiftly disappeared in my mouth. My mother used to be the queen of cooking, and the kitchen was the place she reigned. When my father left, it was as if he'd taken away her joy of making meals. Was it returning to her now? As I stood up to leave, I glanced at her bright face across the table.

"I love you." Words that hadn't come out of my mouth since I was a child, spilled out with ease. Why had it been so hard to say them before? Was it the stone again?

"Oh, Gracie, I love you too." She sprang up and gave me a hug.

"By the way, Julie booked the tickets today. She's flying in on my birthday," I said.

My mother's face lit up with joy.

BACK IN MY ROOM, I wasn't sure what to do next. I had three more days before I turned twenty-five. I wasn't any closer to accomplishing my goals than when I'd first set my eyes on the mysterious stones. Had they helped or hindered me? Brought progress or confusion? The whole experience allowed me to see my circumstances and the people around me in a different light, but I failed to improve my own situation. If I could only change… the past? I opened the box in a rush and browsed through the labels.

I saw something…

There it was, a drawer labeled "time". I opened the lid that hid a stunning deep blue teardrop-shaped crystal with nothing but a silver ring at the top of the stone. I took it out carefully and watched the rays of blue light spread all over my dimly-lit room. Mesmerized, I observed it for a minute.

Why is it still here? Did nobody want it?

I looked through a booklet.

TIME

זְמָן

(Sapphire)

Ability to look into one's own future or translocate into one's own memories from the past, ability to put one's life into reverse to achieve a different outcome, the capability of increasing the span and duration of time travel. The mastery of the gift depends on the carrier's level of faith and maturity.

Multiple events in my life I wished to go back and change came to my memory.

Well, it sounds like science fiction, but who wouldn't want to do this if it was possible? It might not be an easy power to master. None of them were... Will I even be able to figure out how this one works in one day? Haven't I decided to forget the past and move forward? But what if the things I left behind are still holding me back?

With so many painful memories and questions in my heart, the temptation was too great. Plus, it seemed like the future could be entered as well, and that was a very lucrative possibility, even if limited. With slightly shaky hands, I took the stone of Courage off, placed it back in its drawer and threaded the new one through my tiny chain.

I need to get a less flimsy necklace for treasures like this.

I watched the pendant shimmer on my chest. It seemed proper to have such a glamorous stone represent time—the biggest asset humans ever had. I looked up at my computer desk where, years ago, I'd hung a piece of paper with my favorite quote by Baltasar Gracian: "All that really belongs to us is time; even he who has nothing else has that."

When I had next to nothing, when all that I'd cared for had been snatched away, I still believed that time would heal and restore things. My hope for a better future helped me not to despair, but years later my days still didn't belong to me. My time was claimed by circumstances beyond my control or given away to others out of a sense of duty.

Nobody can buy more time or get it back if it wasn't spent wisely. I've wasted mine long enough. Maybe if I have a little more control over it, I'd accomplish the things I want.

And with that sliver of renewed hope, I curled under the blankets and fell asleep.

PART V
THE INTRINSIC LIFE

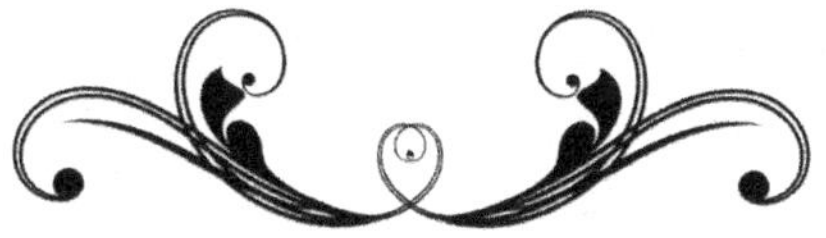

If we take care of the moments, the years will take care of themselves.

—Maria Edgeworth

CHAPTER 18

Friday morning started with an abrupt awakening. My first thought was to throw my alarm out of the window or drown it in the bathtub, but both of these actions required getting out of bed. Instead, I hid under the blankets for a few more minutes, then lured myself into the kitchen with the promise of fresh coffee. My mother made a surprise appearance. She insisted on joining me for a work-out. Only her version of exercise consisted of strolling and chatting with Mr. Kent. Determined to not let the extra pounds catch up, I put in my headphones and jogged on my own. I finished my new routine with a healthy breakfast and a text message from Greg.

What program does a Jedi use to open PDF files?

I smiled and typed: *What?*

Adobe Wan Kenobi, he replied.

I texted back: *Lol, you're pathetic.*

A stream of emojis followed.

At least he wasn't upset about my sudden departure last night.

Back in my room, I read the information about the Time stone again.

Ability to look into one's own future or past... How am I supposed to do this? I bet the influence of each stone depends on the person who wears it. Hopefully, I can get it to work.

With my eyes closed, I sat on the bed and tried to focus on a time from my past where I wanted to be at that moment. My thoughts instantly went back to yesterday's events. There was a sudden pull, as if my body got sucked into the giant vacuum cleaner. A second later, I was in the midst of my tandem jump with the outlines of the ground far beneath me. A blast of cold air prickled my skin, and my chest filled with the euphoria of a free fall. I opened my eyes and landed back in my room.

"Wow, better than virtual reality!"

Closing my eyes again, I transported into a field of wild grasses. Greg's sturdy arms surrounded me, his body supporting my small frame as he drew me close. Instead of running off, I relaxed into his warm embrace without a single worry on my mind.

Wait! No.

I gasped and opened my eyes, forcing myself back into the present time, but his touch lingered on my skin. I got up from the bed and paced the room.

I need to stop going back to yesterday. That's not why I'm doing this! I should probably try to look into the future instead.

I shut my eyes and went over the events of the day ahead. A moment later, my body zipped through the morning and past my workday, as though an invisible hand had pressed the fast-forward button on my life. It switched back to play mode right at the moment when I was walking out of the office building. Instead of going to the tram station, I got into a black Audi A8. No, not with Jason Statham from *The Transporter*, but with Miles Taylor! In complete shock, I opened my eyes and was pulled back into the middle of my bedroom where I stood, still in my undies and bra.

It's just my imagination. This can't be happening.

But the experience felt too real. At the small chance my vision might come to life, I picked out my best dress. Form-fitting black satin slimmed my figure, and delicate lacework on the off-shoulder sleeves complimented my ivory skin. A bright blue scarf hid the sparkly crystal. I arranged my golden locks into the French twist, which I'd looked up online, and spent extra time on my makeup.

If somebody told me a few days ago I would fuss over my image for so long, I would've laughed them off. But here I am, looking great and not feeling the least guilty about it.

I flashed my reflection a killer smile. "Go show everyone what you're capable of."

Satisfied with my appearance and the fact that my bravado hadn't deserted me yet, I left for work.

Outside, my mother and Mr. Kent blocked the apartment entrance, engaged in a lively discussion. I wished them a good day and hurried to the tram with C. S. Lewis book tucked away in my purse. After months of tedious studying, it was nice to read for fun again. Without the stone of Courage to push me into social interactions with total strangers, I looked forward to having some alone time on my ride. Unfortunately, my mind kept mulling over the vision I'd seen earlier, making it impossible to get lost in the book.

After arriving at the office, I was tempted to take a few more trips into the future. Each time I stepped into the car with my boss, my vision ended, as if the stone determined the extent of my time travel. A forecast of that nature made it hard to concentrate on my usual tasks. Paperwork fell out of my hands, documents got displaced, and faxes went out to wrong numbers. Afraid to falter, I avoided Miles Taylor at all costs and prayed that others wouldn't notice my temporary meltdown. It was important for me to do my job well, especially after I asked for a better position.

Mrs. Williamson had to go home early again, and Mr. Bailey pulled me out of my corner to assist. To master the pendant, I practiced rewinding the time and made Mr. Bailey yawn on repeat. The power of the stone wasn't easy to grasp. It only allowed me to return several moments into the past. When I started to question my choice, something unusual happened. I was finishing up a report in Mr. Bailey's office when our accountant, Mr. Patel, stormed in.

"Fred, you've got to look at this! Somebody is meddling in our accounts again."

He was the same age as our boss, had known Mr. Bailey since middle school, and thus reserved the right to call him by his first name. Not seeing me behind the computer, he continued his flustered announcement.

"You've got to call a partners' meeting and get to the bottom of this."

"I can't, Arjun. You know what happened just a few days ago. If I bring this into the open now, these young lawyers will scatter like chickens."

Mr. Bailey got up from his chair at the same time as Mr. Patel noticed my presence. He gave his friend a questioning glance.

"Don't worry, she's the one who saved our behinds," Mr. Bailey said.

Mr. Patel glared in my direction with his big dark eyes, unconvinced. Even his mustache frowned. "We need to talk in private, Miss Ainsworth," he said.

I got up to leave and suddenly flew through time as if carried by a high-speed train. A second later, I stood in the same spot, but my surroundings looked different. Mr. Patel had disappeared, and Mr. Bailey was now pacing by the window. Mrs. Williamson cried in the corner, while several people in the FBI uniforms rummaged through the drawers. One of the agents came up to me.

"Miss Ainsworth, we need to ask you a few questions."

I blinked in disbelief and was instantly propelled to the

present time. Mr. Patel stood in front of me once again with a sour face.

"Miss Ainsworth?" he said, tapping his fingers on the laptop in his hands.

"Y-yes, I'm sorry. I'm leaving."

I hurried out of the office, knocking a pen holder to the floor and tipping over a plant. Once in the hallway, I took a long breath and tried to understand what had happened. Had Mr. Bailey committed a crime? Was he the one to blame for the financial problems Mr. Patel was worried about? Biting my freshly painted nails, I hid in my work corner and decided to do my own investigation. First, I wanted to find out more about Mr. Bailey's connection to Robert Kowalski. I remembered the file Mr. Bailey was reading the day before and typed *Whittaker vs. Kowalski* on my computer search screen. Multiple articles came up. The headlines peppered with words like *corporate fraud, white-collar crime, illicit transactions,* and *money laundering.* I clicked on the article that described a high profile multimillion-dollar case.

The defendant, Tyson Kowalski, a former chief executive of WTLO International, was accused of grand larceny and other charges on behalf of the plaintiff Scott Whittaker, the current company owner. He was convicted of masterminding an accounting fraud that bankrupted Mr. Whittaker's company. Mr. Kowalski is sentenced to ten years in prison by the federal court system. The defense lawyer, Frederick Bailey stated—

"Miss Ainsworth."

I gasped and scrambled to close the search screen. Miles Taylor stood in front of my desk. He was wearing a stylish black suit that sat too well on his masculine figure and once again interfered with my ability to pull myself together. Determined to uphold the image of the confident woman I'd projected yesterday, and with the remnants of courage still surging through my veins, I met his gaze.

"You might've left me with a stutter," I said coolly. "When I asked you to surprise me, that's not what I had in mind."

Miles's raised his eyebrows. "I didn't mean to scare you. It seems you judge me too harshly. I request an acquittal."

He gave me a tight-lipped smile, and my heart plunged into my stomach. Even without supernatural interference, I'd said all the wrong things.

There, you've done it! Happy? Now he's convinced you're a snob. I bet if you look into the future again, you'll be on the tram going home by your lonely self. Oh, why is it so hard? If only I could take back my words...

But I could! I closed my eyes and allowed myself to be pulled a few minutes into the past. When I opened them, Miles came around the corner and stood by my desk again.

"Miss Ainsworth, I'm glad we met here."

I leaped to my feet, tripped on the chair, and fell to the ground. My high-heel shoes were sticking up to the ceiling like a pair of daggers, and my unmentionables were bared for the whole Universe to see.

Really, Grace? Couldn't you at least land gracefully into his arms? Third time's the charm?

I closed my eyes and was back in the chair once again with an unsuspecting Miles Taylor coming around the corner. I remained seated, determined to keep the color of my underwear to myself.

"Miss Ainsworth, I'm glad we met here."

"How can I help you, Mr. Taylor?" I asked.

I folded my arms carefully over the desk and managed a small smile.

"I'm afraid I gave you the wrong impression yesterday and would like a chance to remediate that, especially after everything you've done," he said in a heart-melting tone.

"Mr. Taylor—"

"Please, don't say anything yet. Just look at this when you

have some free time." He handed me a small folder, and I quickly placed it in my purse.

"Of course, Mr. Taylor."

I hoped my voice sounded pleasant instead of uptight. Not wanting to ruin our interaction, I put an imaginary lock between my lips and tossed the key into the Pacific Ocean. What if it was "three strikes you're out" deal with the stone? I sure didn't want to test its limits.

Miles lingered a few seconds longer, but left when I remained mute as a fish. Shaking off a sense of déjà vu from our repeat meetings, I looked back at the computer. It didn't seem like a good idea anymore to do my research in the open area, although the information I'd found perplexed me. Nothing about my vision made sense.

Why would Mr. Bailey want to undermine his own firm? That doesn't make any sense. I wonder if it's all connected to the Kowalski case. But who is Tyson Kowalski?

I tried to jump into Mr. Bailey's doom day again, but the stone must have decided one trip was enough.

Well, if my boss gets arrested, I won't have a job anymore. I better get this thing figured out soon.

Armed with a thorough knowledge of detective books and NCIS Los Angeles episodes, I snuck around the office in an attempt to catch suspicious behaviors. Soon it was obvious that the only odd-acting individual within the firm was me—sliding along the walls and tiptoeing around the corners to listen to conversations were clearly not part of a file clerk's duties. I even ventured out to question Mr. Bailey. Determined to keep the firm from falling apart, I lingered in his office, unsure of what to say without revealing the secret behind my abilities.

"If there's anything I can do…" I hesitated, but boldness fueled my words. "Actually, there're lots of things I can do. I stopped your two partners from leaving, and I might be able to help with these financial difficulties too. I have something that might prevent—"

"Don't worry about it. Just get it out of your head. We already changed all the passwords and restricted access to the accounts. I don't wish to discuss this anymore." Mr. Bailey motioned for me to leave. "Olivia, you need something?"

I swirled around. My supervisor stood at the door, her stare drilling a hole in my head. How much had she overheard?

"Yes, Mr. Bailey. I tried to check the payroll and can't log in."

"We just updated our security system," he said. "Mr. Abeles can get you set up. Go see him right now."

I dashed past Olivia and out of the door.

I should be more careful, at least look behind my back next time I say things like that.

CHAPTER 19

Without the help of the Hearing stone, I soon got tired of my fruitless investigations. I decided that to do some regular old paperwork would be more helpful to the firm at the moment. On my way to pick up files, I passed Mr. Abeles's office and stopped to greet him.

"I see you've returned to your old job." He frowned. "Have you figured out what you want to do with your life yet? I doubt when you were a little girl, you dreamt of putting papers in alphabetical order all day long."

My cheeks burned from his candid words. "Yes, Mr. Abeles, actually—"

"Call me Tzali," the older man suddenly stopped me. His grumpy expression relaxed into a smile. "It's a shorter version of my first name."

He's only trying to be friendly and helpful. You don't need to always put your guard up.

"I actually just got a paralegal certificate and applied for a position here," I continued.

"Eh, you've got to think bigger." His blue eyes looked

through mine as if searching for my soul within. "What inspires you? What makes you excited?"

Why was this person I barely knew asking me questions of that nature? And why was I curious to know what he thought?

"Well, I wanted to teach..."

"No, that's not it. It has to come from here." The older man pointed to his heart. "It has to light your fire. But to find the purpose in life, you have to figure out who you are first. Do you know who you are, Grace?"

He held my gaze for a few seconds, then turned away not waiting for an answer. I continued my paper rounds with his question replaying in my head. Did I know who I was or what I wanted?

I want to figure out how to act around Miles Taylor, get that darn position, bail my sister out of her college debt and somehow save my firm. Plus, I have the pendants to worry about. That's a long enough list for now.

Break time approached, but I wasn't any closer to solving the conspiracy. Alicia overloaded my cell phone with text messages and threatened to show up at my job if I didn't come to our usual place for lunch. I promised to meet with her and hurried out of the office. My friend had already reserved the table at the café downstairs.

"*Que linda eres*—you still look amazing!" Alicia greeted me with a quick hug.

I smiled. "And you always look amazing."

"I can't believe you didn't come for several days! I was dying to know how you've been."

After ordering lunch, I gave Alicia the short version of what'd happened since the last time we'd met, but omitted the troubling information I'd discovered about my firm.

"You know what, *amiga*? These super stones didn't transform you into a different person. They just brought out the true Grace that was hiding inside all these years."

Tears gathered in my eyes and threatened to come out. Why was I so eager to cry lately?

"Thank you, Allie, but let's not talk about me anymore. Tell me about your date instead."

I was glad to hear that Marcos had invited Alicia out. My friend proceeded to give me all the unnecessary details of how she'd managed to entice him on their first date.

"I invited him once, so it was his turn. We're even now." She giggled.

"I'm happy it all worked out well for you."

I opened my purse to grab my wallet. Out dropped the folder Miles had given me earlier. As it landed on the floor, a beige square envelope slid out. Alicia's eyes darted in its direction.

"What's this?"

I shrugged. "Some papers from work."

"Doesn't look like it."

My friend dove down, grabbed the card, and read it before I could stop her. Her mouth gaped open. The nosy girl made a loud squeal and clapped her hands.

"*¡Dios mio!* Grace! Why are you trying to hide this from me?"

"What are you talking about, Allie? Give this to me. I haven't seen it myself yet."

"Well, then you should. And there is nothing work-related about it, trust me."

I grabbed the smooth piece of stationery. The neatly-penned note read:

"Ms. Grace Ainsworth,

I would like to start our acquaintance right and invite you to dinner.

Please, let me know if you could meet me today at the front entrance at 5:30 PM.

Miles Taylor.

A strange sensation filled my head. Was it all a dream? I suppressed the impulse to pinch myself.

A teasing smile played on Alicia's lips. "Miles Taylor? Mr. Hotness? Ha! Didn't expect him to be an old-fashioned romantic who sends hand-written notes to his love interests. Grace, did you use a special stone to make him fall for you? And what's this debt he is talking about? Mm?"

"Don't be silly. There is nothing romantic about a formal invitation. I did something for him at work, and he's just returning the favor." I tried to sound composed and attempted to put a piece of salad in my mouth, but it got stuck in my throat. Coughing, I washed it down with big gulps of water.

Alicia put her hands on her hips and gave me a scornful stare. "Look at yourself, you don't know how to pretend. You can call it whatever you want, but it's clear as day that the guy is inviting you on a date."

"Then I'm not going."

"*¿Por que?*" Alicia gasped. "Is it about Greg?"

"What about him?" I scoffed.

She looked at me as though I had a tree growing out of my head. "*Oye*, Grace, do I have to explain everything to you?"

I considered rewinding our conversation to omit telling her about my adventures with Greg, but instead took another drink of water to wash down my annoyance.

"We're just friends."

"*¡Si, como no!* A guy is tripping over himself to please you, and you think it's just for friendship? Open your eyes, *chica*, or you'll miss out."

"Miss out on what?"

Alicia rolled her eyes. "It's like you fell out of the eighteenth century or have lived in a nunnery all these years.

Don't be so naïve. If I was in your place, I would keep both men around. With your looks…"

An already familiar protest rose up inside of me. "Allie, I don't want to listen to this. Sometimes you're too much for me, really! I just met Greg two days ago, and I'm trying to get the position as Mr. Taylor's assistant."

"So?"

"What do you mean *so*? I don't think I can work for him if he… Anyway, why even talk about it. He's out of my league, and I need to focus on getting the job. At least I have a chance there."

"Think what you want, but I would bend the iron while it's hot or whatever that phrase is."

Alicia flashed me a playful smile, but I gave her a sullen look in return and stuffed the invitation back into my purse.

"I'll do what I think is right. And if I'm mistaken, it will be my own mistake," I finally said.

"You know that I'll always give you my opinion, even if you don't like it," Alicia replied. "I hope you'll put away your excessive sense of responsibility for once and enjoy the evening with the fabulous Mr. Taylor."

ON THE WAY back to work, I thought about my friend's comments. An invitation to dinner from Miles seemed surreal. I couldn't deny that I hoped it was more than a simple act of appreciation for my heroic actions. Either way, it was a chance to spend time together, get to know him a bit more and maybe finally make a good impression. But was it a good idea to accept?

If I don't take a risk, I'll never find out. Allie is right. I should ease up and take my chances.

During the afternoon, I decided not to tempt fate with time manipulations, but the more I thought about the evening, the greater my distress became. How should I behave if I go? What does Miles expect of me? Decisiveness deserted me, and doubts hit me like a hailstorm, crushing any leftover courage. What if Miles discovered that I had an absurd crush on him like all those other foolish women? What if he was just playing me? What if I made a spectacle out of myself and ruined my slim chances of ever being his assistant?

Don't overthink it. It's just one evening out. Use this time to get to know him and to show that you're qualified for the job. Make the best of this.

Five-thirty was fast approaching and sending jitters through my body. It was time to make a decision, but I avoided Miles like I did my favorite pastry shop lately. He finally caught me between two file cabinets and blocked my only escape route.

"Working hard?" he said.

I clenched the files in my hands and tried to remember the next letter of the alphabet that'd suddenly slipped my memory. "Yes, can I help you with something?"

"I came for your verdict about tonight." He leaned closer and my safeguards started to melt.

"Grace?" Greg's voice suddenly boomed next to us.

I jerked back and dropped the stack of papers. Miles straightened and turned towards Greg's tall form, which filled the small aisle. The two men stared at each other, thickening the air with tension.

"What... what are you doing here?" I blinked at Greg who sidestepped Miles and bent down to pick up the files from the floor.

"Came to give the copy of my article to Mr. Bailey and wanted to see you." Greg glanced between me and my boss. His blue eyes darkened like the stormy sky.

Ignoring him, Miles grabbed the last few loose papers and

placed them into my hands. His fingers lingered next to mine.

"I'll be waiting," he said.

I dashed past the two men, mumbling something about the busy day, ran into the spare office, and locked the door. I slid down the wall to the cold floor and sat there until my hands stopped shaking. When I came out, Greg was gone, and Miles had left for the meeting. Not wanting to analyze what happened, I buried myself in work.

CHAPTER 20

Most of my co-workers had already left by the time I snuck out through the back entrance of the firm to avoid meeting James. I didn't want to face more questions from another friend, for somebody else to try to persuade me and give me advice. My mind was made up.

Make a decision and stick to it, I told myself.

After taking a different elevator, I stepped out into the chilly air, tightened my scarf, and scurried down the steps to the sidewalk. The black Audi from my morning vision swung around the corner. The passenger window opened. Miles smiled from his seat and motioned for me to get in. I descended the steps, suppressing a shiver either from cold weather, nerves, or both. Once in the car, I looked back at the building and gasped. Greg stood motionless just a few feet from us. He was well-lit by the street lights, and his eyes locked with mine. Emotion flashed through his features. Was it confusion? Hurt? Worry? I couldn't tell. The tinted window went up, and we drove away.

The lights of the city flew past us. Dozens of other girls would have killed to be with the handsome man beside me. I felt nothing but anxiety. Paralyzed by my insecurities, I struggled to appear natural. It didn't matter whether this was a date or a business meeting, Miles's mere presence sent my hormones into overdrive. Self-conscious, I expected to mess up at any moment.

"I'm glad you decided to accept my invitation," Miles said. "I hoped a written note would carry more weight."

I stared straight ahead, my throat parched, one question burning in my mind: "Why did you invite me?"

"You saved my practice from possible bankruptcy. That's the least I could do."

Of course. What else would it be? You're such a jellyfish! Stop stressing out. Yes, it's unexpected, but relax a bit. Pretend you're a Cinderella who is finally going to the ball. Woo-hoo. Did she freak out? No, she wasted no time getting the main guy charmed before midnight. That's exactly what you should be doing right now. Your goal is to get the job at the castle or the prince. Or both! This is your fairy tale. Go get yourself a happy ending.

In the attempt to break through the swirling thoughts in my head, I turned to my stylish boss and smiled. He rewarded me with a heart-melting grin in return.

"You told me to be myself. I want to accomplish that tonight, but I know so little about you," he said. "Would I be able to uncover at least some of your secrets?"

I gave Miles another silent smile, hoping to appear mysterious and not a nervous wreck too scared to talk. To make matters worse, Greg's distressed face kept flickering in front of my eyes. I couldn't let myself think about that. Not now. It was time to come up with a strategy and win Miles Taylor over. He wanted to get acquainted too, so that should've made things easier. But what could I do? If I had the Beauty stone on, I would've known how to be social and charming. If I'd kept the Hearing stone, I would've understood his thoughts and motives. The Courage stone would've given me boldness to speak up and act with decisiveness. What was the Time stone good for?

It's good for second chances.

Encouraged, I ventured out, made blunders, rewound, tuning up my words and actions until I was able to engage Miles's interest. It wasn't a walk in the park to impress him. Reassured by my ability to redo things, I became bolder and steered our conversation towards the topic of law.

"May I call you Grace?" Miles stretched his arm casually behind my seat. I nodded and moved my restless hands out of sight. His closeness tore at my feeble defenses. "I'm afraid I bored you with my speech about the judicial system."

"Not at all, Mr. Taylor."

"Miles."

"Miles." I licked my dry lips. "I'm very interested in the subject."

"How so?"

There it was—my chance to shine.

"I think it's necessary for any society to function. When I studied the law—"

"A textbook answer? Trust me, things aren't the same in real life."

I was thankful for the dusk that concealed my blush. After recovering, I thought about his question again. Mr. Abeles's words came up to the surface. Was there something that inspired me about the law? Lit the fire in my heart? I closed my eyes and, with the help of the Time stone, returned a few minutes into the past. Miles asked the same question.

"I like the law because I want justice and truth to prevail," I said.

My boss whistled. Had I said the wrong thing again?

"You're an idealist, Grace."

I crossed my arms with sudden determination. That was

the answer I wouldn't change, no matter what my boss thought of it.

"Why do you say that?" I asked.

"The judicial system is more complicated than you might realize. Things aren't always black and white. There're lots of gray areas. But that was a charming thought."

Oh, no, I won't let you take me for a simpleton. I closed my eyes again and let the stone pull me back into the past.

"I want justice and truth to prevail," I repeated after hearing his question for the third time. "But the judicial system is complicated with lots of gray areas..."

That doesn't sound right. I frowned, forgetting that my goal was to have a pleasant conversation. Something deep inside my soul had been provoked, and I wasn't able to let it go. A new conviction rose up and took a hold of me.

"The judicial system isn't always clear cut because we are humans," I continued. "We make mistakes and arrive at wrong conclusions that don't lead to the truth. Like when innocent people get implicated and then released years later. Courts are flawed because they consist of people. Sometimes investigations go wrong. We've even created bad laws, like segregation."

"And how do we fix these injustices?" Miles looked at me with a wry smile.

I cringed. "Oh, I'm not saying that the whole system is corrupt or anything like that, at least not here. I mean, we try our best. It's just on the Earth we'll never have perfect justice because people aren't perfect. Our laws are a mere reflection of our convictions as a society."

"So, that would imply there is no such thing as perfect justice and truth. Then who is to say what is right and what is wrong? If people are fundamentally flawed, then how can we judge each other?"

I peered at my companion. My mouth opened and closed,

and my mind glitched like an old static TV before going blank.

Miles let out a hearty laugh. "You like to think deeply, Grace, but a young pretty woman like you shouldn't burden herself with such heavy concepts. It will age you. Just look at us lawyers. I have gray hair in my thirties, and Mr. Bailey has already lost half of his."

Oh, poodoo! He must take me for an immature child. In that case, aging would be to my benefit. I should definitely become a lawyer.

Before I had a chance to reply, our car stopped, putting an end to *Groundhog Day* and my rising defiance.

"We're here." Miles opened the door and threw the keys to the valet.

I jumped out of the vehicle to give myself a few seconds to simmer down before Miles was next to me again. But walking by that man and leaning on his steady arm made me forget our somewhat unpleasant exchange. We climbed the steps to the stone entrance of the restaurant lit by the warm glow of torches. Columns, arches, and pruned greenery created an illusion of a grand Italian Villa. The host, dressed in a black suit, greeted us at the door and ushered us inside.

Welcome to the ball!

Miles leaned over and whispered into my ear. "This is the best place in the city. You have to try their dessert."

My heart warmed from the intimacy of his tone. We walked through the extravagant interior. Bright chandeliers hung above us and multiplied in the mirrors. Lively music filled the air. Our host escorted us past the large dining room where well-dressed people ate and chatted. We entered a secluded area with a single private table behind an ornamental wall. Afraid to appear clumsy or unrefined, I used the pendant again and again to rewind my actions until I figured out how to sit, what to order, and even which fork to pick up first. My father had been well off, but he'd never taken us to fancy dinners, considering it a waste of time and money. We certainly couldn't afford to eat out after he left, but my boss didn't need to know all that.

"You have great taste," Miles said with delight after I picked the same drink he planned to order just a few minutes later. "I can't wait to learn more about you. Let's leave the heavy subjects alone and talk about Grace Ainsworth."

My heart leaped into my stomach. What could I tell this man about myself? That I was a high school dropout and lived in a small low-income apartment with my mother? I doubted Miles cared to know about my impressive collection of *Star Wars* stamps. The cloud of defeat that'd lifted off in the last three days hovered over my head again, threatening to engulf me.

No, I came too far to give up, I thought with stubborn resolve. *All he needs to know is that I'm capable of handling him and his high-profile clients.*

"Mr. Taylor—"

"Miles, please."

"Miles. I'm afraid, my life is full of riddles, and I'm still figuring it out. All I know at this point is that I work at a great firm and intend to learn all the aspects of running a law office. Hopefully, one day I'll have my own practice. That's why I started from the bottom. Although at this point I'm ready to move up to a paralegal position."

Oh, really, Grace? You want to practice law? Was this hiding in your subconscious mind this whole time, or are you just trying to impress your boss? I thought all you wanted was to make an extra buck.

Miles sipped on his wine. A small smile danced over his lips. "That's one way to do it, I guess. I don't have that much patience. That's why I started at the top."

I choked on my drink and had to use the stone to rewind.

"I'm interested in knowing your story," I said. "You're

such a great lawyer. What made you choose this profession? How did you end up working with Mr. Bailey?"

I'd hit the jackpot. He was eager to talk. Over the next hour, all I had to do was travel back in time on a few occasions to come up with a better question. The flow of information continued. I relaxed and enjoyed the view in front of me. Miles's handsome face was animated. His dark eyes reflected the soft glow of candles and hypnotized me. He talked about his well-to-do family, his prestigious education, his connections that'd helped him land a job with a top law firm, his hobbies, and his wealth. We sat across a small table but seemed to be thousands of miles apart, so different were our upbringings.

As Miles launched into yet another story, his features and the rich décor around us suddenly faded away. I got pulled through time and space. Another face appeared in his place with blue eyes and a warm smile. Endless fields stretched all around us, and the faint fragrance of wild grasses filled the air.

What's happening?

I blinked and was thrown back to my seat. The change of scenery was so unexpected that I jumped up and knocked the glass off the table. It hit the marble floor and shattered. As if in slow motion, I watched waiters hustle to my aid.

"I'm so sorry." I bent down to help.

One waitress shot me a curious stare. "It's not a problem, ma'am. Please, sit down, you'll cut yourself."

"Grace, let them do their job," Miles said, still glued to his chair.

My ears must have illuminated like Christmas lights. I stood by our table not knowing what to do next. In the commotion, I'd forgotten about my ability to rewind and instead excused myself to the restroom. For a minute, I studied my flustered reflection in the mirror.

What are you doing here, Grace?

I needed a friend. Asap. Reaching out to Alicia didn't sound like a good idea. She would've bombarded me with a flood of questions and advice to the likes of "lower your cleavage and he'll forget about your clumsiness". James wasn't a good candidate in this situation either. And what would I tell Greg if I called him? That I needed help to win a guy I'd drooled over for two years? Somehow I didn't think it would sit right with him.

Greg would've told me to be myself.

I lingered in the ladies' room and counted the tiles on the marble floor until my mind cleared. With the stone's help, I tried a few versions of a graceful return and was eventually back at the table. To my relief, I soon found another point of connection with my boss.

"Do you like art?" I asked, already knowing what the answer would be.

"Well, I don't consider myself an expert by any means, but I have a small private collection. What about you?"

"I studied art history. It's amazing how things have changed over the years. So many styles. Expressionism is still my favorite."

"So is mine."

Oh, wow! What a surprise! I guess, we have the same taste. How convenient. Who are you kidding, Grace?

"I never have enough time to catch the art exhibits here in town," I said, ignoring the onslaught of mockery in my head.

"I have a brilliant idea," Miles said. "My apartment is close by and I'd love to show you the new piece of art I acquired a few weeks ago."

It's a good opportunity to converse in a less formal atmosphere. Maybe I'll relax enough to have a genuine conversation, I told myself, but the voice of reason perked up and dampened my perfect logic. *Is that what you think he's inviting you for? To have a cup of tea and talk about art?*

I glanced at my phone. There were no messages or missed

calls, nobody else to claim me for the evening. After a short struggle, my heart won over my head.

"I would love to see your art," I said.

∿

WE CONTINUED to talk about the importance of modernism and surrealism on the way to Miles's place. He acted nonchalant about the whole ordeal and chatted away while I pacified my nerves by chewing on the inside of my cheek. We got off the I-5 in the downtown area and parked inside a skyscraper on Pine Street. The luxury apartment building had a large reception area and an elevator with forty numbered buttons. I stared at them in disbelief until Miles led me out, his hand burning the skin on my back through the thin dress.

Miles's enormous penthouse was full of modern furniture and the latest high-tech accommodations. I admired the floor to ceiling windows and gaped at the stunning views of the Downtown area, Seattle's giant Ferris wheel, and pier. With my cell phone still clenched in my hand, I wondered how many times my tiny apartment would fit into his living room. In the reflection on the glass, I watched Miles—he took off his jacket, loosened his tie, and strolled to the minibar.

Was it all an illusion? Just a few days ago I would've been happy with only one glance from Miles Taylor, and now I stood in his condo. My mind flooded with questions. Was he truly interested in me? Would I keep his interest once the stones' influence ended? Should I forget about the job and take my chances with the relationship if he was to offer?

There must be another way. Perhaps, Mr. Bailey could find a different paralegal position for me, then I wouldn't have to torture myself and try to hide that I'm head over heels for Miles. I can even work for a different firm.

I closed my eyes to control my internal restlessness. Suddenly, my mind fast-forwarded, and I was in a different room with Miles standing next to me. He drew me close, then took the phone out of my hand and turned it off.

"You're the most fascinating piece of art I've ever seen," he said, wrapping his arms around me.

His lips found mine, weakening my knees. My body trembled, and I melted into his embrace. The image blurred again, and an invisible force propelled me further into the future. I was now in an upscale hotel room. Miles was putting on his jacket a few feet away. He turned to leave, his expression hard as a stone. I grabbed his arm with tears running down my cheeks.

"Don't be ridiculous," he said coldly. "You couldn't expect this to last."

Pain ripped through my insides. It was a familiar sensation. An old wound from a long time ago resurfaced, reminding me of a time when another man had walked out of my life.

I opened my eyes and was back by the window. The same downtown lights flickered in the distance, but the world around me had changed. A shadow had fallen over my hopes and expectations. It crashed them into millions of pieces. The glass slipper hit the pavement and shattered before I had a chance to try it on. My gift was now the cause of my affliction.

I touched my lips, still sensing the kiss that was not meant to be. The fog that covered my mind dissipated, and I saw with clarity that the person a few feet from me was the source of my future humiliation. My prince had turned into a dragon and his castle into a dungeon. I tried to get my thoughts together, but my mind was on fire.

Such a fool to fall for his charm. What did I expect? If it wasn't for the Beauty stone, if it wasn't for all of this...

Afraid to reveal the mayhem in my heart, I fixed my eyes

on the window while Miles approached. I bit my lip until the metallic taste of blood filled my mouth. My feet remained glued to the floor, hindering my escape. I was trapped in my reality, seemingly unable to alter the inevitable. My heart still ached to be with Miles. Was my obsession deep enough to throw me into his hands despite the impending heartache? I had to do something fast, but only one thing came to mind.

"Where's your restroom?"

I ran out as soon as I knew the direction. Splashing cold water into my face, I tried to gather all the leftover rational thoughts and come up with a plan. Makeup ran down my cheeks, and I spent the next few minutes fixing my raggedy image. Bathrooms have been a good hiding place lately, but I couldn't stay there forever. I dragged my feet back into the living room and sat on the edge of the plush sofa. Miles moved in my direction, but I got up to answer my phone, which finally showed some signs of life. It was Mr. Kent.

"Grace, you need to come quick! Your mother is sick. I called the ambulance. They took her to the hospital."

In a shaken voice he told me the address. I hung up the phone, worried yet relieved to have a legitimate excuse to leave.

"I'm curious, how did you know our partners planned to leg it?" Miles's voice made me look up. He stood next to me with the drinks. "Is something wrong?"

"My mother's in the hospital." I jumped to my feet, nearly causing the man to lose his balance. "I have to go. Thanks for dinner."

I dashed past him and out of the apartment, wondering why he wanted to question me about the problems at the office.

CHAPTER 21

The elevator took forever. Once out of the building, my first thought was to call Greg for a ride, but I didn't want him to question why I'd left with Miles Taylor. Did he even live in the area? James didn't pick up his phone, and Alicia lived too far. Out of options, I called a taxi. On the way to the hospital, I rubbed away the creases from my forehead, and my personal struggles disappeared into the background as they'd done so many times in the past. I couldn't let my mother see my heartache. It was a good excuse to not deal with the havoc in my own life. At the hospital emergency department, I met a distressed Mr. Kent in the waiting area and followed a volunteer back to the room. My mother lay in bed, attached to the monitor and the IV. She gave me a feeble smile and waved for me to sit down.

"They're poking and prodding me here. Thank goodness you came to save me from all of this," she said. "And this gown has a terrible color. Doesn't suit me at all. I feel sicker just being here."

"You should've called me right away." I sat down and took her hand.

"I called John, and he called the ambulance, and now I'm in this mess." She groaned. "I should've waited it out."

She tried to untangle the cords and made the monitor beep. The nurse came in and silenced it. The doctor followed to let my mother know she needed to stay in the hospital overnight. Her lips trembled, but she tightened them into a bow.

"I thought I was doing better, and now it's all ruined. Just let me go home and die."

"There is nothing life-threatening going on at the moment, Mrs. Ainsworth. However, because you had chest pain and one of the tests came back slightly elevated, we want to monitor you a little longer," the doctor said.

"Chest pain?" I frowned.

"There are different reasons for chest pain. It might be stress or muscle pain. We recommend you stay overnight for a few more tests to rule out a more serious cause."

My mother agreed to be admitted to the hospital after a lot of coaxing, and I sent Mr. Kent home. She demanded to walk to her new room upstairs instead of getting transferred on a stretcher, refused to step on the scales and criticized the food. She must have exhausted herself with so many things to protest because the minute staff left her alone, she fell asleep. Trying to make myself comfortable in the reclining chair, I listened to her quiet breathing. In the dark room, all the thoughts I'd pushed back earlier came back with a vengeance. Inside my heart was a gaping emptiness, and it devoured everything like an enormous black hole. I felt disappointed with myself and my choices. To rewind the whole day and start over would have been ideal, but the stone only allowed me to backtrack a few minutes at a time. I tried to return to an earlier time in the day and change my decisions. But no matter how hard I tried to revisit the memory, the pendant was silent. Bitter tears escaped down my cheek. It seemed that I'd wasted the gift on things that left me hollow. Had I thrown away the only chance I had to alter my life? What would happen if I failed to put Aunt Lou's gifts to good use?

I'd be a good candidate for a reality show. Like the one about lottery winners who squandered all their money. Here is a story about a girl who used a supernatural gift to get a man who'll dump her. How pathetic is that? That blue-blanket guy, what's his name, he was right. This seems to be more than I can handle. I should've just given him the stones.

My mother woke up and reached her hand out to me. "Gracie, why are you still here? Are you ok?"

"I'm fine, mom. You need to get some sleep." I gave her a weak attempt to a smile.

"And you need to go home and rest. I have plenty of people to look after me here. I'm sorry I ruined your evening."

"You didn't. I should've been home. If something happened—"

"Nonsense. I'm not that old or that sick to have a grown daughter be my sitter. I decided I've caused enough trouble for you. Plus, Mr. Kent was kind enough to keep me company over the last few days. I just overdid it with activities, that's all. If you want me to sleep, you need to go home."

That was a new line of thinking for my mother. Slightly shocked, I tried to object, but she insisted I take a taxi and promised to call me first thing in the morning.

"Grace," she called out when I was already at the door. "I'm sorry."

"For what? There is nothing—"

"For not being there for you and your sister after your dad left." Her voice cracked.

"Mom, let's not talk about this right now." I tightened my lips. It was the last thing I wanted to discuss after everything that'd happened earlier, but she motioned for me to sit back down.

"Let me say it. When the paramedics took me, and I didn't know how all of this would turn out, I promised myself to... Anyway, when your dad left me for another woman, I felt like my life was over. All those years I'd lived for him, left all my friends, my family, and he discarded me like an old rag—"

"Mom, please. You shouldn't think about this now." I moved closer and touched her arm, but she composed herself and continued.

"It was too painful to stay in the same city with him, to be alone in that big house, so I fled. I decided to move back to Seattle where I'd spent a happy childhood. But it made things harder for you girls. You had no support." She sniffled.

"Didn't you say that Father left us some money? Wasn't he supposed to pay for child support?"

"I was too clueless and too distraught to fight for it, plus just the idea of talking to him again... Mark probably thought the money he left in my account after the divorce would be enough, but I had no idea how to manage it. The funds disappeared so fast, especially with the cost of living here."

"Yeah, I remember you were so depressed, you didn't even get out of bed for days." I shook my head trying to shake off the memory.

"I realize now how selfish it was for me to shut the world away. You girls lost two parents instead of one." She choked up, and I hugged her.

"Mom, there is no point in blaming yourself for it now. It's not your fault."

She cupped my face with her hands. "I know that you had to step up and take my place. You, Gracie, became a parent to both me and your sister. You pulled us through. You had to be strong where I'd failed. It's very hard for me to admit. Today all I prayed about was a chance to live a little longer and make it up to both of you."

∼

I LEFT the hospital with conflicting emotions raging in my chest. Our apartment was a few blocks away. There was no rain, and I decided to take a walk in hopes of cooling down my fuming thoughts. Murky light from the street lamps and passing cars lit the sidewalk. I moved along the road, deep in my thoughts.

My mother's apology was bittersweet. She couldn't really change the fact that she'd let herself fall apart and turned me into an adult at sixteen. I was betrayed by the father I'd idolized but had to keep my pain bottled inside because of an emotionally drained mother. The wound in my heart had never healed properly. I had covered it up and never looked under the dressing.

That's so not fair. My mother just needed to calm her own conscience. She didn't ask if I was ready for this conversation. It's not like she can go back to the past and undo the damage or change what happened to us.

I stopped in the middle of the street with a daunting realization—I had the ability to do exactly that. I touched the gem under the scarf. My heartbeat increased beneath it. Could I really go back so far into the past and alter the outcome? Would the pendant even let me?

Exhausted with my ruminations, I finally tuned into my surroundings. It got dark and chilly, and I began to regret not spending money on the taxi. Our neighborhood in South Tacoma was not the safest to stroll around at night. The streets were nearly empty of pedestrians when I noticed that the same man had been following me for a while. The stranger kept his distance, his face hidden under a hood, but no matter how many corners I turned, his dark silhouette was still behind me. Panic gripped my insides.

Should I go straight home or pretend I live somewhere else? Call the police? And what would I tell them? That my paranoia went into overdrive?

I walked as fast as I could without tripping and falling on

my high heels. My achy feet longed for a pair of flats, but adrenaline gave me enough energy to move forward. One block from our street I called Mr. Kent.

"I'm sorry to bother you so late. Would you please come out and meet me at the entrance? I might need your help."

Having an older but fit man around was better than going inside the building by myself. All the dark alleys, empty staircases, and creepy elevators I'd ever seen in the movies or read about came into my mind, making my heart beat desperately against my chest wall.

As long as this guy doesn't take my pendant, I can rewind enough times to punch him in all the right places if he dares to approach.

Fortunately, I didn't have to practice my Jedi moves. Mr. Kent met me at the main entrance to our apartment complex and my pursuer, whoever he was, disappeared.

"I'm sorry to bug you," I panted. "I just… didn't feel safe by myself."

"I understand. That's not a problem." He eyed a group of idle men that'd started a yelling competition in a parking lot nearby, sparing me any need to confess my binge-watching tendencies of Criminal Minds.

"You should've let me pick you up from the hospital. How's your mother?" he asked while we climbed up the stairs. "I'm so worried about her."

"She's good. They just want to watch her a little longer. The doctor said—"

I stopped mid-sentence and froze when I opened the door to my apartment. Behind it was a complete disaster. The place looked like a hurricane had gone through it. Dishes were in disarray on the kitchen counter and broken on the floor. Furniture was either out of place or overturned. Clothes and decorations had been scattered all over.

The stones!

I rushed to my room before Mr. Kent had a chance to stop me. My bedroom didn't have a lot of items, but they'd all been ravaged through. My vintage original *Star Wars* poster was ripped in half, my lamp was broken, and my mattress was turned over. My closet was wide open and all the contents had been dumped on the floor. Everything was out except for the wooden box. It stood untouched on the empty shelf, right where I'd set it down. The thieves had ripped off the blanket that'd covered it, but for some reason left Aunt Lou's present behind. I took the key out of my wallet and opened it. Everything seemed to be in place. If the intruders were not able to break into my treasure, why hadn't they taken the box with them?

I stood up and turned to face a distraught Mr. Kent.

"I should call the police," I said with a sigh.

It took several hours after the police arrived for them to ask their questions, take notes, look through each room, and leave. Nothing of value was missing. It looked as though somebody had thrown a wild party at our place and left. Were these people searching for something?

I tried to send Mr. Kent home to bed, but he insisted on helping me clean. My mother's room took the longest. By the time we'd organized my place, both of us were exhausted. We sat at the kitchen table, and I brought tea with leftover cookies. The sugar boost was duly justified and quite necessary. Stretching out my legs, I sank my teeth into the baked goodness.

"I rarely eat at this time," Mr. Kent said, biting into a cookie. "But we had an extra workout today."

"I guess there are benefits to being robbed." I snorted. "The house looks more organized than it ever was. I can tell mom I decided to do a little cleanup before her return."

"Oh, Grace, I'm sorry you had to deal with this after spending your evening at the hospital. You must be so tired. I sure won't be able to sleep well until I buy you a new lock for the door. You should stay at my place tonight, or I can sleep here in the living room."

"No, no, you don't need to worry about it. I'm fine, really. I doubt these people will return. You've already done so much for us."

I strained to pull my cheerfulness back on, but with Mr. Kent's sympathetic eyes on me, my smile faltered.

"I haven't done anything yet," he said. "It was Lara who was kind enough to let me spend time with her. Please, call me if you need anything at all."

Mr. Kent got up but lingered by the table. He shifted his feet around, rubbed his forehead, and cleared his throat several times.

"I know that the timing is off, but I don't want to miss this opportunity to talk to you one-on-one."

I nearly choked on a piece of cookie. Two confessions in one evening?

The older man sat back down and stared at the tablecloth like a reluctant schoolboy. He finally spoke again.

"I don't know if your mother told you. You see, when we were young, your mother used to come to our house all the time and play with my sister. I... I fell in love with her. She was such a carefree, happy girl and so beautiful, but she was five years younger than me. I didn't think she would take me seriously. So I waited, content to keep her company as a friend, a big brother of sorts."

Mr. Kent paused. Was he gathering more courage to continue? He smoothed the tablecloth with his fingers and refused to look at me.

"At twenty-one, I joined the military to help pay for my education. Lara kept in correspondence with me through my sister. Then I took a leave and came home for her birthday. She turned eighteen. We shared a kiss. It was the best few weeks of my life, but I had to return to the base, and she was leaving for college. I didn't want to tie her up with any promises..."

I peered at my neighbor with my mouth half ajar. My mother had never mentioned this story. "So, what happened?"

"I got deployed overseas for a year. Back then it was hard to stay in touch. When I came back and got discharged, I tried to connect with Lara, even flew out to her college but couldn't get enough courage to talk to her. I saw her with another man, watched them from a distance for a few days. She looked so happy with him. I didn't want to interfere. I found out through my sister that they got engaged shortly after. It was too late for me." Mr. Kent sighed. "Life doesn't wait for anyone."

He paused and looked up from under his dark eyebrows. My throat was tight.

"We lost contact after Lara got married," he continued. "Her husband didn't want her to talk with my sister or any of her other old friends. We had no idea that she'd gotten divorced and moved back to the area. She never reached out."

Mr. Kent rubbed his eyes, but I kept quiet. Was there more to the story?

"When my sister met her a few months ago at the store, she was excited and upset at the same time," he said. "She came and told me how Lara had changed and how lonely she seemed. I couldn't stand it another minute. You see, my wife died six years ago, and we didn't have any kids, so I was alone too. I decided to leave my empty house, move next to Lara, and take my chances. But she was so rarely outside, it proved impossible to meet her until you invited me. I didn't want to just barge into her life."

It was hard to comprehend what he'd told me, but I was even less prepared for what came next. Mr. Kent looked up at me again. His eyes glistened.

"It might be too early to talk about this, but when the time is right and your mother feels she's ready... or if she wants it at all, I intend to tell her how I feel. After what happened today with this health scare, I was in such agony. I couldn't stand the thought of losing her again. The more time I spend with her, the more I want to be by her side. I promise to do everything in my power to make her happy and to take care of you and your sister."

The events of that day had depleted me of all my inner strength. The waterfall of emotions that I'd trampled down and hidden over the years bubbled from the depths of my soul. All the uncertainties, all the hurts, all the deficiencies that my heart had suffered through, poured out in a salty flood of tears. I covered my face and broke down, sobbing. Poor Mr. Kent seemed unsure of how to react and for a few minutes just sat in silence.

"There, there, dear. Don't cry." He gave me an awkward pat on the shoulder and stroked my hair. "I'll never ask your mother to be with me if it upsets you so."

"That's not why I'm crying." I sniffled. "I'm crying because I wish you'd come earlier. And what if you change your mind? It's only been two days. My mother is not easy to deal with. She's not the same person you used to know. She's been hurt and needs lots of attention."

"Even better. I have all the time in the world to give her. I was afraid my relocation here would look strange. I don't want any of you ladies to think that I'm somehow intruding. And I'll leave if that's what Lara wants."

For some reason the whole situation became amusing, and we cracked a few jokes about Mr. Kent's stalking tendencies. After a good laugh, I tried to come up with a plan of how Mr. Kent could open his heart to my mom. He was out of practice, and I was out of experience. My sister's arrival was approaching and would bring its own difficulties. In the end, we both decided that it would be best to let things take place naturally. I reassured Mr. Kent of my support for his decision and promised to do everything in my power to facilitate their relationship. After seeing how happy my mother was in his company, I was determined to fend off all the obstacles that might stand in their way.

Mr. Kent tried to convince me a few more times to come over to his apartment. I couldn't. There was one more thing I had to do that evening, and no robbers could stop me. He made me promise to keep my phone close by.

"I'm sorry if I burdened you with all these stories," Mr. Kent said after we got up and walked to the door.

"I'm so glad you did. It was brave of you to get it off your chest."

"I'm finding that speaking the truth requires courage, but it always turns out for the best at the end. I should have done this a long time ago."

"You couldn't be more right." I sighed. "I don't know if I'm as brave as you, but I'm glad you came into my mother's life. Or else I might have completely lost hope that there are any good men out there."

CHAPTER 22

After Mr. Kent left, I went back to my room, puzzled about what to do next. The emotional explosion left me drenched like a patch of dry earth after the rain.

I should schedule weekly crying sessions. It sure helps after a crazy week like this.

I sat on my bed and rubbed my fingers over the polished multifaceted surface of the stone on my chest. Watching it shimmer, I thought about all the things I wanted to change in my past. But was it safe? Would it make things better or worse? Was it even possible? And how would it affect my present? A million questions raced through my mind.

What if I accidentally alter the lives of others? I can't think only of my own needs, especially with Mr. Kent in the picture. But maybe I could make things easier for everyone.

Not wanting the stone's power to go to waste, I decided to do an experiment. With my eyes closed, I tried to remember something from my childhood. Immediately, I was back in my bright big bedroom decorated by my mother and, therefore, full of pink and glittery things. I was sitting on the sofa with my father's guitar in my lap. It was too bulky for my small frame. My fingers pulsated with pain from hard strings, but I stubbornly mastered the chords. An instrument of my father's youth, it'd collected dust in the corner until I decided to give it a try.

My mother's distressed voice from the hallway outside my room startled me. "Mark, where are you going again? You're never home. Please, talk to me!"

"I already told you I have a business meeting. Please, don't start—"

"But you don't let me go anywhere, I can't just sit at home by myself like a piece of furniture and wait for you!"

"Well, do something useful with your time. I work in the office, you work at home. I don't want my wife to mope around with some no-good friends and gossip all day. By the way, I am off tomorrow, and Mitchells invited us for dinner. Make sure you wear something nice."

"I don't want to go there. Can't we just spend the evening together?"

My mother's pleas were followed by the slamming of the front door.

The memory ended, time flew by again, and I now stood in the office in front of my father. He sat behind the large mahogany desk, his pale blue eyes focused on the work in front of him. Impeccably dressed, with carefully combed ash blond hair and neatly trimmed mustache, he always looked too formal to approach.

"I want to show you something. It's a surprise," I said. He nodded without looking up, and I perched on the stool with his guitar in my hands. The instrument was still too large for me, and I had a hard time holding on. I started to play a melody, stumbled, but continued all the way through. After the last chord, I lifted my head only to find the man in front of me glued to the computer screen. I sat there for a minute, waiting for his response.

"Did you like it, dad?" I asked. "It's your favorite song."

"It can be better," he answered, never turning in my direction.

Disappointment washed over me all anew. The emptiness. The rejection. The longing. Would I ever be good enough? I swallowed hard and kept the tears from escaping my eyes. The time fast-forwarded once again.

It was several years later. I stood in the hallway. Mother cried in the living room while Father meticulously went through the house, gathering his things. Julie followed his every step and pulled on his sleeve, only to be shooed away. I stood still, unable to move, unable to speak, frozen like a statue. I watched my father's every move with resentment, my heart slowly turning into stone. Familiar thoughts from my past filled my mind, and my fists clenched inside my pockets.

I won't cry over this. You won't see me cry, ever. I don't care that you're leaving.

Realization washed over me—I couldn't do anything to stop him. Did I even want to? He had always been a distant idol I'd worshiped as a little girl, trying to please him, to get his attention, but never able to deserve it. He never wanted anything to do with me.

I'd always wished I'd done something different on the day he'd walked out of our lives. The scene had played out in my mind so many times. How could I make him look me in the eyes and realize the pain he'd caused? It was my chance, and my voice came out loud and clear.

"You don't deserve me!"

My father stopped by the door and turned around. I met his surprised gaze with a new realization of my own sense of worth.

"You don't deserve any of us."

Suddenly, I was back to the present time. Cold sweat covered my body. I shivered in the dark room. My eyes burned, but I had no more tears left to shed. With clarity, I realized that I couldn't change my father's mind about leaving us for another woman. I couldn't make him regret what he did. I couldn't even stop my mother from falling apart. The only thing I had any control over was how all of that affected me.

As if in a trance, I took off the beautiful but cold stone. It had brought me nothing but pain. It had caused nothing but unfulfilled expectations that left me empty. I was about to crawl into a ball under a pile of blankets and hibernate there until the end of times when my phone rang. The long-awaited unidentified number blinked on the screen. I answered in a flash.

"Lou!"

"How's it going, kid?" Swooshing sounds raged in the background. Was she in the middle of a windstorm?

"I'm contending with your gift." Tears threatened to break through the layer of sarcasm.

"Good. I'm hoping you lose," she said with laughter in her voice.

"What? Why? What does all of this mean?" I spilled out in one breath. "It's too hard. I hate this. I don't understand what to do. I've never felt so lost, so out of control."

"Don't fight it, silly. Give up your control and let it do its work."

"What kind of work?"

"You'll find out soon."

The connection broke before I could ask more questions. I didn't even have a chance to tell her about my visitor and his offer. But her words left me even more confused. Was I somehow missing the point? One thing was clear—I needed to deal with my past and leave it alone. But would it let go of me? Would I ever feel good enough about myself? Would I ever believe that men could be anything but distant and selfish?

All I have in my power is the present moment, and I intend to make the best of it.

Determined, I sat down at the table and grabbed a piece of paper. A few minutes later, it was filled with a list of things I wanted to accomplish. It was past midnight when I returned the pendant to its place in the box. Right next to it was a section labeled "Truth". I remembered what Mr. Kent said earlier about facing the truth and opened the drawer. A round stone, similar to a large alabaster pearl, sat in an open seashell of white gold. Was I brave enough to wear it? Did I have enough willpower to deal with the truth? I took the booklet out and read:

T R U T H

אֱמֶת

(Onyx)

Wisdom to detect the truth and differentiate it from deception or lie in other people's words and actions, ability to make other people say the truth or sense the root of their true intentions, ability to see yourself and others in a true light, empowerment to speak the truth.

Another chance to make things right. Would this stone help me find what I was looking for? I put the pendant on, barricaded my door with furniture, and tried to fall asleep.

PART VI
THE MEANINGFUL LIFE

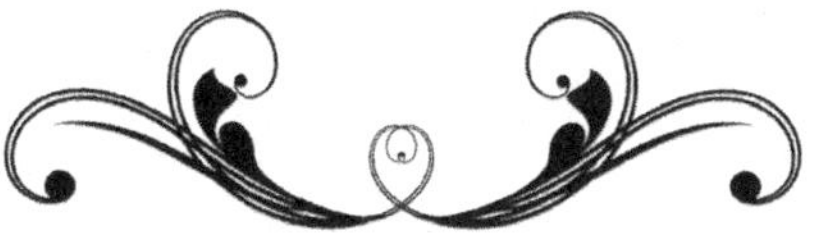

You will know the truth, and the truth will set you free.

—Jesus Christ

CHAPTER 23

On Saturday, I woke up to my phone ringing and the realization that I'd slept through the alarm. My mom was on the other end of the line.

"All the tests came back normal," she said. "The doctor agreed to let me go home this afternoon. He said my heart needs regular exercise, a good diet, and to fall in love."

She laughed, and I breathed a sigh of relief.

Well, that's easy. I have an idea who can provide all of these things.

I called Mr. Kent to share the good news and asked him to pick up my mom. He was excited to oblige.

"Appreciate this, Grace. I'll take you up on any chance to see her."

I chuckled at his eagerness. "You might have to remind me once in a while. It will take time to get used to somebody else caring for her."

"I'll do as much as you ladies let me. Don't want to impose."

"You're not. And I want to apologize for my outburst yesterday. I don't usually fall apart like this. It was just a hard day."

A hard week, a few hard years...

"I don't mind. Anytime you need a shoulder to cry on, you know where to find me." Mr. Kent's voice became somber. "I worried about you staying in the apartment alone after what happened. This whole neighborhood is questionable at best. If only I found Lara a few years earlier..."

"There's no point to regret what can't be changed," I said.

Trust me on that...

"You're right." His voice brightened. "I need to take it one day at a time and enjoy what I have."

"That sounds like a plan. I'll try to do the same."

"Great! Well, on that note, I have to confess that I already bought you a new lock this morning. We should install it before Lara gets home."

I hung up the phone and smiled. It was exciting to think that my mom got a second chance at love. In just a few days, I'd already seen big changes in her, and I was sure Mr. Kent could find a way to her heart. Hopefully, with him around, she'd let go of the past. We all needed a fresh start.

As far as my personal life, I decided to take advantage of my boyfriend-free status and spend time by myself. My plan was slightly derailed with the appearance of Mr. Kent who came to replace the locks. After convincing him not to order a security system or otherwise booby trap our apartment, I sent him to get my mother and went back to my room. It was time to figure out how to use the new pendant. I stopped in front of the mirror and admired the elegant crystal on my neck.

What kind of truth do I need in my life? Mr. Abeles... Tzali said I need to know the truth about myself. That seems like a good place to start.

It was the last day before my birthday, and I wanted to make it count. To slow down and reflect on my life sounded like a perfect plan. During the night, I had a dream of being put on a scale. Did that mean my life needed more weight?

Or did I just have to evaluate some things? I sat at the table and looked at the list of goals I'd written down last night.

Can I accomplish all of this?

A strong assurance that it was all possible filled my heart.

The first item on the paper was to take care of my health.

I need to do this for myself. It's nice to feel good about the way I look. Should I join a gym?

The idea intimidated me. I imagined myself fumbling with the equipment next to a Sports Illustrated swimsuit model. Or falling off the treadmill and knocking out my front teeth in front of a buff heartthrob.

You don't need to look like a movie star to be attractive. Just let what's inside of you shine. Find somebody who'll appreciate your strengths, accept your weaknesses and will love you the way you are.

These thoughts were so refreshing that I wanted to write them down, but my sarcasm took over.

Sure. And where can I find a guy like that? On Mars? All men are after good looks. Even Cinderella ran off once the fancy clothes disappeared, and I'm not exactly princess material without the pendants."

I frowned and chewed the tip of my pen, but next to the first item I wrote: "be the best version of yourself, don't compare."

The second thing on my list was to take steps towards a better job. Should I still continue my education to become a teacher or pursue a career in law? Were the things I told Miles last night about my aspiration to become a lawyer true? I decided to meet with a college counselor and apply for financial assistance.

I want to move in the right direction, even if it'll take me years to complete my degree. Maybe I'll make it into the Guinness records for being the oldest graduate.

I smiled and looked over my third goal—to have fun and to meet new people.

Almost like three wishes... Well, if I learned one thing, it is that I can't hide under the blanket with a good book forever. Oh, Bilbo Baggins, I feel you! I don't want to go on an adventure either. I'd rather stay home and hoard snacks.

"It's a dangerous business, going out your door," Bilbo said, and it rang true in my life. To step through the door of my limitations was just the beginning. Where would I be swept off to next? What new roads waited for me? The few days I'd spent outside of my comfort zone had brightened my existence and helped me to find my voice, but was there more?

It's definitely a stretch. I'm sure Alicia will be thrilled about my decision to be more sociable... Umm, probably not a good idea to tell her about my plan. She'll end up dragging me to the craziest parties.

While I tried to figure out how to spice up my social life, my mind began to talk to me again.

You tell yourself that you prefer to be alone, that you don't need others. In reality, you're afraid to get hurt again, to be misunderstood and rejected like you were by your own father.

That new realization caught me by surprise. A painful tug on my heart pushed me out of my chair. I paced the room, assailed by my own thoughts. Was I hiding all these years to avoid heartache? Intentionally staying numb? Keeping men at a distance because I thought they'd leave me when I wasn't needed?

Didn't the vision about Miles prove me right?

Tears welled up in my eyes. The brutally honest conversation with myself was too gut-wrenching to handle. My mind stubbornly resisted the voice of truth.

Don't fight it... Aunt Lou's words echoed in my memory.

"So, what do I do about this?" I said out loud. "Let's say, I was wrong and want to change. What's next? How do I step out without getting hurt again?"

The strange thoughts rose inside of me again.

You have to take the risk. Do what you're afraid of. Instead of walking away, face it. Instead of staying silent, speak up. Instead of hiding, reach out. If you want to see changes in your life, do things differently. Do the opposite.

A minute later, I was on the phone with Alicia and James, asking them what their plans were for Saturday. They both agreed to meet with me.

"Well, that was easy. Are you happy, little stone? See, I did the opposite of what I wanted and checked off wish number three at the same time."

There is one more person you need to call.

I groaned, reluctantly scrolled through my short list of contacts, and stared at Greg's number. Nail biting, lip chewing, and rehearsals of cheesy lines didn't help me get over the wall of doubts that stood between us. Was Greg still interested in a friendship with me? Was it what I wanted? Was it what he wanted? Would I be willing to complicate my life again after the turmoil with Miles if he decided to be more than a friend? And what if he didn't want anything to do with me at all after seeing me leave with my boss?

I can deal with Greg later. Today I'll hang out with my old friends and, hopefully, clear my head.

Soon, my mother called to tell me Mr. Kent was at the hospital and would take her home.

"Don't worry about anything. Go out and enjoy yourself. I'll just go home and rest."

I couldn't believe this was Lara Ainsworth speaking. Our neighbor most likely had something to do with how easily she let me go. My absence would give them a chance to spend time alone.

I got up. A familiar pulling sensation surged through my body. The leftover power of the Time stone transported me to the future once again. Miles stood in front of me, but our surroundings were blurred. He seemed distraught and covered his mouth with both hands, but the vision disappeared before I could figure out what was happening.

Half an hour later, James picked me up in his car. It took him a few minutes to get over the shock of seeing the upgraded version of me and regain his ability to speak. Even though the weight kept creeping up, with my overall makeover, I was no longer the same Grace. James poked me with his finger to make sure I was real after I got into the passenger's seat next to him.

"I forgot you haven't seen my new image yet." I grinned. "I should've warned you. So, what do you think?"

"I think you look beautiful, and it's harder for me to accept the fact we're still friends," he said.

I grimaced.

Shoot, I should be more careful what kinds of questions I'm asking with this darn Truth stone on me.

"I'm sorry."

"No apologies needed. This topic is closed. Not sure where that came from." James scratched his head.

I searched his face. If he was hiding how he truly felt, he did it well. "Thank you… And, yes, I'd like to keep you as a friend, please. You're way too valuable to downgrade you to boyfriend status."

He finally peeled his eyes off me and started the car. "So, what are we up to? Don't tell me we have to pick up your goofy friend Alicia next."

I gave him a big cheesy smile. "That's exactly what we'll do."

CHAPTER 24

We drove to Renton to meet with Alicia and Marcos. Her new love interest turned out to be a pleasant fellow, and his presence had an additional benefit—it prevented my friend from questioning me about my disastrous evening with Miles Taylor.

"Let's all go eat lunch first. I'm starving," Alicia said once everyone settled in the car.

James gave me a pointed look. I interpreted it as "when is she not starving?" and shot a pleading glance back at him.

"Well, in that case, I know a nice restaurant near Lake Washington. It's close by, and we can go to the park too," he said.

"I bet everyone is outdoors right now," Alicia chirped from behind. "First nice weekend this year!"

We all agreed that since James was driving, we would let him pick the place to eat, and his somewhat sour mood lightened up. He spent the next fifteen minutes updating me on the latest discoveries in the world of technology until excessive giggles from the back seat made him frown again. Marcos and Alicia's silly talk and mutual squeezing caused poor James to roll his eyes. He did it so many times, I was afraid they'd get stuck in the upward position.

"Hey, have some respect for the single people in the front seat!" he yelled at the pair.

"Don't be jealous," Alicia shot back. "Tell him, Grace."

"Leave them alone, James. Be happy we're both independent individuals," I said.

"Well, I'm warning you, Grace, if they don't quit this nonsense, I'll have to get obnoxious with you."

We stopped at a light not too far from the Downtown area, and James reached his long arms to pull me into a side hug. I froze, remembering his earlier comment, but things quickly escalated into a harmless banter with Alicia and Marcos joining in. James even leaned in for a pretend kiss. Laughing, I turned towards the window to save myself and caught Greg's surprised stare from the car in the next lane. His co-worker, Sandra, talked excitedly about something in the front seat. I gave James a hard shove and rolled the window down, but the light changed to green, and we turned in different directions.

Oh, sithspit! What in the world is he thinking about me now? Every time he sees me, I'm with a new guy. And what is this glue stick, Sandra, doing with him again?

I didn't want to make the wrong impression on anybody, especially Greg. Why did everything have to be so complicated when it came to men?

You do care about him, Grace, more than you're willing to admit.

I cut that thought short by apologizing to James who rubbed his sore shoulder and demanded compensation for his injury in the form of ice cream.

As we got closer to our destination, I recognized little shops and restaurants by the Marina.

"I came here years ago," I exclaimed. "It used to be my favorite spot. Took Jules here for ice cream."

"Perfect," James pitched in. "Remember, you owe me one."

"Usually people take their dates here." Marcos winked at Alicia.

We got out of the car, and I took Alicia by the arm. The men followed behind. I lifted my head and drank in the morning sunshine. It was a perfect day for an outing, and I wanted to forget all the trouble from the past week. The park around the lake was full of people who'd come there to spend the weekend. They strolled on the pathways by the water and sat in groups on the grass sunbathing and chatting.

My phone rang, displaying an unknown number. Was it my aunt again?

"Hey, Grace," Miles's smooth baritone echoed in my ear and pierced through my heart.

"How did you get my number?" I lowered my voice and stepped away from Alicia.

He let out a pleasant laugh. "All I had to do was log into the database at work. With all your secrets, I half-expected your number to be disconnected."

I swallowed hard. What kinds of secrets did he want to uncover? And why was he calling?

"Something happened?" I said, ignoring Alicia. She gestured in front of me, demanding to know who I was talking to.

"No, not yet. But I would like for *something* to happen." His voice deepened and sent a shiver down my spine. "You know I fancy you."

Why was I so weak when it came to Miles? My heart ached. Would I still let him into my life despite the warning I'd received? Was that vision even real or just a product of my own fears? And what if my future wasn't set in stone?

"I'd like to see you," he continued.

"Sorry, I'm kind of busy. I have to go."

At that point, we came up to the restaurant entrance. Alicia sent me impatient stares, rubbed her belly, and demonstrated her hunger with other mimes. I mouthed "sorry" but didn't hang up.

Miles continued to talk. "Listen, let me invite you on a real date tonight. Forget all these work formalities. Go out with me."

"Wouldn't it complicate things?" I attempted to sound reasonable.

"It already did. The minute you stormed into my office a few days ago, you ruined me for all the other women. If you say no, I'll have to live like a recluse for the rest of my days."

I laughed. "That would be a terrible waste. I can't let that happen."

"I'll take that as a yes. I'll pick you up at seven."

"Wait. You know where I live?"

"Cheers." Miles chuckled and hung up.

No, no. Call him back and tell him you can't go. Plus, you can't let him see the dump you call home...

I groaned but caught myself under Alicia's prying eyes.

"It's from work." I tried to sound dismissive.

Alicia narrowed her eyes. "On the weekend?"

"Ok, fine, it was Miles. He invited me on another date. Said I ruined him or something like that. Don't know if I believe him."

I should call him back and ask him a few truth or dare questions. Only he'll have to pick the truth.

It looked like Alicia was ready to question me instead, but Marcos came to my rescue to tell us that they'd already gotten a table. Soon my friend was too distracted by food to conduct her interrogation.

We had a great lunch with enjoyable conversations that made the time fly. I kicked Alicia under the table a few times when she started to say something about my aunt and her present.

"Well, all I want to mention, *chica*, is that I'm glad you're finally enjoying your life," she said after correcting herself for the fourth time. "It always amazed me how strong and self-reliant you are, although, a little stubborn. But I also knew there was a happy person underneath all that seriousness. You're so much more animated now than before. You smile more. It's like you've fallen in love or something."

My friend winked and set my cheeks on fire, but she was right. Since my father's departure, I'd never felt so alive. Despite all the chaos that the stones had caused, it had been the most exciting and eventful week of my life.

"I agree, but please don't change anything else. You're different from all these other women who talk too much and laugh too much." James gave Alicia a meaningful glance. "I appreciate your ability to listen and think before speaking. Those are rare finds these days."

Alicia pouted. "*Oye*, James, you're such a pill. It's called having good social skills. Although, I can't imagine that Grace will ever enjoy small talk with a bunch of random people. Not everyone is outgoing like me."

"Thank goodness," James muttered.

Marcos glared at James and put his arm around Alicia's shoulders. "You are the best, *mi amor*."

"Hey, guys! You should stop arguing over me," I pleaded. "If you know me so well, you should've realized this conversation makes me super uncomfortable. Yes, I'll never enjoy crowds, but I do appreciate spending time with a few good friends like you… given that you don't try to kill each other."

"Ok, I'll spare his life for your sake." Alicia bared her teeth and surrendered her table knives. James stuck a white napkin on the fork and waved it over his head with a sad expression. We all laughed, but the peace treaty soon turned into a napkin ball fight, at which point we nearly got kicked out of the establishment.

After our meal, we decided to get some fresh air and walk along the lake. With more distance between James and Alicia, things quieted down. The spring weather gifted us with warmer temperatures that afternoon. People ran and biked along the water, but we opted for a slow stroll. Unfortunately, our peaceful outing soon came to an abrupt end. Several feet in front of us, I spotted Miles Taylor. Leaning on the railing, he looked out at the lake as if posing for a photo shoot. His casual outfit didn't diminish his smoldering looks one bit. For a second I wondered if he'd somehow tracked me down, but my temporary excitement dwindled when Victoria ran up to him and jumped into his arms.

"Grace!" Alicia gasped. "Is that not your Mr. Taylor?"

"Sure is. Only he isn't mine." I tried to sound lighthearted, but my insides were heavy as lead.

Miles put his arm behind Victoria's back and leaned in to say something into her ear. She beamed and laughed. It didn't take much imagination to understand they weren't discussing work-related topics. He didn't look one bit "ruined" for other female species. On the contrary, he seemed quite content squeezing Victoria's curvy waistline at the moment.

I blinked a few times to make sure it wasn't a figment of my imagination. The park was close enough to Downtown Seattle and a popular area, but for him to be so reckless! He clearly didn't care about the possibility of being caught. And that was only a few hours after inviting me out!

I tried to suppress the disappointment that bubbled up in my heart.

Why should this bother me? It was foolish to even think I could compete for his attention. It's all for the best. Seems like I can't avoid facing the truth today one way or the other. What was I even trying to accomplish with the guy?

My throat tightened. "Looks like he's working on his next conquest."

Alicia swore in Spanish; at least it sounded like a few angry epithets. "C'mon, let's teach this bastard a lesson."

She took me by the arm and marched towards Miles and Victoria.

"Alicia, wait," I pleaded.

She didn't slow down. "Listen, if you don't say something, then I will."

I stiffened inside. We were now just a few steps away from the unsuspecting pair.

Now or never. May the Force be with me.

"Miles!" My loud greeting made my boss jump and pull away from his companion. They both turned and stared in our direction.

"Miles?" Victoria scoffed. Her lips curved down. She looked me over like a nuisance, then gave our boss a questioning glare.

"Victoria, what a surprise. Didn't know you work on the weekends." I might have overdone it with the amount of elation in my voice.

"Didn't expect to meet you here, Miss Ainsworth." Miles ran his hand through his hair. A look of disappointment crossed his features, as if he just lost a game of golf.

"Oh, so we're back to formality? Last night you insisted we be on a first-name basis." I was surprised at the amount of mockery in my tone. Miles either coughed or choked. "So what's the plan for tonight? You'll finally show me your art collection? Or was there something else you wanted to show me, Mr. Taylor? I guess I did ask you to surprise me."

Miles clenched his jaw, his eyes darted around like a trapped animal in search of an escape. Victoria glanced between us. Her perfect eyebrows came together in a frown, and I could tell she'd connected the dots. Alicia stood close by with her arms crossed, ready to pound the man into the ground at the first opportunity. He was outnumbered and surrounded.

Well, Miles Taylor, you think there is no such thing as perfect justice and truth? We'll see about that. Now you'll say the truth and nothing but the truth and then face some justice. Screw this job opening.

Filled with determination, I touched the stone on my chest. At that moment I didn't care who else was around me or what the consequences would be. The truth took precedence and begged to be brought out into the open.

"Mr. Taylor, why did you invite me last night and today?" I said.

"Miss Ainsworth… Grace. All I was planning is to…"

"Is to what?"

"Is to get something…" His eyes became big and mouth tightened into a line. "Listen, can we talk about this in private?"

"No, I want to hear it now, Mr. Taylor. It sounds rather interesting. What did you want to get?" I raised my eyebrows and locked eyes with him.

"Information. I was curious how you knew so much about our partners."

My concern peaked. Was he plotting to undermine Mr. Bailey and take over? "What did you plan to do with it?"

"Use it to strengthen my position at the firm." He looked puzzled, as if the words had been pulled out of him by force.

Imagining myself as a private investigator, I continued. "Is that all?"

"No, I wanted to do something else." Miles tensed.

"What is it? Enlighten us."

"I wanted to get you into my bed."

Something close to reverence passed through Miles's features. Victoria gasped. Alicia swore under her breath. And, to my shock, I burst into a fit of laughter. It all felt like a play that had been staged in front of me, and I was a spectator in the first row. I'd expected to be crushed but was relieved instead. My heart was finally free.

At that point my sarcasm took over and kicked out any

remnants of civility. "Let me clarify this. Did you want to demonstrate the new Tempur-Pedic mattress you bought?"

Miles shook his head.

"Hmm, let's see. Did you want to add me to your list of conquests and satisfy your ego?" I enunciated every word.

"Yes. What the..." Miles's gaze helplessly darted from me to Victoria, but nobody came to his rescue. By that time James and Marcos had joined us and looked at our little group with confusion.

"That's what I thought, Mr. Taylor. So glad I left before getting your 'surprise'. Is that what you're planning to do to poor Victoria?" I turned to my boss again. He covered his mouth with both hands, but his head moved up and down in agreement, an image I'd seen earlier in my vision. "Mr. Taylor, how cruel of you. She probably expects a promotion and maybe even a diamond ring."

For a minute everyone held their breath, waiting for an explosion. Suddenly, Victoria growled and pushed Miles away.

"I'll see you in Mr. Bailey's office," she hissed at him. "You'll have to explain yourself."

She swore loudly, stormed passed him, and disappeared into the crowd. Miles wanted to say something, but his mouth opened and closed without producing any sounds. He looked like a fish out of water. Had he found himself incapable of saying anything in an honest enough way? He gave me another perplexed look, mumbled something through his teeth, then ran off in the same direction. I turned to my stunned friends.

Alicia was the first to break the silence. "I can't believe this man! So much drama, *madre mía*."

"More like a comedy. Ladies and gentlemen, I present to you a very honest Miles Taylor." I bowed and waved my hand toward the two runaways.

"Shame." Alicia pouted her lips. "He was so busy catching

all the ladies that he got caught himself. Was his goal to date all the young girls at your firm?"

"Then I guess I ruined his perfect record."

Alicia and I laughed, then she turned to Marcos.

"Did you see that, *mi alma*," she said, pulling her boyfriend close. "Don't ever try to lie to me, or I'll have my friend question you."

"*Sí, mi princesa*." He kissed her, but his smile was strained.

James only scratched his head.

"I am proud of you, Grace." Alicia turned to me again. "You're finally standing up for yourself. That probably means we'll argue more, but I'll love you all the same."

I shook my head. "Let's just forget about it. I don't want this to ruin our day."

Alicia huffed. "Agreed. He doesn't deserve any more of our time."

I put my hand around James's elbow, and we continued our walk along the lake. Listening to my friends chat, I pushed my anxious thoughts away. How could I go back to work on Monday after what'd just happened? Would I be able to face Miles again? I wanted to forget about that for a moment and enjoy my time with friends.

CHAPTER 25

We spent the rest of the afternoon strolling around, eating ice cream, and chatting. Thankfully, I didn't have to use the "truth serum" on anybody else.

"Grace, what are you doing for your birthday tomorrow?" Alicia asked. "We have to plan something. I won't let you skip the celebration like you did last year."

"I have to think about it."

"Don't think too long, or I'll take over."

"You know what, let's get together tomorrow at my place. Just a few people."

"Perfect! I'm coming early to put up the decorations. And you can't argue with me about that."

We decided to meet on Sunday at noon. I called my mom to tell her the plan and to invite Mr. Kent. Since he was right next to her, that was an easy task. I called Mrs. Williamson and a few more of my co-workers. Mrs. Jones was next. Even the girl I'd met on the tram agreed to come. When I made it to Greg's number, my fingers refused to listen. Could my heart take another disappointment? That wasn't a risk I was willing to take at that moment, but I couldn't skip on inviting him after everything he'd done. I had no reason to avoid the guy.

The moment I sent Greg a text message, everything around me suddenly blurred away. I got pulled through the time tunnel. Greg's voice echoed in the distance, but I couldn't make out the words or see him. All I could focus on were my blood-covered hands. I stared at my shaky red fingers. Panic crept up my spine, but the image disappeared and I was back at the park.

"Are you ok, Grace?" Alicia searched my face.

"Yeah, just… Just felt faint all of a sudden." I blinked and touched my sweaty forehead. My hand was ice cold.

"You want to sit down?"

I nodded and dropped on the closest bench.

"You're not pregnant, are you?" Alicia's eyes narrowed. I gave her an exasperated stare. "Ok, ok, just checking."

"Let me rest for a sec. I think fresh air is toxic after spending so much time indoors." I gave Alicia a feeble smile, but my insides continued to tremble.

James and Marcos were busy discussing something and thankfully didn't notice my distress. In a few minutes, James spotted a group of people from his work and waved them over. They got into a long conversation about the latest computer applications, and Alicia walked away with Marcos to look at the lilies that grew by the shore. I wanted to get away from others and think through my strange vision. Restless, I got up and took a short walk by myself. Leaving the busy crowd behind, I wandered into the wooded area of the park.

The stillness of the stately aspens surrounded me on every side. In an attempt to calm down, I ran my fingers over their smooth white trunks and looked up at the twisted empty branches that reached all the way to the sky. The air stood still, infused with the barely noticeable fresh fragrance of occasional fir trees. I followed the path, preoccupied with my thoughts. They had settled down on my chest like a heavy piece of concrete. Anxious questions filled my mind. Whose blood was on my hands? Why was Greg there? What does it mean? Was the pendant warning me? There were no answers.

A short distance ahead a small stone building peeked through the trees. It looked like an old medieval country church and took my imagination to the times of knights. Thankful for a small diversion from my dark ruminations, I walked closer. The whole area seemed abandoned. Moss-covered brick walls crumbled in many places. Gothic style windows had broken glass and peeling molding. Weeds took over a small cemetery next to the structure. The front door was missing, and the dark arch of the entrance lured me inside.

As I stepped inside, the hollow sounds of my shoes against the concrete floor startled the birds. They flew up and hid in the wooden arches and beams of the high ceiling. Sunlight that peeked through the broken glass panels painted uneven streaks of color on the stone benches and across the dusty floor. The room was rectangular in size with an empty altar at the farthest end and a humble wooden cross hanging behind it. Carefully, I walked towards the front, trying not to stir the tangible stillness inside. I sat in a pew and watched particles of dust sparkle as they settled in the rays of the sun.

"What is the truth?" I whispered. Instantly an overwhelming sense of peace filled my heart. Somehow, in that moment of time, I understood that my life was not an accidental tiny spark of dust in the vast cosmos. No, it had meaning and purpose. I'd been carefully crafted and intentionally placed. I was meant to be. My life was interconnected with others around me, as if invisible hands orchestrated my existence with attention to every detail. The truth that I was important and created to make a difference saturated my innermost being.

Empowered by this new realization, I closed my eyes and let that belief settle deep in my heart. It didn't matter anymore what my father, Miles, Greg or any other man thought of me. I didn't need another human's approval to feel complete and capable. We were all limited by our hurts and expectations. How could I blame others for not knowing what I needed or not being able to give me what they didn't have?

I took a deep breath. "Father… I forgive you."

Something cracked inside of me, as if a stone table in my soul had been broken by Aslan. The chains could no longer hold me. I was finally free to be my own person.

"Whatever happened to me in the past, I'll use it to be stronger and wiser in the future."

My voice echoed through the room. I stood up and turned to leave. An image of the crucifixion on a half-broken window panel caught my eye. Under it was a small sign. I walked over and wiped the dust off the rusty words: "Come to Me, all who are weary and heavily burdened, and I will give you rest." There was my answer. There, I laid all my burdens and deceptions to follow the path of truth.

I WALKED out of the building with my heart full of silent gratitude. It was time to get back to my friends. Alicia had already overloaded my phone with frantic text messages. Outside, a lonely stranger stood by one of the graves.

"Life is so short, it flies by," he mumbled.

Not wanting to disturb him, I kept walking, but suddenly he turned around and faced me. It was the same homeless person I'd met several times. I froze mid-stride. Was he following me around?

"Did you find what you were looking for?" He smiled, but

his eyes pierced me with their intense stare, as if all my thoughts had been exposed and handed on a plate to him.

"I… I think so." My throat became dry. I backed away and stumbled on the uneven ground.

The stranger's expression hardened. "Your time is running out. Did you make a decision?"

Is this where my hands get bloody? Was he sent to eliminate me and take away the stones?

"You don't recognize me?" The man unwrapped the blue scarf from his neck and placed it over his head. "I am Bongani."

I instinctively covered the stone on my chest with both hands and took a few more steps back. Did he come to claim his treasure?

"Did you discover the answer to the question?" He persisted, moving closer. His eyes seemed to shine brighter than the sun. His stare blinded me.

"What question?" Adrenaline surged through my veins. I was ready to fight or flee.

"Whether there is perfect justice and truth?"

My stunned vocal cords refused to work. Instead of answering, I turned around and stormed away. Glancing behind a few times to make sure he wasn't following, I broke into a run until the secluded area was behind me.

How did that person know about my conversation with Miles? Why did he ask me that question? Was he a friend or a foe? Was he the one who ransacked my apartment? My imagination ran wild. There were too many coincidences for one day. First Greg, then Miles, now my queer stocker. Had they been intentionally thrown my way?

So much for a relaxing day.

But the peace that'd settled in my heart in the abandoned chapel returned and soothed my ruffled nerves. It surrounded me like a powerful force field that could not be penetrated, and my heartbeat slowed down.

Next time I go around exploring unknown territories, I should take somebody else. Preferably somebody with more muscles than me. And this guy should stop freaking me out. I need to ask Aunt Lou about him or report him to the police.

I found James, Alicia, and Marcos combing the park in search of me.

"Why did you disappear? You nearly passed out!" Alicia fussed as soon as she laid her eyes on me. "And now you look like you just came out of a Zumba class."

"I needed a moment by myself," I said, looking behind my back, but there was no sign of pursuit. "Let's get out of here."

"She's a grown woman and doesn't need your constant supervision," James muttered, at which point Alicia temporary forgot my existence and switched her attention to him. Marcos sighed and stepped away as the two of them jumped into another heated argument. Their silly bickering distracted me from my worries, and I even offered to place bets with Marcos on who would win, but he only shook his head.

As we walked to the car, loneliness settled into the pit of my stomach. The new feelings and thoughts born in my soul among the ruins of the chapel begged to be shared. My mysterious pursuer wasn't a good candidate for it, even though he'd tried to chat. James was normally eager to engage in abstract discussions about the meaning of life, but he was too busy trying to prove something else to Alicia. I longed to talk with Greg, to look into his pensive blue eyes, even to have him tease me.

Grace, you're so illogical. You always want what you can't have. Just forget about him for one day. And that vision? Who knows what kinds of trouble meeting him again would bring.

There was something else on my mind—I wanted to share with Greg the peace I'd received about my past. He needed it too. I took out my phone and sent him a long text message.

CHAPTER 26

The ride back had been quiet. We were all lost in our thoughts. Even Alicia wasn't as chatty. She looked out of the window and pouted. I caught James looking at her through his rearview mirror, but decided to leave them be. We dropped Alicia and Marcos off at five in the evening. After they left, James wanted to stop by his work to pick up a few items, but I was eager to get home and check on my mother. I called Mr. Kent.

"Your mother is taking a nap," he said. "The night in the hospital must have worn her out. I have nothing better to do, so I'll stick around and read a book until you come back. No need to hurry."

I turned to my friend after hanging up. "Ok, James, we can go to your office, but make it quick."

Twenty minutes later, we parked on the street and entered the building. The main entrance was open on the weekends, but we only had one hour until the whole structure would be locked for the night. Since James and I worked on the same floor, I took a seat in the hallway by our law firm and waited for my friend to come back. There was no point to check my phone for a tenth time because Greg hadn't responded. Had he found my message too intrusive? What did I know about the things he'd witnessed anyway? Did I even have the right to speak into his life? Would he come to my birthday? My thoughts were interrupted when I spotted Olivia Peterson. She snuck out of the side door further down the corridor, rushed across the hallway and disappeared through the staircase entrance without noticing me.

What is Olivia doing here? That's strange...

I took my shoes off to minimize the noise and followed her down the concrete stairs, staying a few steps behind. She slipped through the emergency exit a few seconds before I reached the ground floor. My heart raced as I pulled the handle and slowly cracked open the heavy metal door. A red Maserati sped up and turned the corner of the building. Olivia must have left in that car. But who was the driver?

I came out and put my hand over my eyes to shield them from the rays of the setting sun.

"Looking for something?"

I yelped and jumped like a startled cat. Olivia stood on the other side of the door with her arms folded, lips tight and eyes narrowed.

"Are you spying on me?" The enmity in her voice made me wince.

"No... noo!" I let out a nervous giggle that didn't sound too convincing. "I'm just waiting... for a friend."

"Hmm, with your shoes off?"

Olivia glanced at my feet, her mouth creased in a mocking smile. All legitimate explanations evaporated from my brain. I could only think of pathetic excuses like "I always go barefoot down the steps" and "My friend and I played tag at his work party". Instead of answering, I covered the pendant with my hand and locked my eyes with Olivia.

Now, you will tell me the truth...

"What are you doing at the office on Saturday?"

"Checking the accounts." My supervisor's face flushed. "It's none of your business, what I do!"

I had to think of a better question.

"Are you giving away our financial information to Mr. Kowalski?"

"Yes." Olivia froze. "What? What in the world! Where did you get this name?"

"I know more than you give me credit for, *Miss Peterson*. Soon Mr. Bailey will know too."

Olivia smirked. "I'm not sure who you imagine yourself to be, but you're obviously not very smart. You work at a law firm, but know nothing about the burden of proof. You have no evidence, sweetheart. And I tell you what." Olivia's tone changed from mocking to threatening. She leaned towards me and lowered her voice: "If you don't resign from your job on Monday, I'll produce plenty of evidence that will implicate you in stealing funds from the firm. Let's say, you broke into Mr. Bailey's personal computer while you had access to his office this week. How will I validate this claim you may ask? Trust me, I have my ways. Better not mess with me."

She took a step away and took her cell phone out.

"Come back here and pick me up! It's just that stupid girl from work. No, no need to do anything. She'll behave. Won't you?" Olivia gave me a loaded look and hung up the phone. "I want to see your resignation letter on my desk on Monday. I have your address, so consider our brief visit to your place last night a warning to help you keep your mouth shut. Unless, of course, you want to end up in jail… or worse."

I gasped. "What did you search my place for?"

"You've been bragging to Mr. Bailey about having something that could help him. Who knew that you were just faking it to get on his good side."

I'm doomed either way, so let's see what you're up to.

"And how do you plan to sabotage Mr. Bailey?" I said.

"By taking the money out of the firm's accounts and

framing him for it," Olivia said. Confusion creased her features. She frowned and grabbed my arm. "Show me your phone!"

"I left it in the car." That was the unfortunate truth. Did Olivia think I was recording her? That would've been a great idea. She patted me down and frantically glanced around.

"If you say a word about any of this, you'll be implicated as Mr. Bailey's accomplice. What do you think about that?" She hissed.

I wanted to ask why and how she planned to do it, but Olivia had already stormed away. The red luxury car I'd seen earlier returned. My supervisor opened the front door and sat next to Robert Kowalski. She gave me the "I am watching you" gesture before they sped away.

How do they know each other?

I plopped down on the dirty sidewalk by the exit and covered my face. There was no doubt in my heart that Olivia would go through with her threats. The truth was costing me too much. Despair filled my heart.

Oh, Grace. You've gotten yourself into trouble again for sticking your nose where it doesn't belong, and now you'll have to pay for it big time. It was so much better when you sat quietly in your corner and didn't try to save the world. Poor Mr. Bailey! There's nothing I can do to help. Who would ever believe me? Now even Miles will be against me after what I did to him today.

I got up and made my way back to the hallway where James was already waiting.

Don't be afraid, you're doing what is right, my heart said, but I was too distraught to pay attention.

"Is everything alright? You're so pale. Are you sick?" James put an arm around my shoulders and touched my forehead.

"Just take me home. I'm tired," I replied.

~

I SAT QUIETLY in the car all the way back home. When I arrived, Mr. Kent was still in our living room reading a book. I thanked him for his help and sent him home to rest. My mother was sleeping peacefully. I opened the door and watched her for a minute.

At least my mom has a chance to be happy. As for me, I might be the unluckiest person ever.

That is not true... the thought came to me as I entered my room and took the necklace off. I wasn't in a mood to have any more conversations that evening, even if it was with my own conscience. Exhausted and defeated, I put the stone back in its drawer and hid the box in the furthest corner of my closet. I wasn't sure if my aunt's present was a blessing or a curse. I wanted to get it out of my sight and mind.

There is no point in trying to jump in over my head. I only make everything worse. I should've accepted things the way they were and made the best out of it instead of trying to change something. It's about time to stop living in a dream world.

Since it was too early to go to sleep and I didn't want to dwell on my fruitless thoughts, I decided to lose myself in re-watching *The Lord of the Rings: The Two Towers.* Mother woke up and joined me. Over the next several hours, all my misfortunes were forgotten until I got to the part where Frodo broke down and told his servant, Sam, that he couldn't go on anymore. So many times I'd listened to Sam deliver his speech, heard him say: "There's some good in this world, Mr. Frodo and it's worth fighting for," but that evening it hit close to home.

I won't watch an innocent person get hurt. I'll have to talk to Mr. Bailey, even if it doesn't end well for me.

With that decision, the tension inside me eased, and the peace settled back in my heart.

PART VII
THE FULFILLED LIFE

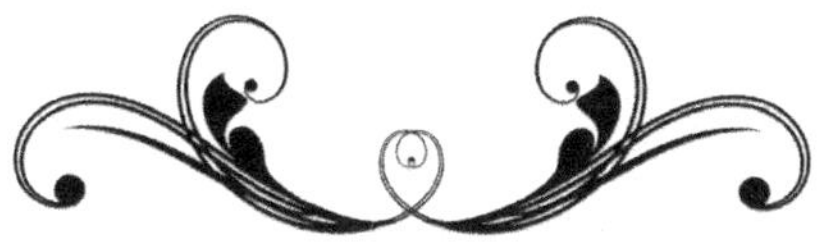

The journey of a thousand miles begins with a single step.

—Lao Tzu

CHAPTER 27

Sunday came faster than I was ready for it. Had I really just turned twenty-five? Technically, I was still twenty-four until one minute before midnight. That's when, according to my mother, I made my first appearance in this world. I wasn't too eager to leave my comfortable existence inside the womb and had to be coaxed out with labor-inducing medications. Now, all these years later, I wasn't enthusiastic about leaving the safety of my blankets either.

The night was restless and full of strange dreams about a person in an orange turban. He followed me around and asked the same question repeatedly, but I couldn't remember a single word.

I groaned and covered my face with my pillow. My consciousness wanted to be in denial that this day existed, that I existed. If I was a figment of somebody's fleeting imagination, maybe they would've wished me away. Then there would be no evil supervisors to deal with, no heartache, no unhappy endings, just blissful non-existence. But the remnants of the Truth stone didn't agree with my line of reasoning.

Be brave, you're here for a reason.

The buzzing of my phone brought me back to reality and reminded me that my world was very much real. I opened the screen with a text message from my aunt.

Happy birthday to my extraordinary niece. I believe in you. Discover who you are and stand by it. Louise.

Aunt Lou wouldn't have approved of my sulking state of mind. But what could I do about my situation? Did I even have a choice?

For now, I chose to get up and get ready. My mother was still asleep when I left to meet my sister at the airport. On the way there, I received a text from Greg with an animated card. Darth Vader and stormtroopers danced to a happy birthday song and brightened my mood.

Inside the airport terminal I spotted Julie in a crowd at the baggage claim area. She wore a white knit sweater, black skinny jeans, and cute boots. Flirting with a young man she'd probably met on the plane, Julie tossed her short blond hair around and swung her curvy hips with each step. I waved to get her attention. A spark of recognition lit her face. She stopped, dropped her carry-ons, and covered her mouth with both hands. Running up to me, she circled around a few times like I was a famous landmark.

"Holy smoke! Is this really you?"

"Finally, I'm able to impress my little sister," I teased. Her awe-stricken stares made me laugh.

Julie squealed and patted me down. Laughing, I tried to catch her hands. The passersby turned in our direction, and my cheeks started to burn.

"Jules! What are you doing, silly girl? We're in public."

"Ah-ha! That sounds like my sis." She gave me a triumphant grin. "For a moment, I thought you got replaced by some hot chick."

"Thanks. I had to dress up for my birthday, you know." I flashed her a playful smile and straightened the skirt of my floral print lavender dress. It was the last and boldest of my new outfits. Sleeveless, with a deep v-neck, it floated down to my ankles, enveloping me in the soft silk. The shapewear corset I bought magically hid my stubborn muffin top and smoothed out the rolls, accentuating my ample hips. All the other "pastries" I carried with pride.

My sibling proceeded to sing "Happy Birthday" for the whole Seattle airport to hear while I attempted to cover her mouth. Despite the embarrassment, I was happy to see Julie's cute animated face.

I took my sister out for a quick breakfast to spend some time alone with her before heading home. Even though facing the truth brought nothing but calamity, I was determined to do it again with Julie. No matter the consequences, it was a wiser choice than sweeping things under the rug. Even my confrontation with Miles and Olivia had been a better option than not knowing.

After we got our food at a small breakfast bistro saturated with the smell of fried eggs and biscuits, I started to talk.

"Jules, a lot happened while you were gone."

"Mmm." She made an approving sign for me to continue while stuffing half of the buttery cinnamon bun in her mouth. It always amazed me how she could eat so much and not add a single pound to her adorable plumpness.

I took a gulp of my black coffee. "There're some serious things we need to talk about."

"Pleeease, not now." My sister dropped the remainder of the gooey treat back on the plate and grimaced. "I know. I messed up big time, but can't we chill at your birthday first?"

"Oh, it's not about school… Although, we do need to talk about that too." The weight of the world settled on my shoulders once again. How would I help my sister now when I was practically jobless? That problem had to be put on the back burner until I could figure something out. I shoved the unpleasant thoughts to the "later" shelf in my mind and attempted to smile.

"What I want to discuss is nothing bad."

"Hmm, don't know if I believe it. You always say that and then end up giving me a lecture." Julie licked her sticky fingers. I wrinkled my nose and handed her a napkin.

"You can trust me this time. In the last few days many things changed and not just with the way I look."

"Oh, so we're talking about you and not me? Phew. I'm all ears then." She leaned over the table and propped her chin on her hands, then narrowed her pretty eyes. "Are you sure you won't flip it around and tell me what to do with *my* life instead?"

"I'll try not to."

"Ok, fire away."

The undercurrent of mockery in my sister's voice was not helping, but I cleared my throat and continued in the same even tone. "This week I thought a lot about us... and decided that maybe I was a bit too harsh with you all these years."

"Maybe? A bit?" Julie's perfect eyebrows shot up. She sat back and crossed her arms.

"Ok, I was a lot stricter than necessary and pushed you too much, but that's because I wanted you to succeed, I wanted our little family to succeed." My voice was almost pleading.

"You wanted everything to be perfect! Perfect grades, perfectly clean house, perfect budget. It sucked the life out of me!"

Her defenses rose higher, but I was determined to get through. "I was also hard on myself. But it wasn't... it was a mistake. You're right. I didn't know how to enjoy life, how to relax."

"Ooooh!" Julie exclaimed so loud that people sitting at the neighboring tables threw sideways glances in our direction. "Grace, you weren't kidding! This isn't bad news at all. That's actually a biggie! What made you change your mind about being a bookworm for the rest of your life? Did you finally meet a decent guy?"

I tried to ignore her blunt comments and her sudden outburst of excitement. As much as I was reserved, she was outspoken and melodramatic, and we usually ended up on opposite sides of the argument. Despite our difference, that morning I was determined to mend things.

"It's been a crazy week. I discovered a lot about myself, even jumped off a plane with a parachute. Not willingly." I smiled at Julie's shocked face. "And there's something I have to tell you about mom, too."

"What happened to her? Did she go bungee jumping?"

I laughed, then let her in on the secret about Mr. Kent. My sister was ecstatic and even teared up hearing about his long wait to get back together with our mother. We both decided that the romantic love story deserved a good ending. It was hard to predict what Lara Ainsworth would do, but we hoped she could move on. We all needed some closure regarding my parents' divorce. It was not an easy topic to bring up with my sister, but that was exactly what I planned to do. And since her mood had lightened up, I went out on a limb.

"Jules, there is something else important."

"More? My goodness, sis, you've got to spread this shocking news out a bit or you'll fry my brain."

"I have to do this. Please, let me."

"Wait a minute." My sister stuffed another chunk of cinnamon goodness in her mouth, then waved for me to continue. "I want to make sure I can enjoy this first. In case you're planning to say something that would ruin my appetite."

I shifted uncomfortably in my seat, my own meal sitting untouched.

"You know, when our father left, we all felt confused and

betrayed. At least, I did. We suddenly went from a sheltered life to not knowing what to eat for dinner—"

"Well, he was a jerk for leaving us," she interrupted. "Why talk about it now? Did he finally remember his parental responsibilities? That would've been handy right now."

"No, this is not about him. It's about us. I can't change what he did, or whether he'll decide to be in our lives or not. But I realized that by being angry at him, I'd held myself hostage. So I made a choice to forgive and let him go."

Julie sat in silence for a while, then sighed and shook her head. "I don't know if I can ever forgive him. He doesn't deserve it."

"I know, but you need to do this for yourself, not for him." I searched her face, hoping my words sunk in.

"I'll think about it," she said.

I didn't want to press further, but there was one more thing that had to be cleared. "Will you at least forgive me for being such a stickler? I wanted to be strong for you, but somehow it came out wrong."

My sibling poked the straw around in her slushy without answering.

"Jules?"

She looked up at me, then leaned back on the chair and chewed on her lower lip—a habit we shared.

"I've always wanted you to say this," her voice faltered. "Now it doesn't sound right. You know, I used to be so mad at you for all these stupid rules and for being this major killjoy. I wanted to have a sister who I could share secrets with and laugh with."

Her eyes glistened. I took her hand, swallowing my own tears, but she wrestled it out and loudly sipped the rest of her drink.

"Dang, I wasn't planning to get all mushy." She furrowed her eyebrows and pursed her glossy lips. "Ugh, screw this, I'll say it. I wanted you to be proud of me but could never be so well put together like you, always messed up. I guess I was more upset with myself than you."

She fanned her flushed face with the menu and glared at the waiter who came to inquire if we needed anything. Her words cut deep into my heart. Not realizing it, I'd been like my father, setting the bar for her so high, it could never be reached.

I tried to claim her hand once again. "I am so sorry. You shouldn't measure yourself against me, Jules. And don't let other people's expectations weigh you down, even if it's your own sister. Be yourself. If anything, I should be more like you. I always adored your love for life, your ability to put all the hardships behind and have fun. I'm sorry, I didn't know how to handle you."

"Stop apologizing already! Just give me a hug."

Julie pushed the plates aside, stretched across the table, and wrapped her arms around my neck. I held her tight, not caring anymore what people around us might think. A little crack in the door of mutual connection was enough for my sister to fling it wide open.

"Well, since you admitted that I'm fun and all that, you should let me organize your birthday." She lifted her head from my shoulder. Sparkles of mischief danced in her bright blue eyes. I almost regretted giving her so much praise. Now there was no stopping the troublemaker.

CHAPTER 28

Alicia was already there when we got home. My friend and my sister bonded in a heartbeat and conspired to fulfill their outrageous plans behind my back.

When Julie left to put her luggage away with Mother in tow, Alicia and I sat on the sofa in the living room.

"Where's Marcos? How did he let you out of his sight?" I said.

"I don't know who that is." She clicked her tongue and shook her head with annoyance.

"Something happened? I'm sorry."

"Nothing to be sorry about. The jerk started saying nonsense about you guys, and I showed him the door. He's been texting me all day, *idiota*."

I suppressed a smile. "Well, you got to give the guy some slack. We did act a little crazy yesterday. Confronted Miles, argued—"

"If he can't handle a little tension, that's his problem," Alicia interrupted, crossing her arms. "Mess with my friends, mess with me. I don't take these things lightly."

The doorbell rang, and she jumped. "That must be James, here to take you away."

"What? You asked him to come early for that?"

"Yep. Booked you a full shebang at the spa, so that you can't interfere with our plans here. Happy birthday." She walked off, and a minute later I heard raised voices by the door.

"What's happening?" Julie came into the room and threw concerned glances towards the entrance.

"Nothing. Just the usual. I better go make sure Alicia and James don't strangle each other."

By the time I stepped into the kitchen everything had gotten quiet. The two of them must have moved into the hall outside. I opened the front door and froze. James had Alicia pinned to the wall and was kissing her!

No wonder they'd stopped arguing.

I coughed into my fist and grinned at the startled couple. "I got worried there for a minute, but I see now you two are getting along just fine."

"Since you're here," Alicia said after catching her breath and fixing her ruffled hair. "You guys should probably leave or you'll be late for the appointment."

She glanced at James, then gave me a quick hug and pushed us towards the stairs.

"Sooo, what happened?" I asked as soon as we got into the car.

My friend shrugged and shot me a guilty smile. "Don't know. I wanted us to stop bickering, and it's all I could think of. Then we got carried away."

"Well, according to Tolkien, all's well that ends better." I laughed, watching James's face take on a spotty red hue.

Our drive to the salon was only a few minutes, which saved him from further banter on my part. I relaxed in the chair and let the cosmetologist do her magic. My thoughts drifted to the events of last week.

Let's see. What have I accomplished this week? Pretty much lost my job and my chances to use the newly earned paralegal certificate. Got a threat of jail over my head. Freed myself from my imaginary love for Miles. Got pre-dumped and pre-cheated. Gained and lost a friend in a matter of days. But my family is restored. My mother and my sister are back in my life. I think this tips the scale in the right direction. Aunt Lou would approve.

As I closed my eyes and relaxed in the treatment chair, thoughts of Greg filled my mind. Everything inside me longed for another chance to see him. What passed between us had to be more than just good companionship. Would he give me another chance?

An hour later, I left the place feeling refreshed. Turning twenty-five was a big milestone, and I stepped into the next phase of my life looking my best. Sitting in the car on the way home, I touched the purple triangle-shaped stone on my chest. A perfect match for my dress. I couldn't resist. It was the last day to wear these unique and beautiful jewelry pieces I'd started to get accustomed to.

I'll enjoy this day no matter what happens tomorrow. My future might be uncertain, but one thing I know for sure—I won't hold myself back anymore.

The voice of truth echoed in my heart once again. A faint whisper in the back of my mind. *Then stop holding back love.*

The idea stunned me like a bucket of ice-cold water. I glanced at James. Was it why I'd kept him at arm's length? I was perfectly content to pine for someone out of my reach but ran off when there was a chance at a real relationship. Afraid of getting hurt or abandoned, I'd kept everyone at a safe distance. My heart was under ten locks, but it was time to take out the key and open it.

James let me out of the car at my apartment entrance and drove to the guest parking lot. I stopped in the middle of the walkway as if struck by lightning.

"Greg!" I suddenly said out loud. "I love Greg."

I was oblivious that a few neighbors outside had turned their heads in my direction and smiled at this strange woman who shouted for all the world to hear. They didn't know that I experienced something for the very first time—I gave myself permission to feel, to pursue something real and tangible. Maybe love was too big of a word to use for someone I'd just met, but nothing else resounded so perfectly inside of me. It echoed through my soul with longing.

Slowly climbing the stairs to my apartment, I was formulating a plan of how to get Greg back and show him that I cared.

Ugh, it's so much easier for guys! They can just send a bouquet and a note with a few lines of poetry. What can I do? Show up at his work and ask him to be my accomplice in taking down Robert Kowalski and Olivia? Very romantic, best idea ever... not. Is there a "How to Attract a Guy for Dummies" book?

But I wasn't about to give up. My eyes were finally opened. With sudden clarity, I saw Greg's kind face on the first day we'd met. I recalled his dazzled look when he'd seen me again in the elevator, and how his hands nervously ran through his hair when he'd invited me to the supposed business meeting. The events of that evening flashed across my memory. He'd been so eager to hear my story, such a stark contrast to the self-absorbed Miles Taylor who only talked about himself. How could I have been so blind before? My insides melted at the memory of Greg's protective hand over mine, his bright eyes so intently focused on me. I smiled, remembering our little ordeal at the law firm and how we'd snuck into the law office to get more information. I thought about our last day together when he helped me overcome my fears.

I longed to feel his touch again, to see the laughter dance in his eyes, to hear his voice, to be next to him. I wanted him with all his annoying tendencies, just the way he was. But would he want the real me with all my flaws and shortcomings? Or had the stones created a perfect mirage? Once dissolved, would it carry away any interest Greg had in me?

Desperate to find the answers and determined to get his attention once again, I sent another text.

Hey, thanks for the card. Darth Vader has some nice moves, lol. Hope to see you soon.

Mr. Kent met me by the front door and blocked the entrance with his arms folded.

"I was told to guard it with my life," he said.

Fortunately, he didn't have to hold down the fort for long. My sister popped out a few minutes later, covered my eyes and led me through our tiny hallway. When the blindfold was removed, I was standing in the middle of our living room. It was filled with people and decorations.

"Happy birthday!" The crowd cheered and threw sparkling confetti in the air.

"We can't really yell 'surprise!' because it's not a surprise." Alicia laughed. "But I hope you're still impressed."

The room did look magical with a disco ball hanging from the chandelier and golden streamers descending from the ceiling. Alicia put me in my mother's antique armchair, which had been decorated like a throne, then immediately crowned me and handed me a star-shaped wishing wand.

"Wish away," Julie called out.

"I already have everything I need." Smiling, I got up and drew my sister into a hug, causing mascara to trickle down her face. She ran off to fix the mess, swearing to change all her makeup to the waterproof kind.

I walked around the room, receiving hugs and handshakes from other guests. I was happy that Mrs. Williamson's son felt well enough to join us with his mother. A few of my co-workers came as well. I greeted the young girl I'd met on the tram, whose name was Tanisha. She and my sister had instantly connected and chatted about college life. Mrs. Jones gave me a big warm hug. My mother kissed me, then sat next to Mr. Kent. She looked rested and content. Alicia left my side and was laughing about something with James.

Mr. Bailey showed up with his wife when everyone started to eat. They were both casually dressed and mixed right into our lively bunch, but I was still surprised to see my boss. It turned out Mrs. Williamson had invited him. After a while, she asked to talk to Mr. Bailey and me and drew us to the corner of the room.

"Mr. Bailey, thank you so much for your present and for coming," I said. "I would have invited you, but—"

"You thought I wouldn't come?" he interrupted.

"You can't possibly attend every employee's birthday party. And I'm not—"

"Important?" Mr. Bailey's eyebrow furrowed.

"Something like that." I bit my lip.

"There is this journalist who came to our company a few days ago," Mr. Bailey said, causing my heart to leap. "I don't know if he interviewed you or if you read the article, but based on his research, every person in the company is important. You just demonstrated it by stepping in to prevent a major disaster."

"Speaking of that," Mrs. Williamson jumped in. "I have something to talk to both of you about."

She clasped her hands together. Her gaze drifted towards her son, who sat at the table, then back to us. "Mr. Bailey, I worked for you for a long time and realize that you rely on me a lot."

"I can't survive a day without you," he said.

"But I think it's time for me to retire, so I can take care of Sammy."

"I'm not ready to hear this at all." Mr. Bailey let out a big sigh. "Although I do understand your circumstances. I was afraid that might happen eventually."

"I'll stay long enough to train your new assistant but with one condition," Mrs. Williamson added.

"Tell me what your condition is."

"I want Grace to replace me. I think she'll do well."

"Mrs. Williamson, I cannot agree with you more."

I stood next to the pair, glancing from one speaker to the other, confused by what'd just taken place. Had I been hired on the spot?

"Oh, dear, we didn't even ask your opinion. Grace, what do you think about taking my position?" Mrs. Williamson asked.

"I don't know if I can do this." My heart sank. It wasn't easy to turn down the offer that would've made me ecstatic just a few days earlier.

"Nonsense. You're a sharp girl, and you already proved you can do the job," Mr. Bailey said. "Plus, I'm sure you wouldn't mind an increase in your salary."

How could I accept this and turn in my resignation on Monday? Olivia's words rang in my head. *I have your address... you'll be implicated.* To stay meant putting my family at risk.

"I'm planning to start college soon," I tried to protest.

"I see no problem with that. Education is always good. We can discuss the possibility of our firm assisting with school expenses."

Mr. Bailey and Mrs. Williamson were relentless. I finally

had to give in to their pleas in hopes of buying myself more time. Suddenly, I had an idea.

"I do have one condition as well, Mr. Bailey."

"What's going on with you two and your conditions?" he grumbled. "Ok, I'll consider it as long as it doesn't involve you leaving."

"I know a great person who would love to take my place as a filer."

I introduced Tanisha and Mr. Bailey. He told the excited girl to come on Monday morning for an interview. I was happy to find a replacement for myself. Mrs. Williamson would just have to stay a little longer until someone else got trained for the job. I was sure a swarm of great candidates would apply as soon as the position was posted. As for me, after warning Mr. Bailey, I planned to lie low and find another job. Anything to keep my distance from Olivia.

After stepping away from Mr. Bailey and Mrs. Williamson, I sat in the corner of the room and watched everyone chat, laugh, and eat. I was especially happy for my mom, who blossomed every time Mr. Kent was around her.

He's a good man, he'll take great care of her.

Being single didn't have the same appeal anymore, especially with James suddenly leaving the ranks. I hoped his "opposites attract" chemistry with Alicia would last despite her constantly fleeting affections. Was I destined to be their third wheel? I glanced at the door and at my phone. There was no sign of Greg and no messages to explain his absence.

Mrs. Jones sat next to me and smiled, cheerful wrinkles gathering on her face. "What's the matter, baby girl? Your young man's missing?"

That woman had always read my mind without any magical help. I tried to hide behind a smile, but my flushed face betrayed me. "I'm fortunate to have so many people come. So happy you're all here. Really, I couldn't ask for more."

"You're happier, but you can't fool these old eyes." Mrs. Jones gave me an all-knowing look and patted my hand. "Let me share a secret with you."

"Of course!"

She looked into the distance as if searching for a long-forgotten memory. "Even as a scrawny little girl I dreamed of doing something great in life. Like you. But, oh, my, heaven knows the time I'd lost being unhappy with how things were turning out. But as I got older, I understood one thing—happiness in life is really in the little things. We create it ourselves. Now, if I can make even one passenger smile, I consider it a day well spent."

"Thank you, Mrs. Jones," I said thoughtfully. "I'm also learning to appreciate what I have and to not sulk over what I don't."

"Living a life is like baking a pie, dear—you chose the ingredients. Be creative. Experiment. And don't forget to sprinkle in some sugar." The older woman winked.

Maybe getting a different perspective was all I needed. My circumstances hadn't changed, but I had. There is so much more to look forward to and to be thankful for.

A few hours later, the celebration had ended, and people started to leave. Greg still hadn't shown up or returned my texts. I pushed away the uneasiness that'd crept into my heart and decided to seek him out at his work on Monday.

Hopefully, the clingy brunette hadn't caught him in her snares yet. If only I had a chance to talk to him with the Truth stone on... What if he doesn't care about me the same way? How do I even bring that up? I should probably work on keeping him as a friend first.

Not able to contain it all inside, I broke my silence and told Alicia.

"Should I just let it go? Don't want to be pushy. If he calls me then—"

"You haven't given the poor guy a single clue that he even

has a chance with you! I think he lost all hope after he saw you leave with that rich snob of a lawyer. And now both of you will sit and wait for each other to make the first move?"

"Oh, Allie." I hit my forehead on her shoulder. "What would I do without you."

"You would die an old maid."

I laughed and gave her a shove.

"Give me your phone," Allie demanded. "Let me take a picture of the birthday girl, so you can see for yourself—any guy would be lucky to have you."

She kept my phone in captivity and took a million more pictures. After a few hours, Mother went to Mr. Kent's place to try a new recipe. Julie and Tanisha ran off to the mall. Even Alicia and James deserted me, no matter how much I begged them to stay longer. They must have been eager to sort through the rest of their disagreements in a private setting. My family and friends had even cleaned our apartment and washed the dishes, leaving me with nothing to do.

It was still early in the afternoon. I sat in the living room and stared at my silent phone.

To call or not to call? Chicken. Even if it'll hurt in the end, I won't regret our time together. But why isn't he here? He didn't even bother to give me a lame excuse of some sort. Maybe he's busy. I can't expect him to drop everything for me.

I dialed Greg's number, but no one picked up. To pursue someone instead of watching from a distance was new to me, but my efforts seemed to be fruitless. Frustrated, I threw my phone under the pillow, went into my bedroom, and took out the box with pendants. With all that fretting about Greg, I almost forgot it was the last day to make the final decision about my future. If the book of instructions was true, my time with the gift was on a countdown. I had to pick one gem.

The night before, all I'd wanted was to put the crazy

adventure behind me and return to my normal life. But was that the right decision? The mysterious stones brought out the good, the bad, and the ugly in my life, but despite all the difficulties, they gave me the power to choose my destiny. The only question was—what should it be? *Discover who you are and stand by it,* my aunt wrote in the morning. But which of the gifts reflected my true self?

A knock on the door interrupted my thoughts. I went to open it. Had one of the guests forgotten something?

My heart leaped and got stuck in my throat. Greg stood in the hallway. He looked better in his denim shirt and khaki pants than most men would in a suit. He pulled a bouquet of field flowers from behind his back and looked me over, leaving a trail of heat with his gaze.

"Seems like my gift matches your outfit." A familiar smile curved his lips.

I squared my jaw, grabbed the flowers and marched into the kitchen with Greg following close behind.

"You missed my birthday party. Think you can get off the hook so easily, with some flowers you picked on the side of the road?"

"I picked them from the field we landed in a few days ago," Greg said, his grin widening. "As a token of your accomplishment."

What? Did he drive all the way there? Crazy man. Is that why he's so late? And what is this silly smile about? I'd like to erase it off his face... with a kiss.

That was definitely not what I wanted to think about! Frowning, I took out the vase and filled it with water.

"You owe me at least another parachute jump for being late. And you should've warned me that journalists disappear from time to time. I would've understood. I already have an aunt like that. Just tell me ahead of time when your business magazine sends you on a secret mission where you can't answer your phone. Otherwise, I'll start thinking that you got kidnapped by some big-name company whose dirty deeds you decided to expose."

I was talking up a storm, avoiding looking at Greg until he put his arm on my bare shoulder. His touch burned my skin. I turned and lost my train of thought in the infinite blue of his eyes.

"You have quite the imagination," Greg said playfully. "Unfortunately, it wasn't anything exciting or newsworthy. Just—"

"Yeah, I saw you yesterday," I interrupted.

With that skinny thing who has artificial boobs and probably artificial intelligence, too. Ugh, Grace, please, behave like an adult. You're overreacting.

I turned away before Greg could say anything else and walked into the living room, putting the bouquet on the coffee table. The familiar fragrance of the fields filled the air. Conflicting emotions overflowed my heart, threatening to spill out and take me down with them.

"I'm afraid there is no cake left," I said, just to bridge the silence. "My friends have a big appetite like me."

Great. Let's see how many more awkward comments I can make.

I turned to the window to calm my wired nerves. The man I'd been anxiously waiting for was finally here, yet I was ready to bolt. Only it was my house, and he was my guest. All my determination from earlier evaporated. How was I supposed to break the invisible barrier of misunderstanding between us or bring up the fact that I was falling hard and fast for him? What if he wasn't interested? What if I'd just push him away and embarrass myself? What if it would ruin our friendship?

It'd been so much easier when I wasn't trying to impress him. Love is a complicated thing. Hopefully, I'll figure it out before getting old and wrinkly.

Greg took a few steps in my direction. My traitorous body shivered, sensing his towering presence behind me. A faint scent of sandalwood enveloped me as he gently moved my hair to the side. His fingers brushed across my back. The same electrical current I'd felt in the car a few days ago from his touch passed through me again. All I wanted at that moment was to lean against his steady broad chest and let him shield me from the world.

Darn this open dress! I should've put my fuzzy sweater on.

"Grace." He stooped down, warming my neck with his breath and causing palpitations in my chest. "Could you tell me what's going on? Or at least let me tell you what happened to me."

I let out a ragged sigh. "There's nothing—"

Before I could finish, Greg's arms wrapped around me, catching me by surprise.

"Your friend blew your cover," he whispered in my ear. Like a startled bird, I struggled to get out of his embrace, but he held me tight. "You can't run away anymore, Cinderella."

I turned around in time to catch his mischievous smile in full force.

"You're… you're insufferable, Greg Miller! I don't know what you're talking about."

He only laughed. I shoved him away, but it was like trying to move a boulder. Greg wrapped one arm around my waist, caught my chin with another, and raised my face until our eyes met.

"You know, I promised to not make you do anything you don't want to. Do you want me to let go?"

The intensity in his eyes destroyed all my defenses. I shook my head. "No."

Before I knew what was happening, Greg's mouth connected with mine and a heatwave swept over me. His feverish kiss burned my lips and set my heart on fire. No other words were needed. At that moment, the cup of my life was full to the brim, and my thirsty heart drank the sweet nectar of affection until it overflowed.

CHAPTER 30

I looked up at Greg when he finally let me take a breath. We were still standing by the window, clinging to each other like our life depended on it.

"So, are you going to hold me forever?"

"Uh huh. We'll stand here for the rest of our days." He gave me another long kiss that made my head spin.

"In that case, I can't guarantee my mom wouldn't use us as shelves for some new trinkets she'll buy at a flea market."

I put my head on his chest and relaxed into his embrace, his soft laughter resonating through me. It felt so good to be supported by his strong body.

"Why did you decide to finally come see me?" I asked.

"Well, I planned to sneak in and wish you a happy birthday later in the day. Just didn't want to see you with that rich boyfriend of yours."

I looked up, surprised. "Who? Miles Taylor? He's not my boyfriend."

"That's not what he told me the other day when I was informed to get lost or else."

I groaned. "Was that when you both cornered me at work?"

Greg nodded and held me tighter. "I couldn't care less about his threats, but I didn't want to meddle into your life and cause problems. Who was I anyway? A random guy you met a few days ago? I couldn't offer you what that lawyer could. It wouldn't be fair to you—"

"Greg, he's nothing compared to you."

I stood on my toes and wrapped my arms around his neck. He leaned down and kissed my nose, causing it to wrinkle.

"It wasn't so clear to me, and the thought that you belonged to someone else drove me nuts. I just needed a day to cool my head off before facing you again. That's why I kept my distance yesterday."

"And Sandra was readily available to offer her condolences?" The words escaped before I could stop them. I bit my lip.

Greg cupped my head with his large hands and forced me to look at him, his face serious. "Yes, she was, but her offer was declined."

He sealed his words with another mind-blowing kiss that left me tipsy. Any self-conscious thoughts about not being as good-looking as his co-worker evaporated. He'd chosen me.

"You got to admit, though, that it's all your fault," he said with a teasing sparkle in his eyes.

"Oh, really?"

"Yep. You wrapped me around your little finger from day one but kept me in the dark about how you felt. On that first evening in the café, I had to restrain myself from leaning over the table to wipe away the tears you struggled to hide. You were so vulnerable, so open… Then on Friday, all I wanted was to hold you in my arms, but you pushed me away. If that wasn't enough, you ran out like my car was on fire when I dropped you off. I was confused about what to make of it but decided to just enjoy getting to know you. Didn't feel like I had to rush or anything."

"Oh, yeah? Then what changed today?"

He wrapped a strand of my hair around his finger, a sly smile playing on his lips. "Today required extreme measures."

I arched one brow. "What happened?"

"Your friend Alicia called me from your phone and told me that I'm an idiot, and I'll be the biggest loser if I don't come to you right away."

I laughed. "That sounds like Allie. That's why she deserted me, little schemer! She must have talked everyone else into leaving me early too."

Greg pressed his forehead to mine. "She said that I'll never find another girl like you and would regret it for the rest of my life. And she was totally right. So I had to snatch you away while I could… and now you have to put up with all my quirks and my corny jokes."

"I could use a corny joke right now."

"Ok. You asked for it." Greg fought to keep his expression neutral. "A man went up to the movie theater's ticket window and said: 'I need one more ticket, please.' The ticket vendor asks: 'For the Hobbit?' The man replies: 'No, that's my girlfriend.'"

I groaned and tried to push Greg away, but he put me over his shoulder like a sack of potatoes and carried me to the sofa despite my loud protests. Hanging upside down, I thanked myself for wearing a tight bra. He dropped me on the cushion and let me give him a few pathetic hits with a pillow which satisfied my somewhat injured ego.

"I think your height is perfect. There are lots of benefits of having a short girlfriend," he said with a laugh, blocking my attempt to slap him upside the head. "You're very compact. I can take you anywhere. I won't even have to pay for a separate air ticket. You'll fit on my lap."

That resulted in another pillow assault.

"I won't ever fly with you," I pouted.

"So how are we going to travel the world?"

"What do you mean?"

"I read your message yesterday," he said, his face turning somber. He smoothed my hair, which at the moment resembled an angry haystack. "I thought about it all evening. Even prayed for the first time in years… You're right. I blamed myself, blamed others, even blamed God for all the injustice I witnessed and couldn't fix. But my bitterness is not helping anybody."

"Greg…" I inched myself closer and dipped my hands into his soft, unruly hair.

He sighed, caught my wrist, and pressed his lips to my palm. "So, I decided to let go, to forgive and to do what I can. And what I can't, I would have to leave it in God's hands for someone else to step in and tackle the problem."

"So, you'll be a reporter again?"

"I don't know yet. Although I do want to visit other countries and help make this world a better place." Greg interlaced his fingers with mine, his eyes bursting with delight. "You made a dreamer out of me again."

"I have to tell you something too, before we get carried away." I took my hand away and hid it under my leg. My stomach tightened into knots. Would Greg understand?

I told him about Aunt Lou's present and how the beauty stone had changed me, giving me the power to attract other people. It was harder to explain how the pendants gave me the ability to hear the thoughts, act with boldness, predict the future, re-visit the past, and know the truth. My heart grew heavier with each word.

"I think your infatuation might be with a person who isn't really… who isn't really me." I choked on the last sentence and searched Greg's face. But he was distant, lost in thought. Did he think I was crazy? Or did he believe me and feel manipulated, tricked by the magical gems into something that wasn't real?

Whatever happens, I don't want our relationship to be based on a lie.

Greg rubbed his forehead and finally looked at me, his handsome face puzzled. "I don't know what to tell you."

My heart ached, but I was going to finish what I'd started, even if it meant losing Greg. My eyes filled with tears. "The girl you saw on Monday, that wasn't me being sick—that was me being myself… before the Beauty stone."

We sat in silence. I stared at the stitched up surface of the sofa cushion between us, but the unruly tears streaked down my face no matter how much I fought them. Greg's rough fingers brushed my cheeks.

"I'd understand if you want to leave…"

I didn't get to finish the sentence because Greg pulled me into his lap and wrapped me in his arms. How many times had I wanted to be held like this when my insides ached from the heavy burdens and loneliness? Now my wish had finally come true. Even if it only lasted a moment, I was thankful and let myself relax while Greg gently stroked my hair.

"You want to tell me that the woman in my arms right now isn't real?" Greg asked.

I hid my face in his shirt.

"Let me say something, and then you decide whether I believe the lie or not," he murmured. "I met this girl a few days ago. She turned my world upside down. She is not perfect. At times she's bossy, and saucy, and stubborn. She doesn't like others to see her weaknesses and hides her tears, but she doesn't know her own worth. I've seen her take risks for others and stand up for what's right. She has been through some hard stuff and stepped in to take care of her family. She values honesty above all else. She's smart, hard-working and thoughtful, and I'd like to know her better. I'm drawn to her curious mind, her smile, her kind eyes, her curves… Did the stones give you all that?"

He paused and lifted my face. A teasing smile slowly stretched his lips. "If so, I hope at least the curves stay."

"You're such a dork!"

He laughed while I struggled to get out of his bear hug and ended up surrendering to another kiss.

CHAPTER 31

Now that Greg was with me, I was ready to fight for my dreams again. I had somebody strong and steady next to me to turn to for support.

"Greg, I might need your help with something," I said, standing up from the sofa. "It's about my work."

"Oh, no, here we go again. Detective Ainsworth is up to something." He leaned back and relaxed as if ready to watch a TV show.

"C'mon Greg! This is serious. I found out who leaked the information from our office to the other firm."

"You did?"

"And unfortunately, she knows that I know. She threatened me yesterday, told me to resign from my job or she'd get me arrested."

"You've got to be kidding me!" Greg stood up, his eyes full of concern.

"I wish I was kidding. She has the means to do that too, and I don't have any proof or any power to stop her. But if I get her to confess while we record her—"

"How are you going to do that?" Greg interrupted, his

voice tense. "Why don't you just tell your boss and let him handle it?"

"I want to make her talk first, to find out what she's planning. If I don't, Mr. Bailey and the whole company might be in trouble. Even if he believes me and fires Olivia, there might be other people in the office working for Robert Kowalski. If their scheme is successful, she might implicate me in the theft of office funds either way. Unless I have something to stop her."

Greg's face hardened, his eyes turned dark. "I really don't like the idea of you messing around with these criminals. Some things are better left alone."

"I have to do this. How will I live with myself if I don't at least try? Please, I need your help."

Greg ran his hand through his hair and sighed. Was he remembering his hopeless situation in Sudan? But we were here in the States, and I wasn't in the same amount of danger. Or was I?

"Ok, but you're not going anywhere without me," he said after a long pause. "What do you want to do?"

"I need to figure out a way to meet with Olivia, but I don't have her contact information."

"That's not a problem. I can get it. Next."

"I want Mr. Bailey to hear our conversation when we meet but not be in the same room."

"Done."

"Ok, then I'm ready. Let's do this."

Greg squared his jaw and folded his arms. "I think you left out one little tiny detail. How are you going to make her confess?"

"I have my ways." I winked, but Greg only shook his head, his expression grim.

After a few phone calls, he handed me Olivia's number, then called Mr. Bailey and talked him into coming in for a fake televised interview in the evening. The older man huffed and puffed about having to leave his favorite recliner on Sunday, but Greg's persuasion skills prevailed.

Pacing the room, I tried to formulate what to tell my supervisor. The truth was, I didn't really have a clear plan. All I had was an idea based on my vivid imagination, detective stories, and crime shows. It just had to work. The first step was easy—to contact Olivia. Everything else after that was a fuzzy mess. But I had to do at least something.

Not trusting my voice to stay steady and convincing on the phone, I sent Olivia a formal text message:

This is Grace Ainsworth. I have proof that you had illegal access to the information inside our company, and that you were giving this information to your accomplice from the competing firm."

Olivia was quick to respond: *I don't know what you're alluding to.*

I typed the reply: *If you don't meet me promptly, I'm going to take the evidence to Mr. Bailey and the police tonight. I would prefer we reach an agreement on the side. Bring ten thousand dollars.*

Olivia was quick to respond: *Are you threatening me???*

Was she seething with anger or frantically calling her accomplice asking him what to do? Maybe both. After a few long minutes, she texted again: *I'll meet you at the Freeway Park at seven. Don't bring anybody else. I'll know.*

Greg looked over the text messages, then called a few of his contacts and took me to his friend's house. Within an hour, the place swarmed with different people and activities that looked like a scene from an action movie. It sure felt like we were getting ready for an impossible mission, only I was no Ethan Hunt. Nonetheless, I was wired with a hidden audio recorder and fit with a tiny communication device that was placed into my ear. One of my shirt's buttons was replaced with a camera.

"Where in the world did you get all these things and people?" I questioned Greg.

He winked and kissed my nose. "Remnants of my previous employment."

I frowned, determined to pester him later, but for now, I needed to focus on the task ahead. Olivia's request to meet in the park presented a challenge. Built over the highway, it was small and filled with irregular concrete platforms that were stacked together like a labyrinth. Secluded enough to hide two people from prying eyes and with the loud rumbling of the interstate below to obscure our conversation, it was an ideal spot for my supervisor but not for Greg's team. Olivia warned me not to bring anybody else, and I couldn't risk raising her suspicion. I had one shot at this.

Equipment that would broadcast and record our conversation was placed in a mobile van, close enough to the park but out of everyone's sight. After lots of arguing about where Greg should be, he finally agreed that it would make more sense for him to usher Mr. Bailey into the van than to pretend to walk a dog or read a newspaper. Plus, he didn't have a dog, and Olivia might have recognized him from his visits to the firm if he was spotted. To hide behind a newspaper on the bench was proclaimed archaic, which led to a heated debate among the present media professionals whether paper news was a dying form of art. In the end, a few of Greg's friends signed up to be random passersby.

By the time everything was put in motion, it was almost six-thirty, just a few minutes after sunset. I picked a spot that was cleaner and quieter than the rest and sat down on one of the concrete blocks to wait for Olivia. I rubbed my sweaty hands over my jeans and willed my mind to focus on the things I'd say. My thoughts wandered off to Greg. He was probably meeting with Mr. Bailey and convincing him to step into the van to witness my meeting with Olivia from the distance.

Pigeons busied themselves near the waterfall, which cascaded down large blocks of concrete into a small pond at the bottom. I watched them for a minute and tried to relax. Homeless people roamed by, and city kids jumped around on the park's uneven structure, but my corner remained relatively hidden. The air was pleasantly warm despite the light rain that'd drizzled throughout the day. Spring, young and fresh, was finally free from the oppression of winter. But even with the nicer weather, I couldn't stop shivering. An unpleasant sensation twisted my gut.

A man came around the corner. He seemed vaguely familiar. I couldn't see his face under his cap, but his presence made the hair stand up on the back of my neck. He lifted his head and met my gaze. My breath caught in my throat. It was the same person I'd seen by the restaurant and in the parking lot on Thursday! Did he also follow me to my apartment on Friday night? For a brief moment, his bright eyes kept me captive, and I was pulled into their endless depth. He turned away and disappeared around the corner a second before Olivia came looking for me.

My thoughts raced. Was this person stalking me, or was it another coincidence? I had no time to dwell on that because Olivia had spotted me and was quickly approaching. I licked my dry lips, lifted my chin and willed my mind to focus.

"Grace," I heard Greg's voice in my ear. "Olivia's coming, and she's alone. I had one of my guys trace her. They saw her drive into the parking garage and walk out by herself. I'm close by. Finish this soon or Mr. Bailey will eat me alive here."

Olivia was now standing over me with her arms crossed. I wondered if she could hear the pounding of my heart or see uncertainty in my eyes. Ever so subtly, the hunger for justice rose in my chest and replaced my nervousness. No matter what, I was determined to bring her down.

"Please, be careful," Greg whispered in my earpiece.

Olivia looked around and sat next to me with her usual look of disdain.

"What's the meaning of all of this?" She barked.

"Well, since you want me to leave my job, I've got to make money some other way now." I gave the woman a cold stare, surprised at my even tone of voice.

"Are you threatening me?"

"You didn't leave me a choice, did you? Now I have to play by your rules."

"I see. Your true nature finally came out. You hid it well, greedy little slu—"

"I didn't come here to listen to your insults," I cut her off. "Did you bring the money?"

"First, show me the evidence you claim to have."

Our conversation was going nowhere. I had to make Olivia mention her connection to Robert Kowalski, or this battle would soon be lost. But how could I pose the question without raising her suspicion? While I agonized over it, my supervisor was checking her watch and glancing around.

"I think you're bluffing out of desperation," Olivia snapped. "Show me what you've got or I'm leaving. I've had enough of this nonsense."

Not knowing how else to appease her, I took the flash drive out of my pocket. "On this flash drive, I have the recordings of your conversations with Robert Kowalski."

Olivia moved closer and opened her right hand. "Now, give it to me. I'll go home and see what you've got in there. I'm sure a smart girl like you made a copy."

To give Olivia an empty flash drive would be the end of our conversation. It was clear I hadn't thought it through well enough.

"I need the money upfront." I stubbornly clenched the device in my fist and scooted back to the edge of the seat.

Olivia sneered. "Wow, are you so stupid that you brought

the original? Well, either way, you're going to hand it to me now, and then I'll decide what to do next."

I shook my head.

Olivia swiftly leaned over and moved her left hand next to my side. A hard object pressed into my ribs. A large purse sat on her knees. It covered a small gun from the view of anybody who might happen to walk by.

I froze as if in a bad dream.

"Now put the flash drive in my purse," Olivia demanded.

"Grace, what's going on?" Greg's concerned voice was lost in the whooshing sound of blood that rushed through my veins. I opened my hand and dropped the device in Olivia's bag.

"That's a good girl. I don't like to be told what to do. Next time, think twice before trying to pull something off like this. I don't have time for your stupid games. If I hear from you again, or if you try to meddle in my affairs, you'll be fined for blackmailing me, to say the least. And I do have the evidence now thanks to your lovely text message." She got up. My face was no doubt whiter than the starched bedsheets, but I gathered all my runaway brain cells and looked Olivia in the eyes.

"I know what you're up to," I forced out through clenched teeth. "Robert Kowalski, older brother of Tyson Kowalski. Olivia Peterson, or should I say Olivia Kowalski, wife of a criminal…"

"Stop! Where did you—"

"I have my ways. And I know what you're up to. This game is over." Thankful that Greg had friends who could dig up information on anybody in the world, I continued. "Are you trying to avenge your husband by going to jail yourself? That's not very smart."

Olivia's palm landed on my face so fast I didn't even see it coming. I covered my stinging cheek.

"Shut up!" The woman spat out.

"What's going on here?" Mr. Bailey roared, running up to

us. He must have lost his patience and decided to take things into his own hands. Greg was right behind him, covering the distance in a few swift steps, his eyes shooting deadly arrows at Olivia. She leaped to her feet, ready to bolt.

Oh, no. I almost had her!

"Give me that flash drive right now!" Mr. Bailey commanded. He stepped between Olivia and me, grabbing the strap of her purse.

"Back off!" Her eyes narrowed, her lips tightened to a thread on her pale face. The miniature silvery gun was in her hand again, pointed at our boss.

"Mr. Bailey, please, don't." I took a hold of his sleeve.

"Be reasonable, Olivia. Hand me the evidence and I'll let you disappear."

Olivia laughed. "I'm not going anywhere until you pay for what you've done to my husband!"

I couldn't believe they were fighting over the empty flash drive! All I could think about was getting Mr. Bailey away from the danger. Greg was next to me in a split second and pushed me behind his back.

"Grace, get out of here," he commanded.

"Ok, that's enough," Mr. Bailey said in an irritated tone as he grabbed Olivia's hand with the gun and pulled harder on her purse. On an impulse, I stepped forward and stood between the two people struggling for control.

"Please, stop, there is nothing there!"

All I remember was a loud snap and a sharp pain in my left ribs. Everything went still. The world around me got awfully quiet, and all I could hear was an annoying ringing in my ears. As if in a fog, I saw Olivia's and Mr. Bailey's terrified faces in front of me. A moment later, I fell backward into somebody's strong arms. Greg was above me now, his eyes full of terror.

Why is everyone freaking out?

Confused, I touched my left side and brought my hand

up. It was covered with blood. My vision was coming to pass. Olivia ran and Mr. Bailey frantically dialed his cell phone. Greg leaned closer. His lips were moving, but I couldn't understand what he was saying. A few seconds later, everything disappeared, and my world turned black.

CHAPTER 32

m I dead?

Am I dead?
I tried to open my eyes but could barely lift them enough to make a small crack. The world outside was blurry and white.

White is good. I must be in heaven. Wait, I can't die yet! I just found Greg. And my mom... well, she'll be fine with Mr. Kent. He can take care of my sister too. But Greg...

"I think she's waking up," I tried to move my head in the direction of the pleasant voice, but it wouldn't obey. Through my half-open eyelids, I could make out the shapes of three people who stood above me.

"Good. The darkness had finally retreated and the danger is over," another voice said. He sounded familiar. I tried to concentrate on the face of the speaker. Was it... was it Mr. Abeles?

"And I think she passed the test," the third person said.

I turned my head slightly, the small movement taking all of my energy, and focused on the last speaker. It was Bongani! I blinked a few times but couldn't move or make a single sound, as though paralysis had taken over my whole body. Slowly, my vision cleared. I could see that the three

256

men wore similar clothing with long-sleeved white robes and golden belts. Purple shawls rested on their shoulder. Turbans of similar colors covered their heads.

Son of a blaster! I'm dead for sure. These men look like they ride camels and live in tents.

"I watched her the most," the first person spoke again. I recognized him as my nameless stalker. He was the youngest of the three. A kind smile spread over his bronzed face. His dark eyes sparkled like stars in the night when he looked in my direction. "What I observed was reassuring. She's been stepping out, finally enjoying her life, taking risks."

"I've listened to her the most," Bongani said. "She's compassionate and cares for the well-being of others. When I challenged her, she didn't back away. When I pretended to be homeless and let her read my thoughts, she didn't hesitate to help. Most importantly, she's a seeker of truth and is ready to stand up for her believes."

"I agree. Although, I think you two scared her more than helped." Mr. Abeles chuckled.

"At least she kept the pendants on." Bongani smirked. "Even if just to spite me."

"Next time try to be more discreet. Well, Grace is not without her faults either. But I think after some nudging, she's finally ready to step into her destiny. Let's not forget she only had a week to get ready for a decision that usually takes years."

"But, Tzali, she did have the advantage of tapping into the dreams. Although, I don't think she always heeded the warning," the younger man interjected.

"You're right, Amir, but she did realize the value of the gifts," Bongani added. "After the robbery, it's what she checked on first. Of course, she didn't know the treasure could protect itself. Thankfully, nobody can take it without the owner's consent."

"One less thing for us to worry about," Amir said. "Did

you notice she picked out all the stones that are in the foundation of the Heavenly City?"

"Indeed!" Tzali exclaimed. "And she is a smart girl to choose the amethyst today."

"Oh, yes, the stone of Invincibility, מָעוֹז—protection from all harm and the gift of healing. It saved her life. As soon as I saw it on her neck, all my worries dissipated." Amir smiled, and I remembered his watchful eyes minutes before meeting Olivia.

Tzali nodded. "I think the gifts of our God are in good hands."

"But she still needs to make her final choice."

"Yes, she does."

"And she only has until midnight to do that."

"Oh, like Cinderella! My favorite story."

"Seriously, Amir?"

"What?"

"Cinderella lost everything at midnight. Grace's life is only beginning."

"Stop it, you two. Her time is running out soon."

"But why midnight?"

"That's when she turns twenty-five."

"Then let us hurry."

The men gathered around my bed. White clouds of steam with a pleasant aroma spread above me. My eyelids became heavy again and obscured my vision. I fell into a deep sleep until my consciousness returned once again.

"We can't explain this, Mr. Miller."

"What do you mean? I watched blood pour out of her!" Greg raised his voice. "It was all over the place. Paramedics had to hold pressure on her wound when they took her, they thought her spleen was ruptured or something. Didn't you see all the stains on her clothes?"

"We couldn't find the source of the bleeding," the nurse continued calmly, as if she was explaining something to a small child. "We examined and scanned her, but there are no internal injuries. Her blood count is only slightly low, nothing serious."

The stone of Invincibility...

With all the threats above my head, the pendant I put on last night was a clear choice.

"But look at her! She's so pale and still not awake."

"We're definitely going to keep her in the hospital for observation, but I can't answer your questions beyond that."

She only has until midnight... The words echoed in my head.

"No! I can't stay!" I sat up in bed with eyes wide open. The nurse and Greg rushed to my side and tried to lay me back down, but I was already tearing the monitor wires off. Alarms filled the room with obnoxious beeping.

"Miss Ainsworth, please, relax. You're still not well. Just rest a bit and I'll go get the doctor to talk to you about the plan." She turned to Greg. "Please, keep an eye on her, I'll bring something to calm her down."

No! I can't go back to sleep!

The nurse left in a rush and a second later I was squeezed senseless in Greg's embrace.

"If you don't stop hugging me so tightly, I might pass out again," I croaked.

"I'm sorry!" Greg let go but continued to hover over my stretcher. "You scared me."

"Does my family know?" I asked while peeking under the gown to check my left ribcage. There was no wound from the bullet that'd seared through my body.

"No. I didn't have enough sense left in my brain to call anybody. All I could think of was you."

"Good. Don't tell them. You said you were with me the whole time?"

"Yes. I followed the ambulance. They rushed you to the trauma room first, then moved you here. I thought I was going to lose it with all these nurses and doctors swirling around you. They wouldn't let me get close at first."

"Did you see the three men in long robes and turbans come to visit me?" I looked around the small room.

"No, nobody came besides Mr. Bailey and police. He's still in the waiting area. Police questioned us and already left." Greg looked at me with concern.

"Did Olivia get arrested?" I asked to change the subject.

"I don't know. Police came to the park as soon as the ambulance arrived. Mr. Bailey probably told them everything. But now I'm not sure what will happen because apparently you're bulletproof." Greg smiled.

I started to question him again, feeling the need to catch up and orient myself. "What time is it?"

"Ten thirty."

"In the evening?"

"Yes."

"Listen, I have to be home," I said with urgency in my voice. "My mom and sister probably already called a million times and are worried. Where's my phone? I have to do something."

"There's nothing for you to do today besides rest. I'll call them and explain everything, but it's better if you stay in the hospital until they make sure you're ok."

"I'm totally fine." I sat up. "Trust me. I have to be home."

"I don't like the sound of it. Don't you think we've had enough craziness for one day? Maybe when you feel better and I'm less of a wreck." He ran his hand through his messy hair and sighed. "I just can't get over the fact that I was standing right there and couldn't protect you."

His features creased in pain. He held my face with his hands and planted a tender kiss on my lips.

"The stone protected me."

Greg reached out and touched the jewelry piece on my chest. "Everyone tried to take it off when they were checking you, but they couldn't. I still think it's safer for you to stay here overnight."

I crossed my arms. "If you don't help me, I'll leave by myself. I need to be home by midnight."

Greg rubbed his bloodshot eyes. "I guess I'll have to sneak you out. Let's see. Your clothes got cut up by paramedics. You can't go out wearing just a necklace. Although, under other circumstances—"

"Greg!" I gave him a pleading glance that did nothing to erase the teasing grin that brightened his weary face. "Concentrate, please."

"I might have some extra clothes in my car. It'll probably fit three of you, but it's worth a try."

He came back ten minutes later with a blanket and a shirt that went down to my mid-thighs. Time was running out. Greg pulled the IV out of my arm, and the small hole it left behind instantly closed up without him needing to hold pressure. Slightly lightheaded, I sat on the edge of the bed, but before we had a chance to escape someone knocked on the door.

"Can I come in?" Mr. Bailey's concerned face peeked out from behind the curtain.

"Of course. Maybe you can talk some sense into this stubborn woman," Greg grumbled, pulling the blanket protectively over my shoulders. My boss came in and sat on the chair next to my bed.

"If you were my daughter, I would've put you under house arrest for a few weeks, then let you out with a leash on," Mr. Bailey said, but a smile broke through his stern expression. "I'm glad you're better. Sure didn't need you to risk your life, silly girl. Would've believed you regardless. I'd rather lose the company than have somebody put themselves in harm's way."

"Speaking of arrests, what happened to Olivia?" I interrupted.

"I just spoke with the Chief of Police, who is my personal friend. Olivia disappeared, but they'll keep searching."

"What will they do? Nobody could locate the bullet, and Grace doesn't have a single scratch on her body," Greg said, but I sent him a silent plea to be quiet.

"That's hard to believe!" Mr. Bailey exclaimed.

"It was… it wasn't real blood," I interjected.

"Well, then you sure tricked everyone. But since Olivia left her purse, her phone, and a flash drive behind, there shouldn't be a problem to find enough evidence regarding their little scheme. I bet Mr. Kowalski is closing down his practice as we speak and running out of the country."

"I had no evidence. It was all a hoax to get her to talk." I sighed.

"But she doesn't know it," Greg said. "Plus, she probably thinks the police are hunting her down for attempted murder."

I moaned. "And what will police think of my text message to her?"

"Don't worry, my friend took care of it as soon as Olivia threatened to use it." Greg put his arm around my shoulders and kissed my head. I looked at him with surprise. What else were his friends able to do? "Plus, we recorded the whole ordeal."

"I gave police access to our office. They'll search her desk and computer," Mr. Bailey continued. "Her home, too. Hopefully, by the time they discover you're okay, they'll dig up enough proof about her shady dealings with Robert Kowalski."

"I hope so," I said thoughtfully. "That means we can't leave without being released first. Don't want to raise any suspicion. Greg, can you get me the doctor?"

"Good thinking." Mr. Bailey patted my hand when Greg ran out of the room. "You'll make a great lawyer one day,

Grace. I sure hope you still want to be my assistant. Although, you'll make a fine bodyguard too."

I chuckled. "Not sure if I'll ever get the hang of this whole legal thing, but it's worth a try."

～

After a lot of begging and even doing jumping jacks to demonstrate that I was in perfect health, the emergency physician finally agreed to release me. We walked out and got into Greg's car at eleven twenty-five. Zipping through an empty freeway, we drove to my apartment. I chewed my nails and begged Greg to speed up.

"I see you conquered your fear of fast-moving cars," he teased.

At eleven-fifty we were finally inside my apartment complex. I jumped out of the car as soon as Greg parked, ran up the stairs and knocked with all my strength. Hurried footsteps sounded on the other side, the door opened and my mother's worried face appeared in the hallway.

"Hi, Mom. We'll talk later," I blurted and ran past her into my room. After closing the door, I took out the golden key, dashed to my closet, flung it open, and pulled the wooden box out. I took a ragged breath in and looked at the clock. Eleven fifty-five. Which stone should I choose?

I knew in an instant.

EPILOGUE

I sat at my mahogany writing desk near an open window, my hair no doubt resembling an abandoned bird's nest, but I didn't care. An unruly strand kept getting in my way, and I finally pinned it behind my ear with the pen. After rubbing my tired eyes, I readjusted my glasses and stared at the last page of a small hardcover notebook. In the last twenty-four hours it got covered with my messy handwriting. I was barely surviving on coffee, but there could be no rest until my mission was accomplished and the danger passed. Willing my mind to concentrate, I skimmed over the last paragraph:

> *My spunky Cathy, you might ask why I have decided to put all these details of my life on paper. I'm writing my story to help you learn from my experience. Like Mark Twain said: "The two most important days in your life are the day you are born and the day you find out why." I hope my openness and this gift I'm passing on will help you discover your purpose.*
>
> *Since you're the oldest girl among your Ainsworth cousins, our family legacy is yours to carry. I'm hoping to be next to you at the moment you receive it, but no matter what happens in the future,*

Closing the notebook, I stood up and walked over to a tall metal safe in the back of the room. The large map of the world hung on the wall behind it with multiple pins marking the spots Greg and I had visited over the years. Pictures of smiling kids and people who'd supported our efforts around the globe were taped in haphazard fashion. Their faces covered the oceans and parts of the continents. Memories warmed my anxious heart.

It will be okay, Grace. You can do it… for them.

I stood for a minute, looking over the display, lost in my thoughts. Finally, I sighed, entered the combination, and opened the safe.

Struggling under its weight, I pulled out the large wooden box with intricate carvings and sat it on the coffee table. I took a small golden key off my neck, opened the top of the container, and placed the notebook inside.

Ever since the three Magi advised me to move the pendants to another location for everyone's safety, the task of securing and passing on the treasure had been at the forefront of my mind. After watching over me for the duration of one week and up until my twenty-fifth birthday, they disappeared for eleven long years. What sort of danger forced them to come knocking on my door again in the middle of the night? Magi would not disclose, and I didn't even want to think about it. But when I caught somebody following my car and watching me on the street, getting the treasure out of my home became the priority.

I frowned.

Nobody can take the pendants against my will!

Yes, I was the sole protector of the gifts, and only I had the power to assign the ownership. But would I not let go of the precious gems if the lives of my family members were put on the line? That was not a situation I ever wanted to be in. The last time I was threatened with a gun, it'd taken years for justice to catch up, putting Robert and Olivia Kowalski behind bars. Whatever was the source of this new threat, I was determined to do everything within my power to keep my family safe.

I'd worked hard to go after my dreams. Although moving to sunny California and becoming the top attorney in the area was not my end goal, but it had given us enough money and influence to do what we loved most—help the less fortunate around the world. It was my duty to safeguard what we'd accomplished.

I picked up the box and carried it down the winding stairs of my cozy home. Maneuvering around the suitcases that had occupied the open foyer since our recent return from Thailand took some skill. No time to unpack. Gone were the days of excessive order. My life was hectic at times, but I wouldn't trade it for anything else.

Finally, after nearly tripping over the toy truck and stepping on a few Legos, I made it to the door in one piece.

I swear, these little things are secret parent-torture devices!

I glanced at my watch. Seven-thirty in the evening. I made it on time. Should have been ready years ago. I opened one side of the double front door and came face to face with a person in a plain blue uniform that was waiting outside. A white armored truck was parked nearby.

Here we go again. Safe travels.

I handed the box to the stranger and watched as she got into the vehicle and drove away. A light breath of air flew by and played with my hair. I put my hand above my eyes and looked out at the horizon, squinting from the light of the setting sun. An orange hue spread over the heavens above and reflected in the ocean shore below. I took a full breath of the salty fresh air and stepped back into the house.

My ten-year-old daughter, Cathy, and my seven-year-old son, Michael, ran down the hall as soon as I walked in. They shouted over each other and jumped around me.

"Mommy, Michael is touching my stuff again!"

"You're stingy!"

"Leave your mom alone, you rascals." My husband, Greg, strolled in from the kitchen, squeezing himself between me and the kids. He pretended to fight them off using the rubber spatula as the sword. Our son laughed and tried to climb on him, which resulted in a wrestling match on the floor.

After getting up, Greg put one arm around my waist and smoothed down the mess on my head with another. "Hey, shush, kids. Can't you see? Mommy has the 'I am super tired' hair-do today."

Greg was still as good-looking as when we first met, even with that unruly beard he grew every time we traveled. He smelled like grilled chicken, which made my stomach growl.

"Is everything okay now?" he asked, worry etched around his bright eyes. "You've been locked in that office for hours."

I wrapped my hands around his neck. "Everything will be perfect… as soon as I get a hold of some food and take a bath."

"Yep, you're definitely overdue for one," Greg arched his brow, but held me even tighter when I tried to push him away. He nuzzled my neck, tickling me with his mane of a beard.

"And you're overdue for a shave!" I made a face.

"Ok, fine, I'll do it, so that your mom won't say I've gone wild."

I rolled my eyes. He knew my mother adored him,

bearded or not. "Remember, she and John are flying in next week."

"Oh, yeah, Grandpa John's coming!" Michael jumped around, but Cathy crossed her arms and pouted her pretty lips.

"Mom, ask Michael if he ate the candies Grandma Lou sent me from Brazil! I can't find them anywhere and he won't admit it." Cathy narrowed her eyes at her younger brother.

"Oh, no, buddy. I don't envy you right now." Greg made exaggerated faces at our son and made him giggle.

I bent down to my son's level and took his hand. "Honey, you know that in this house honesty is valued the most. Tell your sister what you did with her candy."

Michael furrowed his blond brows, wrinkled his little nose, then said, "I hid them in my pillowcase."

Cathy dashed upstairs. I kissed Michael's rosy cheek, but he wiggled out and ran after her.

"Cathy, you need to share!" he yelled.

I straightened, laughing, but got captured in Greg's arms again.

"How do you do this?" he inquired after kissing me.

"How do I do what?" I replied with a teasing smile.

"Make people always tell you the truth."

"Greg, you know how…"

"I still find it hard to believe. Seems like it's part of who you are. No wonder you're such a good lawyer."

"Oh, no, I definitely can't take full credit for that. It's all because of Mr. Bailey's support. He believed in me, and I'll never forget that."

"You should probably apply for a position as a judge next."

"Maybe I should."

I leaned into his broad chest. Securely wrapped in his arms, I could finally relax. The last rays of the setting sun peeked through the horizon. They washed over our embrace, revealing the outlines of a white onyx stone inside the seashell imprinted on my right shoulder—the gift that was etched into my skin and my heart, the Truth that was intertwined with my soul.

Thank you for reading!

**If you enjoyed the story, please, leave a short review on Amazon or GoodReads.
I would love to hear from you.**

DOWNLOAD EXCLUSIVE **FREE NOVELLA** AT THE LINK BELOW
~A LOVE STORY THAT STARTED IT ALL~

The Healer's Choice

https://www.subscribepage.com/healer's_choice

RECEIVE A COMPLIMENTARY GUIDE
TO THE BOOK:

7-day Journey of Self-discovery
www.subscribepage.com/sevendayjourney

All the proceeds from the sale of this book will be donated to non-profit organizations that support and empower underprivileged women around the world.

BE THE FIRST TO KNOW WHEN THE **NEXT BOOK** COMES OUT: https://www.subscribepage.com/nextreading

I am thankful to God, my family, friends, fellow authors, editors, early readers, and Self-Publishing school for supporting me through the process of writing and releasing this book.

If you have a story that lived for a long time in your heart and mind, a story that begs to be released into the world, don't hold it back.

Contact me at **elenashelestwriter@gmail.com** if you don't know where to start. I want to support your dream.

Made in United States
North Haven, CT
24 April 2023